SPADEWORK

A COLLECTION OF "NAMELESS DETECTIVE" STORIES

BILL PRONZINI

INTRODUCTION BY MARCIA MULLER

CRIPPEN & LANDRU PUBLISHERS NORFOLK VIRGINIA 1996

Cover copyright © 1996 by Crippen & Landru, Publishers

Cover painting by Carol Heyer; cover design by Deborah Miller

Crippen & Landru logo by Eric D. Greene

ISBN (limited edition): 1-885941-06-4

ISBN (trade edition: 1-885941-07-2

FIRST EDITION

10 9 8 7 6 5 4 3 2 1

Printed in the United States of America on acid-free recycled paper

Crippen & Landru, Publishers
P. O. Box 9315
Norfolk, VA 23505
USA

♠ CONTENTS ♠

INTRODUCTION:
MY TWO BEST FRIENDS
by Marcia Muller

I MAY as well admit it right up front: This is the most biased intro-duction to a collection of short stories that you're ever likely to read. For years Bill Pronzini and his "Nameless Detective" have been my two best friends. Bill and I have collaborated on novels, stories, and anthologies—much as "Nameless" and my series character, Sharon McCone, have collaborated on two cases. Four years ago, with the blessings of "Nameless" and Sharon, Bill and I were married. Last year, with our blessings, "Nameless" married his long-time love, Kerry Wade.

Fiction imitating life? Perhaps.

Actually, I've known "Nameless" far longer than I've known his creator. We met in the mid seventies in a San Francisco thrift shop. I'm not all that clear on what he was doing there, but as an aspiring crime writer, I was in search of inspiration and a good read.

The used book I pulled off the shelf was "Nameless's" second case, *The Vanished*. In those days, publishers didn't follow the practice of brand-naming series as they do today, so Random House had simply labeled it "a novel of suspense." I was three quarters through it before I realized I didn't know the detective's name, so I paged backwards, think-ing I'd either missed or forgotten it. No, no name. How could that be? I knew the man as well as I knew many of my friends. He was real to me, but I didn't know his name!

I decided that in order to pull off such a feat, this Pronzini person must be a very skilled writer, and proceeded to hunt up his other titles.

Over the years I've watched "Nameless" develop from a "sloppy over-weight Italian guy" who had terrible trouble with some perfectly dreadful women, to a more svelte Italian guy who has a terrific relationship with a special woman. Of course, he doesn't understand her any more than he did the others; some character traits must remain constant. I've also watched him face danger and his own private demons, as well as grow and change as a result of those confrontations. And I've watched his creator face the horror of the blank page, as well as grow and change as a writer—

refining his considerable talents and probing ever more deeply into his concerns about the human condition. (This trait of the author's that remains constant is the same as "Nameless's," and for my own sake, I hope this continues.)

Needless to say, I'm delighted to see this collection of the more recent "Nameless Detective" short stories. The fifteen tales that make up *Spadework* display their author's full range of talent. We have humor: the character-and-cat-generated type represented in "Bedeviled," the side-splitting situational sort exemplified in "Here Comes Santa Claus," and the kind that is used to convey a serious message, found in a new story written expressly for this collection, "Zero Tolerance."

Throughout we have the classical locked-room puzzles and well clued deductive stories that are a Pronzini trademark—and drive me to distraction because I can neither create them nor figure them out beforehand. In such stories as "Cat's-Paw," "Incident in a Neighborhood Tavern," "Twenty Miles from Paradise," "Ace in the Hole," "Something Wrong," and "One Night in Dolores Park," the solutions to the crimes hinge on a deceptively simple fact or set of facts that, when revealed, will provoke the reader to exclaim, "Why didn't I see that?" "Bomb Scare," a complete detective story in less than one thousand words, and "Worried Mother Job" similarly present situations that seem to be one thing when they are quite another.

Bill's fine characterization proves that the mystery short story need not merely be well constructed and clever, and the tales that best illustrate this deal with the dark side of human nature. "Skeleton Rattle Your Mouldy Leg," "Souls Burning," and "Home Is the Place Where" are haunting and powerful, bringing the reader face to face with terrible secrets, private pain, and feelings of frustration and helplessness. The most thought-provoking of Bill's stories deal with a theme that recurs throughout all his work: the often tragic consequences of human beings' intolerance and attempts to control and manipulate others. The spectres these stories raise and the questions they pose linger long after reading them.

One final reason I'm happy to see this collection appear: Its publication marks the twenty-fifth anniversary of "Nameless's" first appearance in book form—his first novel-length case, *The Snatch*, published in 1971. It's a tribute to Bill that he's been able to continue developing him over all that time, keeping him ever fresh, human, and appealing.

But enough of praising; it's never a good idea to spoil one's spouse. Time to let the work stand on its own merits. And time for you, the reader, to begin turning the pages. You'll enjoy *Spadework*—I guarantee it.

Petaluma, California
December, 1995

CAT'S-PAW

THERE are two places that are ordinary enough during the daylight hours but that become downright eerie after dark, particularly if you go wandering around in them by yourself. One is a graveyard; the other is a public zoo. And that goes double for San Francisco's Fleishhacker Zoological Gardens on a blustery winter night when the fog comes swirling in and makes everything look like capering phantoms or two-dimensional cutouts.

Fleishhacker Zoo was where I was on this foggy winter night—alone, for the most part—and I wished I was somewhere else instead. *Anywhere* else, as long as it had a heater or a log fire and offered something hot to drink.

I was on my third tour of the grounds, headed past the sea lion tank to make another check of the aviary, when I paused to squint at the luminous dial of my watch. Eleven forty-five. Less than three hours down and better than six left to go. I was already half-frozen, even though I was wearing long johns, two sweaters, two pairs of socks, heavy gloves, a woolen cap, and a long fur-lined overcoat. The ocean was only a thousand yards away, and the icy wind that blew in off of it sliced through you to the marrow. If I got through this job without contracting pneumonia, I would consider myself lucky.

Somewhere in the fog, one of the animals made a sudden roaring noise; I couldn't tell what kind of animal or where the noise came from. The first time that sort of thing had happened, two nights ago, I'd jumped a little. Now I was used to it, or as used to it as I would ever get. How guys like Dettlinger and Hammond could work here night after night, month after month, was beyond my comprehension.

I went ahead toward the aviary. The big wind-sculpted cypress trees that grew on my left made looming, swaying shadows, like giant black dancers with rustling headdresses wreathed in mist. Back beyond them, fuzzy yellow blobs of light marked the location of the zoo's café. More nightlights burned on the aviary, although the massive fenced-in wing on the near side was dark.

Most of the birds were asleep or nesting or whatever the hell it is birds do at night. But you could hear some of them stirring around, making noise. There were a couple of dozen different varieties in there, including such esoteric types as the crested screamer, the purple gallinule, and the black crake. One esoteric type that used to be in there but wasn't any longer was something called a bunting, a brilliantly colored migratory bird. Three of them had been swiped four days ago, the latest in a rash of thefts the zoological gardens had suffered.

The thief or thieves had also got two South American Harris hawks, a bird of prey similar to a falcon; three crab-eating macaques, whatever they were; and half a dozen rare Chiricahua rattlesnakes known as *Crotalus pricei.* He or they had picked the locks on buildings and cages, and got away clean each time. Sam Dettlinger, one of the two regular watchmen, had spotted somebody running the night the rattlers were stolen, and given chase, but he hadn't got close enough for much of a description, or even to tell for sure if it was a man or a woman.

The police had been notified, of course, but there was not much they could do. There wasn't much the Zoo Commission could do either, beyond beefing up security—and all that had amounted to was adding one extra night watchman, Al Kirby, on a temporary basis; he was all they could afford. The problem was, Fleishhacker Zoo covers some seventy acres. Long sections of its perimeter fencing are secluded; you couldn't stop somebody determined to climb the fence and sneak in at night if you surrounded the place with a hundred men. Nor could you effectively police the grounds with any less than a hundred men; much of those seventy acres is heavily wooded, and there are dozens of grottoes, brushy fields and slopes, rush-rimmed ponds, and other areas simulating natural habitats for some of the zoo's fourteen hundred animals and birds. Kids, and an occasional grown-up, have gotten lost in there in broad daylight. A thief who knew his way around could hide out on the grounds for weeks without being spotted.

I got involved in the case because I was acquainted with one of the commission members, a guy named Lawrence Factor. He was an attorney, and I had done some investigating for him in the past, and he thought I was the cat's nuts when it came to detective work. So he'd come to see me, not as an official emissary of the commission but on his own; the commission had no money left in its small budget for such as the hiring of a private detective. But Factor had made a million bucks or so in the practice of criminal law, and as a passionate animal lover, he was willing to foot the bill himself. What he wanted me to do was sign on as another night watchman, plus nose around among my contacts to find out if there was any word on the street about the thefts.

It seemed like an odd sort of case, and I told him so. "Why would anybody steal hawks and small animals and rattlesnakes?" I asked. "Doesn't make much sense to me."

"It would if you understood how valuable those creatures are to some people."

"What people?"

"Private collectors, for one," he said. "Unscrupulous individuals who run small independent zoos, for another. They've been known to pay exorbitantly high prices for rare specimens they can't obtain through normal channels—usually because of the state or federal laws protecting endangered species."

"You mean there's a thriving black market in animals?"

"You bet there is. Animals, reptiles, birds—you name it. Take the *pricei*, the southwestern rattler, for instance. Several years ago, the Arizona Game and Fish Department placed it on a special permit list; people who want the snake first have to obtain a permit from the Game and Fish authority before they can go out into the Chiricahua Mountains and hunt one. Legitimate researchers have no trouble getting a permit, but hobbyists and private collectors are turned down. Before the permit list, you could get a *pricei* for twenty-five dollars; now, some snake collectors will pay two hundred and fifty dollars and up for one."

"The same high prices apply on the other stolen specimens?"

"Yes," Factor said. "Much higher, in the case of the Harris hawk."

"How much higher?"

"From three to five thousand dollars, after it has been trained for falconry."

I let out a soft whistle. "You have any idea who might be pulling the thefts?"

"Not specifically, no. It could be anybody with a working knowledge of zoology and the right—or wrong—contacts for disposal of the specimens."

"Someone connected with Fleishhacker, maybe?"

"That's possible. But I damned well hope not."

"So your best guess is what?"

"A professional at this sort of thing," Factor said. "They don't usually rob large zoos like ours—there's too much risk and too much publicity; mostly they hit small zoos or private collectors, and do some poaching on the side. But it has been known to happen when they hook up with buyers who are willing to pay premium prices."

"What makes you think it's a pro in this case? Why not an amateur? Or even kids out on some kind of crazy lark?"

"Well, for one thing, the thief seemed to know exactly what he was after each time. Only expensive and endangered specimens were taken. For another thing, the locks on the building and cage doors were picked by an expert—and that's not my theory, it's the police's."

"You figure he'll try it again?"

"Well, he's four-for-four so far, with no hassle except for the minor scare Sam Dettlinger gave him; that has to make him feel pretty secure. And there are dozens more valuable, prohibited specimens in the gardens. I like the odds that he'll push his luck and go for five straight."

But so far the thief hadn't pushed his luck. This was the third night I'd been on the job and nothing had happened. Nothing had happened during my daylight investigation either; I had put out feelers all over the city, but nobody admitted to knowing anything about the zoo thefts. Nor had I been able to find out anything from any of the Fleishhacker employees I'd talked to. All the information I had on the case, in fact, had been furnished by Lawrence Factor in my office three days ago.

If the thief was going to make another hit, I wished he would do it pretty soon and get it over with. Prowling around here in the dark and the fog and that damned icy wind, waiting for something to happen, was starting to get on my nerves. Even if I was being well paid, there were better ways to spend long, cold winter nights. Like curled up in bed with a copy of *Black Mask* or *Detective Tales* or one of the other pulps in my collection. Like curled up in bed with Kerry. . . .

I moved ahead to the near doors of the aviary and tried them to make sure they were still locked. They were. But I shone my flash on them anyway, just to be certain that they hadn't been tampered with since the last time one of us had been by. No problem there, either.

There were four of us on the grounds—Dettlinger, Hammond, Kirby, and me—and the way we'd been working it was to spread out to four corners and then start moving counterclockwise in a set but irregular pattern; that way, we could cover the grounds thoroughly without all of us congregating in one area, and without more than fifteen minutes going by from one building check to another. We each had a walkie-talkie clipped to our belts so one could summon the others if anything went down. We also used the things to radio our positions periodically, so we'd be sure to stay spread out from each other.

I went around the other side of the aviary, to the entrance that faced the long, shallow pond where the bigger tropical birds had their sanctuary. The doors there were also secure. The wind gusted over the pond as I was checking the doors, like a williwaw off the frozen Arctic tundra; it made the cypress trees genuflect, shredded the fog for an instant so that I could see all the way across to the construction site of the new Primate Discovery Center, and cracked my teeth together with a sound like rattling bones. I flexed the cramped fingers of my left hand, the one that had suffered some slight nerve damage in a shooting scrape a few months back; extreme cold aggravated the chronic stiffness. I thought longingly of the hot coffee in my thermos. But the thermos was over at the zoo office behind the carousel, along with my brown-bag supper, and I was not due for a break until one o'clock.

The path that led to Monkey Island was on my left; I took it, hunching forward against the wind. Ahead, I could make out the high dark mass of man-made rocks that comprised the island home of sixty or seventy spider monkeys. But the mist was closing in again, like wind-driven skeins of shiny gray cloth being woven together magically; the building that housed the elephants and pachyderms, only a short distance away, was invisible.

One of the male peacocks that roam the grounds let loose with its weird cry somewhere behind me. The damned things were always doing that, showing off even in the middle of the night. I had never cared for peacocks much, and I liked them even less now. I wondered how one of them would taste roasted with garlic and anchovies. The thought warmed me a little as I moved along the path between the hippo pen and the brown bear grottoes, turned onto the wide concourse that led past the front of the Lion House.

In the middle of the concourse was an extended oblong pond, with a little center island overgrown with yucca trees and pampas grass. The vegetation had an eerie look in the fog, like fantastic creatures waving their appendages in a low-budget science fiction film. I veered away from them, over toward the glass-and-wire cages that had been built onto the Lion House's stucco facade. The cages were for show: inside was the Zoological Society's current pride and joy, a year-old white tiger named Prince Charles, one of only fifty known white tigers in the world. Young Charley was the zoo's rarest and most valuable possession, but the thief hadn't attempted to steal him. Nobody in his right mind would try to make off with a frisky, five-hundred-pound tiger in the middle of the night.

Charley was asleep; so was his sister, a normally marked Bengal tiger named Whiskers. I looked at them for a few seconds, decided I wouldn't like to have to pay their food bill, and started to turn away.

Somebody was hurrying toward me, from over where the otter pool was located.

I could barely see him in the mist; he was just a moving black shape. I tensed a little, taking the flashlight out of my pocket, putting my cramped left hand on the walkie-talkie so I could use the thing if it looked like trouble. But it wasn't trouble. The figure called my name in a familiar voice, and when I put my flash on for a couple of seconds I saw that it was Sam Dettlinger.

"What's up?" I said when he got to me. "You're supposed to be over by the gorillas about now."

"Yeah," he said, "but I thought I saw something about fifteen minutes ago, out back by the cat grottoes."

"Saw what?"

"Somebody moving around in the bushes," he said. He tipped back his uniform cap, ran a gloved hand over his face to wipe away the thin film of moisture the fog had put there. He was in his forties, heavyset, owl-eyed, with carrot-colored hair and a mustache that looked like a dead caterpillar draped across his upper lip.

"Why didn't you put out a call?"

"I couldn't be sure I actually saw somebody and I didn't want to sound a false alarm; this damn fog distorts everything, makes you see things that aren't there. Wasn't anybody in the bushes when I went to check. It might have been a squirrel or something. Or just the fog. But I figured I'd better search the area to make sure."

"Anything?"

"No. Zip."

"Well, I'll make another check just in case."

"You want me to come with you?"

"No need. It's about time for your break, isn't it?"

He shot the sleeve of his coat and peered at his watch. "You're right, it's almost midnight—"

Something exploded inside the Lion House—a flat cracking noise that sounded like a gunshot.

Both Dettlinger and I jumped. He said, "What the hell was that?"

"I don't know. Come on!"

We ran the twenty yards or so to the front entrance. The noise had awakened Prince Charles and his sister; they were up and starting to prowl their cage as we rushed past. I caught hold of the door handle and tugged on it, but the lock was secure.

I snapped at Dettlinger, "Have you got a key?"

"Yeah, to all the buildings. . . ."

He fumbled his key ring out, and I switched on my flash to help him find the right key. From inside, there was cold dead silence; I couldn't hear anything anywhere else in the vicinity except for faint animal sounds lost in the mist. Dettlinger got the door unlocked, dragged it open. I crowded in ahead of him, across a short foyer and through another door that wasn't locked, into the building's cavernous main room.

A couple of the ceiling lights were on; we hadn't been able to tell from outside because the Lion House had no windows. The interior was a long rectangle with a terra-cotta tile floor, now-empty feeding cages along the entire facing wall and the near side wall, another set of entrance doors in the far side wall, and a kind of indoor garden full of tropical plants flanking the main entrance to the left. You could see all of the enclosure from two steps inside, and there wasn't anybody in it. Except—

"Jesus!" Dettlinger said. "Look!"

I was looking, all right. And having trouble accepting what I saw. A man lay sprawled on his back inside one of the cages diagonally to our right; there was a small glistening stain of blood on the front of his heavy coat and a revolver of some kind in one of his outflung hands. The small access door at the front of the cage was shut, and so was the sliding panel at the rear that let the big cats in and out at feeding time. In the pale light, I could see the man's face clearly: his teeth were bared in the rictus of death.

"It's Kirby," Dettlinger said in a hushed voice. "Sweet Christ, what—?"

I brushed past him and ran over and climbed the brass railing that fronted all the cages. The access door, a four-by-two-foot barred inset, was locked tight. I poked my nose between two of the bars, peering in at the dead man. Kirby, Al Kirby. The temporary night watchman the Zoo Commission had hired a couple of weeks ago. It looked as though he had been shot in the chest at close range; I could see where the upper middle of his coat had been scorched by the powder discharge.

My stomach jumped a little, the way it always does when I come face-to-face with violent death. The faint, gamy, big-cat smell that hung in the air didn't help it any. I turned toward Dettlinger, who had come up beside me.

"You have a key to this access door?" I asked him.

"No. There's never been a reason to carry one. Only the cat handlers have them." He shook his head in an awed way. "How'd Kirby get in there? What *happened?*"

"I wish I knew. Stay put for a minute."

I left him and ran down to the doors in the far side wall. They were locked. Could somebody have had time to shoot Kirby, get out through these doors, then relock them before Dettlinger and I busted in? It didn't seem likely. We'd been inside less than thirty seconds after we'd heard the shot.

I hustled back to the cage where Kirby's body lay. Dettlinger had backed away from it, around in front of the side-wall cages; he looked a little queasy now himself, as if the implications of violent death had finally registered on him. He had a pack of cigarettes in one hand, getting ready to soothe his nerves with some nicotine. But this wasn't the time or the place for a smoke; I yelled at him to put the things away, and he complied.

When I reached him I said, "What's behind these cages? Some sort of rooms back there, aren't there?"

"Yeah. Where the handlers store equipment and meat for the cats. Chutes, too, that lead out to the grottoes."

"How do you get to them?"

He pointed over at the rear side wall. "That door next to the last cage."

"Any other way in or out of those rooms?"

"No. Except through the grottoes, but the cats are out there."

I went around to the interior door he'd indicated. Like all the others, it was locked. I said to Dettlinger, "You have a key to this door?"

He nodded, got it out, and unlocked the door. I told him to keep watch out here, switched on my flashlight, and went on through. The flash beam showed me where the light switches were; I flicked them on and began a quick, cautious search. The door to one of the meat lockers was open, but nobody was hiding inside. Or anywhere else back there.

When I came out I shook my head in answer to Dettlinger's silent question. Then I asked him, "Where's the nearest phone?"

"Out past the grottoes, by the popcorn stand."

"Hustle out there and call the police. And while you're at it, radio Hammond to get over here on the double—"

"No need for that," a new voice said from the main entrance. "I'm already here."

I glanced in that direction and saw Gene Hammond, the other regular night watchman. You couldn't miss him; he was six-five, weighed in at a good two-fifty, and had a face like the back end of a bus. Disbelief was written on it now as he stared across at Kirby's body.

"Go," I told Dettlinger. "I'll watch things here."

"Right."

He hurried out past Hammond, who was on his way toward where I stood in front of the cage. Hammond said as he came up, "God—what happened?"

"We don't know yet."

"How'd Kirby get in there?"

"We don't know that either." I told him what we did know, which was not much. "When did you last see Kirby?"

"Not since the shift started at nine."

"Any idea why he'd have come in here?"

"No. Unless he heard something and came in to investigate. But he shouldn't have been in this area, should he?"

"Not for another half hour, no."

"Christ, you don't think that he—"

"What?"

"Killed himself," Hammond said.

"It's possible. Was he despondent for some reason?"

"Not that I know about. But it sure looks like suicide. I mean, he's got that gun in his hand, he's all alone in the building, all the doors are locked. What else could it be?"

"Murder," I said.

"How? Where's the person who killed him, then?"

"Got out through one of the grottoes, maybe."

"No way," Hammond said. "Those cats would maul anybody who went out among 'em—and I mean anybody; not even any of the handlers would try a stunt like that. Besides, even if somebody made it down into the moat, how would he scale that twenty-foot back wall to get out of it?"

I didn't say anything.

Hammond said, "And another thing: why would Kirby be locked in this cage if it was murder?"

"Why would he lock himself in to commit suicide?"

He made a bewildered gesture with one of his big hands.

"Crazy," he said. "The whole thing's crazy."

He was right. None of it seemed to make any sense at all.

I knew one of the homicide inspectors who responded to Dettlinger's call. His name was Branislaus and he was a pretty decent guy, so the preliminary questions-and-answers went fast and hassle-free. After which he packed Dettlinger and Hammond and me off to the zoo office while he and the lab crew went to work inside the Lion House.

I poured some hot coffee from my thermos, to help me thaw out a little, and then used one of the phones to get Lawrence Factor out of bed. He was paying my fee and I figured he had a right to know what had happened as soon as possible. He made shocked noises when I told him, asked a couple of pertinent questions, said he'd get out to Fleishhacker right away, and rang off.

An hour crept away. Dettlinger sat at one of the desks with a pad of paper and a pencil and challenged himself in a string of tick-tack-toe games. Hammond chain-smoked cigarettes until the air in there was blue with smoke. I paced around for the most part, now and then stepping out into the chill night to get some fresh air: all that cigarette smoke was playing merry hell with my lungs. None of us had much to say. We were all waiting to see what Branislaus and the rest of the cops turned up.

Factor arrived at one-thirty, looking harried and upset. It was the first time I had ever seen him without a tie and with his usually immaculate Robert Redford hairdo in some disarray. A patrolman accompanied him into the office, and judging from the way Factor glared at him, he had had some difficulty getting past the front gate. When the patrolman left I gave Factor a detailed account of what had taken place as far as I knew it, with embellishments from Dettlinger. I was just finishing when Branislaus came in.

Branny spent a couple of minutes discussing matters with Factor. Then he said he wanted to talk to the rest of us one at a time, picked me to go first, and herded me into another room.

The first thing he said was, "This is the screwiest shooting case I've come up against in twenty years on the force. What in bloody hell is going on here?"

"I was hoping maybe you could tell me."

"Well, I can't—yet. So far it looks like a suicide, but if that's it, it's a candidate for Ripley. Whoever heard of anybody blowing himself away in a lion cage at the zoo?"

"Any indication he locked himself in there?"

"We found a key next to his body that fits the access door in front."

"Just one loose key?"

"That's right."

"So it could have been dropped in there by somebody else after Kirby was dead and after the door was locked. Or thrown in through the bars from outside."

"Granted."

"And suicides don't usually shoot themselves in the chest," I said.

"Also granted, although it's been known to happen."

"What kind of weapon was he shot with? I couldn't see it too well from outside the cage, the way he was lying."

"Thirty-two Iver Johnson."

"Too soon to tell yet if it was his, I guess."

"Uh-huh. Did he come on the job armed?"

"Not that I know about. The rest of us weren't, or weren't supposed to be."

"Well, we'll know more when we finish running a check on the serial number," Branislaus said. "It was intact, so the thirty-two doesn't figure to be a Saturday night special."

"Was there anything in Kirby's pockets?"

"The usual stuff. And no sign of a suicide note. But you don't think it was suicide anyway, right?"

"No, I don't."

"Why not?"

"No specific reason. It's just that a suicide under those circumstances rings false. And so does a suicide on the heels of the thefts the zoo's been having lately."

"So you figure there's a connection between Kirby's death and the thefts?"

"Don't you?"

"The thought crossed my mind," Branislaus said dryly. "Could be the thief slipped back onto the grounds tonight, something happened before he had a chance to steal something, and he did for Kirby—I'll admit the possibility. But what were the two of them doing in the Lion House? Doesn't add up that Kirby caught the guy in there. Why would the thief enter it in the first place? Not because he was trying to steal a lion or a tiger, that's for sure."

"Maybe Kirby stumbled on him somewhere else, somewhere nearby. Maybe there was a struggle; the thief got the drop on Kirby, then forced him to let both of them into the Lion House with his key."

"Why?"

"To get rid of him where it was private."

"I don't buy it," Branny said. "Why wouldn't he just knock Kirby over the head and run for it?"

"Well, it could be he's somebody Kirby knew."

"Okay. But the Lion House angle is still too much trouble for him to go through. It would've been much easier to shove the gun into Kirby's belly and shoot him on the spot. Kirby's clothing would have muffled the sound of the shot; it wouldn't have been audible more than fifty feet away."

"I guess you're right," I said.

"But even supposing it happened the way you suggest, it *still* doesn't add up. You and Dettlinger were inside the Lion House thirty seconds after the shot, by your own testimony. You checked the side entrance doors almost immediately and they were locked; you looked around behind the cages and nobody was there. So how did the alleged killer get out of the building?"

"The only way he could have got out was through one of the grottoes in back."

"Only he *couldn't* have, according to what both Dettlinger and Hammond say."

I paced over to one of the windows—nervous energy—and looked out at the fog-wrapped construction site for the new monkey exhibit. Then I turned and said, "I don't suppose your men found anything in the way of evidence inside the Lion House?"

"Not so you could tell it with the naked eye."

"Or anywhere else in the vicinity?"

"No."

"Any sign of tampering on any of the doors?"

"None. Kirby used his key to get in, evidently."

I came back to where Branislaus was leaning hipshot against somebody's desk. "Listen, Branny," I said, "this whole thing is *too* screwball. Somebody's playing games here, trying to muddle our thinking—and that means murder."

"Maybe," he said. "Hell, probably. But how was it done? I can't come up with an answer, not even one that's believably far-fetched. Can you?"

"Not yet."

"Does that mean you've got an idea?"

"Not an idea; just a bunch of little pieces looking for a pattern."

He sighed. "Well, if they find it, let me know."

When I went back into the other room I told Dettlinger that he was next on the grill. Factor wanted to talk some more, but I put him off. Hammond was still polluting the air with his damned cigarettes, and I needed another shot of fresh air; I also needed to be alone for a while.

I put my overcoat on and went out and wandered past the cages where the smaller cats were kept, past the big open fields that the giraffes and rhinos called home. The wind was stronger and colder than it had been earlier; heavy gusts swept dust and twigs along the ground, broke the fog up into scudding wisps. I pulled my cap down over my ears to keep them from numbing.

The path led along to the concourse at the rear of the Lion House, where the open cat-grottoes were. Big, portable electric lights had been set up there and around the front so the police could search the area. A couple of patrolmen glanced at me as I approached, but they must have recognized me because neither of them came over to ask what I was doing there.

I went to the low, shrubberied wall that edged the middle cat-grotto. Whatever was in there, lions or tigers, had no doubt been aroused by all the activity; but they were hidden inside the dens at the rear. These grottoes had been newly renovated—lawns, jungly vegetation, small trees, everything to give the cats the illusion of their native habitat. The side walls separating this grotto from the other two were man-made rocks, high and unscalable. The moat below was fifty feet wide, too far for either a big cat or a man to jump; and the near moat wall was sheer and also unscalable from below, just as Hammond and Dettlinger had said.

No way anybody could have got out of the Lion House through the grottoes, I thought. Just no way.

No way it could have been murder then. Unless—

I stood there for a couple of minutes, with my mind beginning, finally, to open up. Then I hurried around to the front of the Lion House and looked at the main entrance for a time, remembering things.

And then I knew.

Branislaus was in the zoo office, saying something to Factor, when I came back inside. He glanced over at me as I shut the door.

"Branny," I said, "those little pieces I told you about a while ago finally found their pattern."

He straightened. "Oh? Some of it or all of it?"

"All of it, I think."

Factor said, "What's this about?"

"I figured out what happened at the Lion House tonight," I said. "Al Kirby didn't commit suicide: he was murdered. And I can name the man who killed him."

I expected a reaction, but I didn't get one beyond some widened eyes and opened mouths. Nobody said anything and nobody moved much. But you could feel the sudden tension in the room, as thick in its own intangible way as the layers of smoke from Hammond's cigarettes.

"Name him," Branislaus said.

But I didn't, not just yet. A good portion of what I was going to say was guesswork—built on deduction and logic, but still guesswork—and I wanted to choose my words carefully. I took off my cap, unbuttoned my coat, and moved away from the door, over near where Branny was standing.

He said, "Well? Who do you say killed Kirby?"

"The same person who stole the birds and other specimens. And I don't mean a professional animal thief, as Mr. Factor suggested when he hired me. He isn't an outsider at all; and he didn't climb the fence to get onto the grounds."

"No?"

"No. He was *already* in here on those nights and on this one because he works here as a night watchman. The man I'm talking about is Sam Dettlinger."

That got some reaction. Hammond said, "I don't believe it," and Factor said, "My God!" Branislaus looked at me, looked at Dettlinger, looked at me again—moving his head like a spectator at a tennis match.

The only one who didn't move was Dettlinger. He sat still at one of the desks, his hands resting easily on its blotter; his face betrayed nothing.

He said, "You're a liar," in a thin, hard voice.

"Am I? You've been working here for some time; you know the animals and which ones are endangered and valuable. It was easy for you to get into the buildings during your rounds: just use your key and walk right in. When you had the specimens you took them to some pre-arranged spot along the outside fence and passed them over to an accomplice."

"What accomplice?" Branislaus asked.

"I don't know. You'll get it out of him, Branny; or you'll find out some other way. But that's how he had to have worked it."

"What about the scratches on the locks?" Hammond asked. "The police told us the locks were picked—"

"Red herring," I said. "Just like Dettlinger's claim that he chased a stranger on the grounds the night the rattlers were stolen. Designed to cover up the fact that it was an inside job." I looked back at Branislaus. "Five'll get you ten Dettlinger's had some sort of locksmithing experience. It shouldn't take much digging to find out."

Dettlinger started to get out of his chair, thought better of it, and sat down again. We were all staring at him, but it did not seem to bother him much; his owl eyes were on my neck, and if they'd been hands I would have been dead of strangulation.

Without shifting his gaze, he said to Factor, "I'm going to sue this son of a bitch for slander. I can do that, can't I, Mr. Factor?"

"If what he says isn't true, you can," Factor said.

"Well, it isn't true. It's all a bunch of lies. I never stole anything. And I sure never killed Al Kirby. How the hell could I? I was with this guy, *outside* the Lion House, when Al died inside."

"No, you weren't," I said.

"What kind of crap is that? I was standing right next to you, we both heard the shot—"

"That's right, we both heard the shot. And that's the first thing that put me onto you, Sam. Because we damned well *shouldn't* have heard it."

"No? Why not?"

"Kirby was shot with a thirty-two-caliber revolver. A thirty-two is a small gun; it doesn't make much of a bang. Branny, you remember saying to me a little while ago that if somebody had shoved that thirty-two into Kirby's middle, you wouldn't have been able to hear the pop more than fifty feet away? Well, that's right. But Dettlinger and I were a lot more than fifty feet from the cage where we found Kirby—twenty yards from the front entrance, thick stucco walls, a ten-foot foyer, and another forty feet or so of floor space to the cage. Yet we not only heard a shot, we heard it loud and clear."

Branislaus said, "So how is that possible?"

I didn't answer him. Instead I looked at Dettlinger and I said, "Do you smoke?"

That got a reaction out of him. The one I wanted: confusion. "What?"

"Do you smoke?"

"What kind of question is that?"

"Gene must have smoked half a pack since we've been in here, but I haven't seen you light up once. In fact, I haven't seen you light up the whole time I've been working here. So answer me, Sam—do you smoke or not?"

"No, I don't smoke. You satisfied?"

"I'm satisfied," I said. "Now suppose you tell me what it was you had in your hand in the Lion House, when I came back from checking the side doors?"

He got it, then—the way I'd trapped him. But he clamped his lips together and sat still.

"What are you getting at?" Branislaus asked me. "What *did* he have in his hand?"

"At the time I thought it was a pack of cigarettes; that's what it looked like from a distance. I took him to be a little queasy, a delayed reaction to finding the body, and I figured he wanted some nicotine to calm his nerves. But that wasn't it at all; he wasn't queasy, he was scared —because I'd seen what he had in his hand before he could hide it in his pocket."

"So what was it?"

"A tape recorder," I said. "One of those small battery-operated jobs they make nowadays, a white one that fits in the palm of the hand. He'd just picked it up from wherever he'd stashed it earlier—behind the bars in one of the other cages, probably. I didn't notice it there because it was so small and because my attention was on Kirby's body."

"You're saying the shot you heard was on tape?"

"Yes. My guess is, he recorded it right after he shot Kirby. Fifteen minutes or so earlier."

"Why did he shoot Kirby? And why in the Lion House?"

"Well, he and Kirby could have been in on the thefts together; they could have had some kind of falling-out, and Dettlinger decided to get rid of him. But I don't like that much. As a premeditated murder, it's too elaborate. No, I think the recorder was a spur-of-the-moment idea; I doubt if it belonged to Dettlinger, in fact. Ditto the thirty-two. He's clever, but he's not a planner, he's an improviser."

"If the recorder and the gun weren't his, whose were they? Kirby's?"

I nodded. "The way I see it, Kirby found out about Dettlinger pulling the thefts; saw him do the last one, maybe. Instead of reporting it, he did some brooding and then decided tonight to try a little shakedown. But Dettlinger's bigger and tougher than he was, so he brought the thirty-two along for protection. He also brought the recorder, the idea probably being to tape his conversation with Dettlinger, without Dettlinger's knowledge, for further blackmail leverage.

"He buttonholed Dettlinger in the vicinity of the Lion House and the two of them went inside to talk it over in private. Then something happened. Dettlinger tumbled to the recorder, got rough, Kirby pulled the gun, they struggled for it, Kirby got shot dead—that sort of scenario.

"So then Dettlinger had a corpse on his hands. What was he going to do? He could drag it outside, leave it somewhere, make it look like the mythical fence-climbing thief killed him; but if he did that he'd be running the risk of me or Hammond appearing suddenly and spotting him. Instead he got what he thought was a bright idea: he'd create a big mystery and confuse hell out of everybody, plus give himself a dandy alibi for the apparent time of Kirby's death.

"He took the gun and the recorder to the storage area behind the cages. Erased what was on the tape, used the fast-forward and the timer to run off fifteen minutes of tape, then switched to record and fired a second shot to get the sound of it on tape. I don't know for sure what he fired the bullet into; but I found one of the meat locker doors open when I searched back there, so maybe he used a slab of meat for a target. And then piled a bunch of other slabs on top to hide it until he could get rid of it later on. The police wouldn't be looking for a second bullet, he thought, so there wasn't any reason for them to rummage around in the meat.

"His next moves were to rewind the tape, go back out front, and stash the recorder—turned on, with the volume all the way up. That gave him fifteen minutes. He picked up Kirby's body . . . most of the blood from the wound had been absorbed by the heavy coat Kirby was wearing, which was why there wasn't any blood on the floor and why Dettlinger didn't get any on him. And why I didn't notice, fifteen minutes later, that it was starting to coagulate. He carried the body to the cage, put it inside with the thirty-two in Kirby's hand, relocked the access door—he told me he didn't have a key, but that was a lie—and then threw the key in with the body. But putting Kirby in the cage was his big mistake. By doing that he made the whole thing too bizarre. If he'd left the body where it was, he'd have had a better chance of getting away with it.

"Anyhow, he slipped out of the building without being seen and hid over by the otter pool. He knew I was due there at midnight, because of the schedule we'd set up; and he wanted to be with me when that recorded gunshot went off. Make me the cat's-paw, if you don't mind a little grim humor, for what he figured would be his perfect alibi.

"Later on, when I sent him to report Kirby's death, he disposed of the recorder. He couldn't have gone far from the Lion House to get rid of it; he made the call, and he was back within fifteen minutes. With any luck, his fingerprints will be on the recorder when your men turn it up.

"And if you want any more proof I'll swear in court I didn't smell cordite when we entered the Lion House; all I smelled was the gamy odor of jungle cats. I should have smelled cordite if that thirty-two had just been discharged. But it hadn't, and the cordite smell from the earlier discharges had already faded."

That was a pretty long speech and it left me dry-mouthed. But it had made its impression on the others in the room, Branislaus in particular.

He asked Dettlinger, "Well? You have anything to say for yourself?"

"I never did any of those things he said—none of 'em, you hear?"

"I hear."

"And that's all I'm saying until I see a lawyer."

"You've got one of the best sitting next to you. How about it, Mr. Factor? You want to represent Dettlinger?"

"Pass," Factor said thinly. "This is one case where I'll be glad to plead bias."

Dettlinger was still strangling me with his eyes. I wondered if he would keep on proclaiming his innocence even in the face of stronger evidence than what I'd just presented. Or if he'd crack under pressure, as most amateurs do.

I decided he was the kind who'd crack eventually, and I quit looking at him and at the death in his eyes.

"Well, I was wrong about that much," I said to Kerry the following night. We were sitting in front of a log fire in her Diamond Heights apartment, me with a beer and her with a glass of wine, and I had just finished telling her all about it. "Dettlinger hasn't cracked and it doesn't look as if he's going to. The DA'll have to work for his conviction."

"But you *were* right about most of it?"

"Pretty much. I probably missed a few details; with Kirby dead, and unless Dettlinger talks, we may never know some of them for sure. But for the most part I think I got it straight."

"My hero," she said, and gave me an adoring look.

She does that sometimes—puts me on like that. I don't understand women, so I don't know why. But it doesn't matter. She has auburn hair and green eyes and a fine body; she's also smarter than I am—she works as an advertising copywriter—and she is stimulating to be around. I love her to pieces, as the boys in the back room used to say.

"The police found the tape recorder," I said. "Took them until late this morning, because Dettlinger was clever about hiding it. He'd buried it in some rushes inside the hippo pen, probably with the idea of digging it up again later on and getting rid of it permanently. There was one clear print on the fast-forward button—Dettlinger's."

"Did they also find the second bullet he fired?"

"Yep. Where I guessed it was: in one of the slabs of fresh meat in the open storage locker."

"And did Dettlinger have locksmithing experience?"

"Uh-huh. He worked for a locksmith for a year in his mid-twenties. The case against him, even without a confession, is pretty solid."

"What about his accomplice?"

"Branislaus thinks he's got a line on the guy," I said. "From some things he found in Dettlinger's apartment. Man named Gerber—got a record of animal poaching and theft. I talked to Larry Factor this afternoon and he's heard of Gerber. The way he figures it, Dettlinger and Gerber had a deal for the specimens they stole with some collectors in Florida. That seems to be Gerber's usual pattern of operation anyway."

"I hope they get him too," Kerry said. "I don't like the idea of stealing birds and animals out of the zoo. It's . . . obscene, somehow."

"So is murder."

We didn't say anything for a time, looking into the fire, working on our drinks.

"You know," I said finally, "I have a lot of sympathy for animals myself. Take gorillas, for instance."

"Why gorillas?"

"Because of their mating habits."

"What are their mating habits?"

I had no idea, but I made up something interesting. Then I gave her a practical demonstration.

No gorilla ever had it so good.

SKELETON RATTLE YOUR MOULDY LEG

HE was one of the oddest people I had ever met. Sixty years old, under five and a half feet tall, slight, with great bony knobs for elbows and knees, with bat-winged ears and a bent nose and eyes that danced left and right, left and right, and had sparkly little lights in them. He wore baggy clothes—sweaters and jeans, mostly, crusted with patches—and a baseball cap turned around so that the bill poked out from the back of his head. In his back pocket he carried a whisk broom, and if he knew you, or wanted to, he would come up and say, "I know you—you've got a speck on your coat," and he would brush it off with the broom. Then he would talk, or maybe recite or even sing a little: a gnarled old harlequin cast up from another age.

These things were odd enough, but the oddest of all was his obsession with skeletons.

His name was Nick Damiano and he lived in the building adjacent to the one where Eberhardt and I had our new office—lived in a little room in the basement. Worked there, too, as a janitor and general handyman; the place was a small residence hotel for senior citizens, mostly male, called the Medford. So it didn't take long for our paths to cross. A week or so after Eb and I moved in, I was coming up the street one morning and Nick popped out of the alley that separated our two buildings.

He said, "I know you—you've got a speck on your coat," and out came the whisk broom. Industriously he brushed away the imaginary speck. Then he grinned and said, "Skeleton rattle your mouldy leg."

"Huh?"

"That's poetry," he said. "From *archy and mehitabel.* You know archy and mehitabel?"

"No," I said, "I don't."

"They're lower case; they don't have capitals like we do. Archy's a cockroach and mehitabel's a cat and they were both poets in another life. A fellow named don marquis created them a long time ago. He's lower case too."

"Uh . . . I see."

SKELETON RATTLE YOUR MOULDY LEG ♠ 31

"One time mehitabel went to Paris," he said, "and took up with a tom cat named francy, who was once the poet Francois Villon, and they used to go to the catacombs late at night. They'd dance and sing among those old bones."

And he began to recite:

> *"prince if you pipe and plead and beg*
> *you may yet be crowned with a grisly kiss*
> *skeleton rattle your mouldy leg*
> *all men's lovers come to this"*

That was my first meeting with Nick Damiano; there were others over the next four months, none of which lasted more than five minutes. Skeletons came into all of them, in one way or another. Once he sang half a dozen verses of the old spiritual, "Dry Bones," in a pretty good baritone. Another time he quoted, " 'The Knight's bones are dust/And his good sword rust—/His Soul is with the saints, I trust.' " Later I looked it up and it was a rhyme from an obscure work by Coleridge. On the other days he made sly little comments: "Why, hello there, I knew it was you coming—I heard your bones chattering and clacking all the way down the street." And "Cleaned out your closet lately? Might be skeletons hiding in there." And "Sure is hot today. Sure would be fine to take off our skins and just sit around in our bones."

I asked one of the Medford's other residents, a guy named Irv Feinberg, why Nick seemed to have such a passion for skeletons. Feinberg didn't know; nobody knew, he said, because Nick wouldn't discuss it. He told me that Nick even owned a genuine skeleton, liberated from some medical facility, and that he kept it wired to the wall of his room and burned candles in its skull.

A screwball, this Nick Damiano—sure. But he did his work and did it well, and he was always cheerful and friendly, and he never gave anybody any trouble. Harmless old Nick. A happy whack, marching to the rhythm of dry old bones chattering and clacking together inside his head. Everybody in the neighborhood found him amusing, including me: San Francisco has always been proud of its characters, its kooks. Yeah, everyone liked old Nick.

Except that somebody *didn't* like him, after all.

Somebody took hold of a blunt instrument one raw November night, in that little basement room with the skeleton leering on from the wall, and beat Nick Damiano to death.

It was four days after the murder that Irv Feinberg came to see me. He was a rotund little guy in his sixties, very energetic, a retired plumber who wore loud sports coats and spent most of his time doping out the races at Golden Gate Fields and a variety of other tracks. He had known Nick as well as anyone could, had called him his friend.

I was alone in the office when Feinberg walked in; Eberhardt was down at the Hall of Justice, trying to coerce some of his former cop pals into giving him background information on a missing-person case he was working. Feinberg said by way of greeting, "Nice office you got here," which was a lie, and came over and plopped himself into one of the clients' chairs. "You busy? Or you got a few minutes we can talk?"

"What can I do for you, Mr. Feinberg?"

"The cops have quit on Nick's murder," he said. "They don't come around anymore, they don't talk to anybody in the hotel. I called down to the Hall of Justice, I wanted to know what's happening. I got the big runaround."

"The police don't quit this fast on a homicide investigation—"

"The hell they don't. A guy like Nick Damiano? It's no big deal to them. They figure it was somebody looking for easy money, a drug addict from over in the Tenderloin. On account of Dan Cady, he's the night clerk, found the door to the alley unlocked just after he found Nick's body."

"That sounds like a reasonable theory," I said.

"Reasonable, hell. The door wasn't tampered with or anything; it was just unlocked. So how'd the drug addict get in? Nick wouldn't have left that door unlocked; he was real careful about things like that. And he wouldn't have let a stranger in, not at that time of night."

"Well, maybe the assailant came in through the front entrance and went out through the alley door. . . ."

"No way," Feinberg said. "Front door's on a night security lock from eight o'clock on; you got to buzz the desk from outside and Dan Cady'll come see who you are. If he don't know you, you don't get in."

"All right, maybe the assailant wasn't a stranger. Maybe he's somebody Nick knew."

"Sure, that's what I think. But not somebody outside the hotel. Nick never let people in at night, not anybody, not even somebody lives there; you had to go around to the front door and buzz the desk. Besides, he didn't have any outside friends that came to see him. He didn't go out himself either. He had to tend to the heat, for one thing, do other chores, so he stayed put. I know all that because I spent plenty of evenings with him, shooting craps for pennies. . . . Nick liked to shoot craps, he called it 'rolling dem bones.' "

Skeletons, I thought. I said, "What do you think then, Mr. Feinberg? That somebody from the hotel killed Nick?"

"That's what I think," he said. "I don't like it, most of those people are my friends, but that's how it looks to me."

"You have anybody specific in mind?"

"No. Whoever it was, he was in there arguing with Nick before he killed him."

"Oh? How do you know that?"

"George Weaver heard them. He's our newest tenant, George is, moved in three weeks ago. Used to be a bricklayer in Chicago, came out here to be with his daughter when he retired, only she had a heart attack and died last month. His other daughter died young and his wife died of cancer; now he's all alone." Feinberg shook his head. "It's a hell of a thing to be old and alone."

I agreed that it must be.

"Anyhow, George was in the basement getting something out of his storage bin and he heard the argument. Told Charley Slattery a while later that it didn't sound violent or he'd have gone over and banged on Nick's door. As it was, he just went back upstairs."

"Who's Charley Slattery?"

"Charley lives at the Medford and works over at Monahan's Gym on Turk Street. Used to be a small-time fighter; now he just hangs around doing odd jobs. Not too bright, but he's okay."

"Weaver didn't recognize the other voice in the argument?"

"No. Couldn't make out what it was all about either."

"What time was that?"

"Few minutes before eleven, George says."

"Did anyone else overhear the argument?"

"Nobody else around at the time."

"When was the last anybody saw Nick alive?"

"Eight o'clock. Nick came up to the lobby to fix one of the lamps wasn't working. Dan Cady talked to him a while when he was done."

"Cady found Nick's body around two A.M.?"

"Two-fifteen."

"How did he happen to find it? That wasn't in the papers."

"Well, the furnace was still on. Nick always shuts it off by midnight or it gets to be too hot upstairs. So Dan went down to find out why and there was Nick lying on the floor of his room with his head all beat in."

"What kind of guy is Cady?"

"Quiet, keeps to himself, spends most of his free time reading library books. He was a college history teacher once, up in Oregon. But he got in some kind of trouble with a woman—this was back in the forties, teachers had to watch their morals—and the college fired him and he couldn't get another teaching job. He fell into the booze for a lot of years afterward. But he's all right now. Belongs to AA."

I was silent for a time. Then I asked, "The police didn't find anything that made them suspect one of the other residents?"

"No, but that don't mean much." Feinberg made a disgusted noise through his nose. "Cops. They don't even know what it was bashed in Nick's skull, what kind of weapon. Couldn't find it anywhere. They figure the killer took it away through that unlocked alley door and got rid of it. I figure the killer unlocked the door to make it look like an outside job, then went upstairs and hid the weapon somewhere till next day."

"Let's suppose you're right. Who might have a motive to've killed Nick?"

"Well . . . nobody, far as I know. But *somebody's* got one, you can bet on that."

"Did Nick get along with everybody at the Medford?"

"Sure," Feinberg said. Then he frowned a little and said, "Except Wesley Thane, I guess. But I can't see Wes beating anybody's head in. He pretends to be tough but he's a wimp. And a goddamn snob."

"Oh?"

"He's an actor. Little theater stuff these days, but once he was a bit player down in Hollywood, made a lot of crappy B movies where he was one of the minor bad guys. Hear him tell it, he was Clark Gable's best friend back in the forties. A windbag who thinks he's better than the rest of us. He treated Nick like a freak."

"Was there ever any trouble between them?"

"Well, he hit Nick once, just after he moved in five years ago and Nick tried to brush off his coat. I was there and I saw it."

"Hit him with what?"

"His hand. A kind of slap. Nick shied away from him after that."

"How about recent trouble?"

"Not that I know about. I didn't even have to noodge him into kicking in twenty bucks to the fund. But hell, everybody in the building kicked in something except old lady Howsam; she's bedridden and can barely make ends meet on her pension, so I didn't even ask her."

I said, "Fund?"

Feinberg reached inside his gaudy sport jacket and produced a bulky envelope. He put the envelope on my desk and pushed it toward me with the tips of his fingers. "There's two hundred bucks in there," he said. "What'll that hire you for? Three-four days?"

I stared at him. "Wait a minute, Mr. Feinberg. Hire me to do what?"

"Find out who killed Nick. What do you think we been talking about here?"

"I thought it was only talk you came for. A private detective can't investigate a homicide in this state, not without police permission. . . ."

"So get permission," Feinberg said. "I told you, the cops have quit on it. Why should they try to keep you from investigating?"

"Even if I did get permission, I doubt if there's much I could do that the police haven't already—"

"Listen, don't go modest on me. You're a good detective, I see your name in the papers all the time. I got confidence in you; we all do. Except maybe the guy who killed Nick."

There was no arguing him out of it; his mind was made up, and he'd convinced the others in the Medford to go along with him. So I quit trying finally and said all right, I would call the Hall of Justice and see if I could get clearance to conduct a private investigation. And if I could, then I'd come over later and see him and take a look around and start talking to people. That satisfied him. But when I pushed the envelope back across the desk, he wouldn't take it.

"No," he said, "that's yours, you just go ahead and earn it." And he was on his feet and gone before I could do anything more than make a verbal protest.

I put the money away in the lock-box in my desk and telephoned the Hall. Eberhardt was still hanging around, talking to one of his old cronies in General Works, and I told him about Feinberg and what he wanted. Eb said he'd talk to the homicide inspector in charge of the Nick Damiano case and see what was what; he didn't seem to think there'd be any problem getting clearance. There were problems, he said, only when private eyes tried to horn in on VIP cases, the kind that got heavy media attention.

He used to be a homicide lieutenant so he knew what he was talking about. When he called back a half hour later he said, "You got your clearance. Feinberg had it pegged: the case is already in the Inactive File for lack of leads and evidence. I'll see if I can finagle a copy of the report for you."

Some case, I thought as I hung up. In a way it was ghoulish, like poking around in a fresh grave. And wasn't that an appropriate image; I could almost hear Nick's sly laughter.

Skeleton rattle your mouldy leg.

The basement of the Medford Hotel was dimly lighted and too warm: a big, old-fashioned oil furnace rattled and roared in one corner, giving off shimmers of heat. Much of the floor space was taken up with fifty-gallon trash receptacles, some full and some empty and one each under a pair of garbage chutes from the upper floors. Over against the far wall, and throughout a small connecting room beyond, were rows of narrow storage cubicles made out of wood and heavy wire, with padlocks on each of the doors.

Nick's room was at the rear, opposite the furnace and alongside the room that housed the hot-water heaters. But Feinberg didn't take me there directly; he said something I didn't catch, mopping his face with a big green handkerchief, and detoured over to the furnace and fiddled with the controls and got it shut down.

"Damn thing," he said. "Owner's too cheap to replace it with a modern unit that runs off a thermostat. Now we got some young snot he hired to take Nick's job, don't live here and don't stick around all day and leaves the furnace turned on too long. It's like a goddamn sauna in here."

There had been a police seal on the door to Nick's room, but it had been officially removed. Feinberg had the key; he was a sort of building mayor, by virtue of seniority—he'd lived at the Medford for more than fifteen years—and he had got custody of the key from the owner. He opened the lock, swung the thick metal door open, and clicked on the lights.

The first thing I saw was the skeleton. It hung from several pieces of shiny wire on the wall opposite the door, and it was a grisly damned thing streaked with blobs of red and green and orange candle wax. The top of the skull had been cut off and a fat red candle jutted up from the hollow inside, like some sort of ugly growth. Melted wax rimmed and dribbled from the grinning mouth, giving it a bloody look.

"Cute, ain't it?" Feinberg said. "Nick and his frigging skeletons."

I moved inside. It was just a single room with a bathroom alcove, not more than fifteen feet square. Cluttered, but in a way that suggested everything had been assigned a place. Army cot against one wall, a small table, two chairs, one of those little waist-high refrigerators with a hot plate on top, a standing cupboard full of pots and dishes; stacks of newspapers and magazines, some well-used books—volumes of poetry, an anatomical text, two popular histories about ghouls and grave-robbers, a dozen novels with either "skeleton" or "bones" in the title; a broken wooden wagon, a Victrola without its ear-trumpet amplifier, an ancient Olivetti typewriter, a collection of oddball tools, a scabrous iron-bound steamer trunk, an open box full of assorted pairs of dice, and a lot of other stuff, most of which appeared to be junk.

A thick fiber mat covered the floor. On it, next to the table, was the chalked outline of Nick's body and some dark stains. My stomach kicked a little when I looked at the stains; I had seen corpses of bludgeon victims and I knew what those stains looked like when they were fresh. I went around the table on the other side and took a closer look at the wax-caked skeleton. Feinberg tagged along at my heels.

"Nick used to talk to that thing," he said. "Ask it questions, how it was feeling, could he get it anything to eat or drink. Gave me the willies at first. He even put his arm around it once and kissed it, I swear to God. I can still see him do it."

"He got it from a medical facility?"

"One that was part of some small college he worked at before he came to San Francisco. He mentioned that once."

"Did he say where the college was?"

"No."

"Where did Nick come from? Around here?"

Feinberg shook his head. "Midwest somewhere, that's all I could get out of him."

"How long had he been in San Francisco?"

"Ten years. Worked here the last eight; before that, he helped out at a big apartment house over on Geary."

"Why did he come to the city? Did he have relatives here or what?"

"No, no relatives, he was all alone. Just him and his bones—he said that once."

I poked around among the clutter of things in the room, but if there had been anything here relevant to the murder, the police would have found it and probably removed it and it would be mentioned in their report. So would anything found among Nick's effects that determined his background. Eberhardt would have a copy of the report for me to look at later; when he said he'd try to do something he usually did it.

When I finished with the room we went out and Feinberg locked the door. We took the elevator up to the lobby. It was dim up there, too—and a little depressing. There was a lot of plaster and wood and imitation marble, and some antique furniture and dusty potted plants, and it smelled of dust and faintly of decay. A sense of age permeated the place: you felt it and you smelled it and you saw it in the surroundings, in the half-dozen men and one woman sitting on the sagging chairs, reading or staring out through the windows at O'Farrell Street, people with nothing to do and nobody to do it with, waiting like doomed prisoners for the sentence of death to be carried out. Dry witherings and an aura of hopelessness—that was the impression I would carry away with me and that would linger in my mind.

I thought: I'm fifty-four, another few years and I could be stuck in here too. But that wouldn't happen. I had work I could do pretty much to the end and I had Kerry and I had some money in the bank and a collection of 6500 pulp magazines that were worth plenty on the collectors' market. No, this kind of place wouldn't happen to me. In a society that ignored and showed little respect for its elderly, I was one of the lucky ones.

Feinberg led me to the desk and introduced me to the day clerk, a sixtyish barrel of a man named Bert Norris. If there was anything he could do to help, Norris said, he'd be glad to oblige; he sounded eager, as if nobody had needed his help in a long time. The fact that Feinberg had primed everyone here about my investigation made things easier in one respect and more difficult in another. If the person who had killed Nick Damiano *was* a resident of the Medford, I was not likely to catch him off guard.

When Norris moved away to answer a switchboard call, Feinberg asked me, "Who're you planning to talk to now?"

"Whoever's available," I said.

"Dan Cady? He lives here—two-eighteen. Goes to the library every morning after he gets off, but he's always back by noon. You can probably catch him before he turns in."

"All right, good."

"You want me to come along?"

"That's not necessary, Mr. Feinberg."

"Yeah, I get it. I used to hate that kind of thing too when I was out on a plumbing job."

"What kind of thing?"

"Somebody hanging over my shoulder, watching me work. Who needs crap like that? You want me, I'll be in my room with the scratch sheets for today's races."

Dan Cady was a thin, sandy-haired man in his mid-sixties, with cheeks and nose road-mapped by ruptured blood vessels—the badge of the alcoholic, practicing or reformed. He wore thick glasses, and behind them his eyes had a strained, tired look, as if from too much reading.

"Well, I'll be glad to talk to you," he said, "but I'm afraid I'm not very clear-headed right now. I was just getting ready for bed."

"I won't take up much of your time, Mr. Cady."

He let me in. His room was small and strewn with library books, most of which appeared to deal with American history; a couple of big maps, an old one of the United States and an even older parchment map of Asia, adorned the walls, and there were plaster busts of historical figures I didn't recognize, and a huge globe on a wooden stand. There was only one chair; he let me have that and perched himself on the bed.

I asked him about Sunday night, and his account of how he'd come to find Nick Damiano's body coincided with what Feinberg had told me. "It was a frightening experience," he said. "I'd never seen anyone dead by violence before. His head . . . well, it was awful."

"Were there signs of a struggle in the room?"

"Yes, some things were knocked about. But I'd say it was a brief struggle—there wasn't much damage."

"Is there anything unusual you noticed? Something that should have been there but wasn't, for instance?"

"No. I was too shaken to notice anything like that."

"Was Nick's door open when you got there?"

"Wide open."

"How about the door to the alley?"

"No. Closed."

"How did you happen to check it, then?"

"Well, I'm not sure," Cady said. He seemed faintly embarrassed; his eyes didn't quite meet mine. "I was stunned and frightened; it occurred to me that the murderer might still be around somewhere. I took a quick look around the basement and then opened the alley door and looked out there . . . . I wasn't thinking very clearly. It was only when I shut the door again that I realized it had been unlocked."

"Did you see or hear anything inside or out?"

"Nothing. I left the door unlocked and went back to the lobby to call the police."

"When you saw Nick earlier that night, Mr. Cady, how did he seem to you?"

"Seem? Well, he was cheerful; he usually was. He said he'd have come up sooner to fix the lamp but his old bones wouldn't allow it. That was the way he talked. . . ."

"Yes, I know. Do you have any idea who he might have argued with that night, who might have killed him?"

"None," Cady said. "He was such a gentle soul . . . I still can't believe a thing like that could happen to him."

Down in the lobby again, I asked Bert Norris if Wesley Thane, George Weaver, and Charley Slattery were on the premises. Thane was, he said, Room 315; Slattery was at Monahan's Gym and would be until six o'clock. He started to tell me that Weaver was out, but then his eyes shifted past me and he said, "No, there he is now just coming in."

I turned. A heavyset, stooped man of about seventy had just entered from the street, walking with the aid of a hickory cane; but he seemed to get along pretty good. He was carrying a grocery sack in his free hand and a folded newspaper under his arm.

I intercepted him halfway to the elevator and told him who I was. He looked me over for about ten seconds, out of alert blue eyes that had gone a little rheumy, before he said, "Irv Feinberg said you'd be around." His voice was surprisingly strong and clear for a man his age. "But I can't help you much. Don't know much."

"Should we talk down here or in your room?"

"Down here's all right with me."

We crossed to a deserted corner of the lobby and took chairs in front of a fireplace that had been boarded up and painted over. Weaver got a stubby little pipe out of his coat pocket and began to load up.

I said, "About Sunday night, Mr. Weaver. I understand you went down to the basement to get something out of your storage locker. . . ."

"My old radio," he said. "New one I bought a while back quit playing and I like to listen to the eleven o'clock news before I go to sleep. When I got down there I heard Damiano and some fella arguing."

"Just Nick and one other man?"

"Sounded that way."

"Was the voice familiar to you?"

"Didn't sound familiar. But I couldn't hear it too well; I was over by the lockers. Couldn't make out what they were saying either."

"How long were you in the basement?"

"Three or four minutes, is all."

"Did the argument get louder, more violent, while you were there?"

"Didn't seem to. No." He struck a kitchen match and put the flame to the bowl of his pipe. "If it had I guess I'd've gone over and banged on the door, announced myself. I'm as curious as the next man when it comes to that."

"But as it was you went straight back to your room?"

"That's right. Ran into Charley Slattery when I got out of the elevator; his room's just down from mine on the third floor."

"What was his reaction when you told him what you'd heard?"

"Didn't seem to worry him much," Weaver said. "So I figured it was nothing for me to worry about either."

"Slattery didn't happen to go down to the basement himself, did he?"

"Never said anything about it if he did."

I don't know what I expected Wesley Thane to be like—the Raymond Massey or John Carradine type, maybe, something along those shabbily aristocratic and vaguely sinister lines—but the man who opened the door to Room 315 looked about as much like an actor as I do. He was a smallish guy in his late sixties, he was bald, and he had a nondescript face except for mean little eyes under thick black brows that had no doubt contributed to his career as a B-movie villain. He looked somewhat familiar, but even though I like old movies and watch them whenever I can, I couldn't have named a single film he had appeared in.

He said, "Yes? What is it?" in a gravelly, staccato voice. That was familiar, too, but again I couldn't place it in any particular context.

I identified myself and asked if I could talk to him about Nick Damiano. "That cretin," he said, and for a moment I thought he was going to shut the door in my face. But then he said, "Oh, all right, come in. If I don't talk to you, you'll probably think I had something to do with the poor fool's murder."

He turned and moved off into the room, leaving me to shut the door. The room was larger than Dan Cady's and jammed with stage and screen memorabilia: framed photographs, playbills, film posters, blown-up black-and-white stills; and a variety of salvaged props, among them the plumed helmet off a suit of armor and a Napoleonic uniform displayed on a dressmaker's dummy.

Thane stopped near a lumpy-looking couch and did a theatrical about-face. The scowl he wore had a practiced look, and it occurred to me that under it he might be enjoying himself. "Well?" he said.

I said, "You didn't like Nick Damiano, did you, Mr. Thane," making it a statement instead of a question.

"No, I didn't like him. And no, I didn't kill him, if that's your next question."

"Why didn't you like him?"

"He was a cretin. A gibbering moron. All that nonsense about skeletons—he ought to have been locked up long ago."

"You have any idea who did kill him?"

"No. The police seem to think it was a drug addict."

"That's one theory," I said. "Irv Feinberg has another: he thinks the killer is a resident of this hotel."

"I know what Irv Feinberg thinks. He's a damned meddler who doesn't know when to keep his mouth shut."

"You don't agree with him then?"

"I don't care one way or another."

Thane sat down and crossed his legs and adopted a sufferer's pose; now he was playing the martyr. I grinned at him, because it was something he wasn't expecting, and went to look at some of the stuff on the walls. One of the black-and-white stills depicted Thane in Western garb, with a smoking six-gun in his hand. The largest of the photographs was of Clark Gable, with an ink inscription that read, "For my good friend, Wes."

Behind me he said impatiently, "I'm waiting."

I let him wait a while longer. Then I moved back near the couch and grinned at him again and said, "Did you see Nick Damiano the night he was murdered?"

"I did not."

"Talk to him at all that day?"

"No."

"When was the last you had trouble with him?"

"Trouble? What do you mean, trouble?"

"Irv Feinberg told me you hit Nick once, when he tried to brush off your coat."

"My God," Thane said, "that was years ago. And it was only a slap. I had no problems with him after that. He avoided me and I ignored him; we spoke only when necessary." He paused, and his eyes got bright with something that might have been malice. "If you're looking for someone who had trouble with Damiano recently, talk to Charley Slattery."

"What kind of trouble did Slattery have with Nick?"

"Ask him. It's none of my business."

"Why did you bring it up then?"

He didn't say anything. His eyes were still bright.

"All right, I'll ask Slattery," I said. "Tell me, what did you think when you heard about Nick? Were you pleased?"

"Of course not. I was shocked. I've played many violent roles in my career, but violence in real life always shocks me."

"The shock must have worn off pretty fast. You told me a couple of minutes ago you don't care who killed him."

"Why should I, as long as no one else is harmed?"

"So why did you kick in the twenty dollars?"

"What?"

"Feinberg's fund to hire me. Why did you contribute?"

"If I hadn't it would have made me look suspicious to the others. I have to live with these people; I don't need that sort of stigma." He gave me a smug look. "And if you repeat that to anyone, I'll deny it."

"Must be tough on you," I said.

"I beg your pardon?"

"Having to live in a place like this, with a bunch of broken-down old nobodies who don't have your intelligence or compassion or great professional skill."

That got to him; he winced, and for a moment the actor's mask slipped and I had a glimpse of the real Wesley Thane—a defeated old man with faded dreams of glory, a never-was with a small and mediocre talent, clinging to the tattered fringes of a business that couldn't care less. Then he got the mask in place again and said with genuine anger, "Get out of here. I don't have to take abuse from a cheap gumshoe."

"You're dating yourself, Mr. Thane; nobody uses the word 'gumshoe' any more. It's forties B-movie dialogue."

He bounced up off the couch, pinch-faced and glaring. "Get out, I said. Get out!"

I got out. And I was on my way to the elevator when I realized why Thane hadn't liked Nick Damiano. It was because Nick had taken attention away from him—upstaged him. Thane was an actor, but there wasn't any act he could put on more compelling than the real-life performance of Nick and his skeletons.

Monahan's Gym was one of those tough, men-only places that catered to ex-pugs and oldtimers in the fight game, the kind of place you used to see a lot of in the forties and fifties but that have become an anachronism in this day of chic health clubs, fancy spas, and dwindling interest in the art of prizefighting. It smelled of sweat and steam and old leather, and it resonated with the grunts of weightlifters, the smack and thud of gloves against leather bags, the profane talk of men at liberty from a more or less polite society.

I found Charley Slattery in the locker room, working there as an attendant. He was a short, beefy guy, probably a light-heavyweight in his boxing days, gone to fat around the middle in his old age; white-haired, with a face as seamed and time-eroded as a chunk of desert sandstone. One of his eyes had a glassy look; his nose and mouth were lumpy with scar tissue. A game fighter in his day, I thought, but not a very good one. A guy who had never quite learned how to cover up against the big punches, the hammerblows that put you down and out.

"Sure, I been expectin you," he said when I told him who I was. "Irv Feinberg, he said you'd be around. You findin out anything the cops dint?"

"It's too soon to tell, Mr. Slattery."

"Charley," he said, "I hate that Mr. Slattery crap."

"All right, Charley."

"Well, I wish I could tell you somethin would help you, but I can't think of nothin. I dint even see Nick for two-three days before he was murdered."

"Any idea who might have killed him?"

"Well, some punk off the street, I guess. Guy Nick was arguin with that night—George Weaver, he told you about that, dint he? What he heard?"

"Yes. He also said he met you upstairs just afterward."

Slattery nodded. "I was headin down the lobby for a Coke, they got a machine down there, and George, he come out of the elevator with his cane and this little radio unner his arm. He looked kind of funny and I ast him what's the matter and that's when he told me about the argument."

"What did you do then?"

"What'd I do? Went down to get my Coke."

"You didn't go to the basement?"

"Nah, damn it. George, he said it was just a argument Nick was havin with somebody. I never figured it was nothin, you know, violent. If I had—Yeah, Eddie? You need somethin?"

A muscular black man in his mid-thirties, naked except for a pair of silver-blue boxing trunks, had come up. He said, "Towel and some soap, Charley. No soap in the showers again."

"Goddamn. I catch the guy keeps swipin it," Slattery said, "I'll kick his ass." He went and got a clean towel and a bar of soap, and the black man moved off with them to a back row of lockers. Slattery watched him go; then he said to me, "That's Eddie Jordan. Pretty fair welterweight once, but he never trained right, never had the right manager. He could of been good, that boy, if—" He broke off, frowning. "I shouldn't ought to call him that, I guess. 'Boy.' Blacks, they don't like to be called that nowadays."

"No," I said, "they don't."

"But I don't mean nothin by it. I mean, we always called em 'boy,' it was just somethin we called em. 'Nigger,' too, same thing. It wasn't nothin personal, you know?"

I knew, all right, but it was not something I wanted to or ever could explain to Charley Slattery. Race relations, the whole question of race, was too complex an issue. In his simple world, "nigger" and "boy" were just words, meaningless words without a couple of centuries of hatred and malice behind them, and it really wasn't anything personal.

"Let's get back to Nick," I said. "You liked him, didn't you, Charley?"

"Sure I did. He was goofy, him and his skeletons, but he worked hard and he never bothered nobody."

"I had a talk with Wesley Thane a while ago. He told me you had some trouble with Nick not long ago."

Slattery's eroded face arranged itself into a scowl. "That damn actor, he don't know what he's talkin about. Why don't he mind his own damn business? I never had no trouble with Nick."

"Not even a little? A disagreement of some kind, maybe?"

He hesitated. Then he shrugged and said, "Well, yeah, I guess we had that. A kind of disagreement."

"When was this?"

"I dunno. Couple of weeks ago."

"What was it about?"

"Garbage," Slattery said.

"Garbage?"

"Nick, he dint like nobody touching the cans in the basement. But hell, I was in there one night and the cans unner the chutes was full, so I switched em for empties. Well, Nick come around and yelled at me, and I wasn't feelin too good so I yelled back at him. Next thing, I got sore and kicked over one of the cans and spilled out some garbage. Dan Cady, he heard the noise clear up in the lobby and come down and that son of a bitch Wes Thane was with him. Dan, he got Nick and me calmed down. That's all there was to it."

"How were things between you and Nick after that?"

"Okay. He forgot it and so did I. It dint mean nothin. It was just one of them things."

"Did Nick have problems with any other people in the hotel?" I asked.

"Nah. I don't think so."

"What about Wes Thane? He admitted he and Nick didn't get along very well."

"I never heard about them havin no fight or anythin like that."

"How about trouble Nick might have had with somebody outside the Medford?"

"Nah," Slattery said. "Nick, he got along with everybody, you know? Everybody liked Nick, even if he was goofy."

Yeah, I thought, everybody liked Nick, even if he was goofy. Then why is he dead?

I went back to the Medford and talked with three more residents, none of whom could offer any new information or any possible answers to that question of motive. It was almost five when I gave it up for the day and went next door to the office.

Eberhardt was there, but I didn't see him at first because he was on his hands and knees behind his desk. He poked his head up as I came inside and shut the door.

"Fine thing," I said, "you down on your knees like that. What if I'd been a prospective client?"

"So? I wouldn't let somebody like you hire me."

"What're you doing down there anyway?"

"I was cleaning my pipe and I dropped the damn bit." He disappeared again for a few seconds, muttered, "Here it is," reappeared, and hoisted himself to his feet.

There were pipe ashes all over the front of his tie and his white shirt; he'd even managed to get a smear of ash across his jowly chin. He was something of a slob, Eberhardt was, which gave us one of several common bonds: I was something of a slob myself. We had been friends for more than thirty years, and we'd been through some hard times together—some very hard times in the recent past. I hadn't been sure at first that taking him in as a partner after his retirement was a good idea, for a variety of reasons; but it had worked out so far.

He sat down and began brushing pipe dottle off his desk—he must have dropped a bowlful on it as well as on himself. He said as I hung up my coat, "How goes the Nick Damiano investigation?"

"Not too good. Did you manage to get a copy of the police report?"

"On your desk. But I don't think it'll tell you much."

The report was in an unmarked manila envelope; I read it standing up. Eberhardt was right that it didn't enlighten me much. Nick Damiano had been struck on the head at least three times by a heavy blunt instrument and had died of a brain hemorrhage, probably within seconds of the first blow. The wounds were "consistent with" a length of three-quarter-inch steel pipe, but the weapon hadn't been positively identified because no trace of it had been found. As for Nick's background, nothing had been found there either. No items of personal history among his effects, no hint of relatives or even of his city of origin. They'd run a check on his fingerprints through the FBI computer, with negative results: he had never been arrested on a felony charge; never been in military service or applied for a civil service job, never been fingerprinted at all.

When I put the report down Eberhardt said, "Anything?"

"Doesn't look like it." I sat in my chair and looked out the window for a time, at heavy rainclouds massing above the Federal Building down the hill. "There's just nothing to go on in this thing, Eb—no real leads or suspects, no apparent motive."

"So maybe it's random. A street-killing, drug-related, like the report says."

"Maybe."

"You don't think so?"

"Our client doesn't think so."

"You want to talk over the details?"

"Sure. But let's do it over a couple of beers and some food."

"I thought you were on a diet."

"I am. Whenever Kerry's around. But she's working late tonight—new ad campaign she's writing. A couple of beers won't hurt me. And we'll have something non-fattening to eat."

"Sure we will," Eberhardt said.

We went to an Italian place out on Clement and had four beers apiece and plates of fettucine Alfredo and half a loaf of garlic bread. But the talking we did got us nowhere. If one of the residents of the Medford had killed Nick Damiano, what was the damn motive? A broken-down old actor's petulant jealousy? A mindless dispute over garbage cans? Just what *was* the argument all about that George Weaver had overheard?

Eberhardt and I split up early and I drove home to my flat on Pacific Heights. The place had a lonely feel; after spending most of the day in and around the Medford, I needed something to cheer me up—I needed Kerry. I thought about calling her at Bates and Carpenter, her ad agency, but she didn't like to be disturbed while she was working. And she'd said she expected to be there most of the evening.

I settled instead for cuddling up to my collection of pulp magazines—browsing here and there, finding something to read. On nights like this the pulps weren't much of a substitute for human companionship in general and Kerry in particular, but at least they kept my mind occupied. I found a 1943 issue of *Dime Detective* that looked interesting, took it into the bathtub, and lingered there reading until I got drowsy. Then I went to bed, went right to sleep for a change—

—and woke up at 3:00 A.M. by the luminous dial of the nightstand clock, because the clouds had finally opened up and unleashed a wailing torrent of wind-blown rain; the sound of it on the roof and on the rainspouts outside the window was loud enough to wake up a deaf man. I lay there half groggy, listening to the storm and thinking about how the weather had gone all screwy lately.

And then all of a sudden I was thinking about something else, and I I wasn't groggy anymore. I sat up in bed, wide awake. And inside of five minutes, without much effort now that I had been primed, I knew what it was the police had overlooked and I was reasonably sure I knew who had murdered Nick Damiano.

But I still didn't know why. I didn't have an inkling of why.

The Medford's front door was still on its night security lock when I got there at a quarter to eight. Dan Cady let me in. I asked him a couple of questions about Nick's janitorial habits, and the answers he gave me pretty much confirmed my suspicions. To make absolutely sure, I went down to the basement and spent ten minutes poking around in its hot and noisy gloom.

Now the hard part, the part I never liked. I took the elevator to the third floor and knocked on the door to Room 304. He was there; not more than five seconds passed before he called out, "Door's not locked." I opened it and stepped inside.

He was sitting in a faded armchair near the window, staring out at the rain and the wet streets below. He turned his head briefly to look at me, then turned it back again to the window. The stubby little pipe was between his teeth and the overheated air smelled of his tobacco, a kind of dry, sweet scent, like withered roses.

"More questions?" he said.

"Not exactly, Mr. Weaver. You mind if I sit down?"

"Bed's all there is."

I sat on the bottom edge of the bed, a few feet away from him. The room was small, neat—not much furniture, not much of anything; old patterned wallpaper and a threadbare carpet, both of which had a patina of gray. Maybe it was my mood and the rain-dull day outside, but the entire room seemed gray, full of that aura of age and hopelessness.

"Hot in here," I said. "Furnace is going full blast down in the basement."

"I don't mind it hot."

"Nick Damiano did a better job of regulating the heat, I understand. He'd turn it on for a few hours in the morning, leave it off most of the day, turn it back on in the evenings, and then shut it down again by midnight. The night he died, though, he didn't have time to shut it down."

Weaver didn't say anything.

"It's pretty noisy in the basement when that furnace is on," I said. "You can hardly hold a normal conversation with somebody standing right next to you. It'd be almost impossible to hear anything, even raised voices, from a distance. So you couldn't have heard an argument inside Nick's room, not from back by the storage lockers. And probably not even if you stood right next to the door, because the door's thick and made of metal."

He still didn't stir, didn't speak.

"You made up the argument because you ran into Charley Slattery. He might have told the police he saw you come out of the elevator around the time Nick was killed, and that you seemed upset; so you had to protect yourself. Just like you protected yourself by unlocking the alley door after the murder."

More silence.

"You murdered Nick, all right. Beat him to death with your cane—hickory like that is as thick and hard as three-quarter-inch steel pipe. Charley told me you had it under your arm when you got off the elevator. Why under your arm? Why weren't you walking with it like you usually do? Has to be that you didn't want your fingers around the handle, the part you clubbed Nick with, even if you did wipe off most of the blood and gore."

He was looking at me now, without expression—just a dull steady waiting look.

"How'd you clean the cane once you were here in your room? Soap and water? Cleaning fluid of some kind? It doesn't matter, you know. There'll still be minute traces of blood on it that the police lab can match up to Nick's."

He put an end to his silence then; he said in a clear, toneless voice, "All right. I done it," and that made it a little easier on both of us. The truth is always easier, no matter how painful it might be.

I said, "Do you want to tell me about it, Mr. Weaver?"

"Not much to tell," he said. "I went to the basement to get my other radio, like I told you before. He was fixing the door to one of the storage bins near mine. I looked at him up close, and I knew he was the one. I'd had a feeling he was ever since I moved in, but that night, up close like that, I knew it for sure."

He paused to take the pipe out of his mouth and lay it carefully on the table next to his chair. Then he said, "I accused him point blank. He put his hands over his ears like a woman, like he couldn't stand to hear it, and ran to his room. I went after him. Got inside before he could shut the door. He started babbling, crazy things about skeletons, and I saw that skeleton of his grinning across the room, and I . . . I don't know, I don't remember that part too good. He pushed me, I think, and I hit him with my cane, I kept hitting him. . . ."

His voice trailed off and he sat there stiffly, with his big gnarled hands clenched in his lap.

"*Why*, Mr. Weaver? You said he was the one, that you accused him— accused him of what?"

He didn't seem to hear me. He said, "After I come to my senses, I couldn't breathe. Thought I was having a heart attack. God, it was hot in there . . . hot as hell. I opened the alley door to get some air and I guess I must have left it unlocked. I never did that on purpose. Only the story about the argument."

"Why did you kill Nick Damiano?"

No answer for a few seconds; I thought he still wasn't listening and I was about to ask the question again. But then he said, "My Bible's over on the desk. Look inside the front cover."

The Bible was a well-used Gideon and inside the front cover was a yellowed newspaper clipping. I opened the clipping. It was from the Chicago *Sun-Times,* dated June 23, 1957—a news story, with an accompanying photograph, that bore the headline: FLOWER SHOP BOMBER IDENTIFIED.

I took it back to the bed and sat again to read it. It said that the person responsible for a homemade bomb that had exploded in a crowded florist shop the day before, killing seven people, was a handyman named Nicholas Donato. One of the dead was Marjorie Donato, the bomber's estranged wife and an employee of the shop; another victim was the shop's owner, Arthur Cullen, with whom Mrs. Donato had apparently been having an affair. According to friends, Nicholas Donato had been despondent over the estrangement and the affair, had taken to drinking heavily, and had threatened "to do something drastic" if his wife didn't move back in with him. He had disappeared the morning of the explosion and had not been apprehended at the time the news story was printed. His evident intention had been to blow up only his wife and her lover; but Mrs. Donato had opened the package containing the bomb immediately after it was brought by messenger, in the presence of several customers, and the result had been mass slaughter.

I studied the photograph of Nicholas Donato. It was a head-and-shoulders shot, of not very good quality, and I had to look at it closely for a time to see the likeness. But it was there: Nicholas Donato and Nick Damiano had been the same man.

Weaver had been watching me read. When I looked up from the clipping he said, "They never caught him. Traced him to Indianapolis, but then he disappeared for good. All these years, twenty-seven years, and I come across him here in San Francisco. Coincidence. Or maybe it was supposed to happen that way. The hand of the Lord guides us all, and we don't always understand the whys and wherefores."

"Mr. Weaver, what did that bombing have to do with you?"

"One of the people he blew up was my youngest daughter. Twenty-two that year. Went to that flowershop to pick out an arrangement for her wedding. I saw her after it happened, I saw what his bomb did to her . . . ."

He broke off again; his strong voice trembled a little now. But his eyes were dry. He'd cried once, he'd cried many times, but that had been long ago. There were no tears left any more.

I got slowly to my feet. The heat and the sweetish tobacco scent were making me feel sick to my stomach. And the grayness, the aura of age and hopelessness and tragedy were like an oppressive weight.

I said, "I'll be going now."

"Going?" he said. "Telephone's right over there."

"I won't be calling the police, Mr. Weaver. From here or from any-where else."

"What's that? But . . . you know I killed him. . . ."

"I don't know anything," I said. "I don't even remember coming here today."

I left him quickly, before he could say anything else, and went downstairs and out to O'Farrell Street. Wind-hurled rain buffeted me, icy and stinging, but the feel and smell of it was a relief. I pulled up the collar on my overcoat and hurried next door.

Upstairs in the office I took Irv Feinberg's two hundred dollars out of the lock-box in the desk and slipped the envelope into my coat pocket. He wouldn't like getting it back; he wouldn't like my calling it quits on the investigation, just as the police had done. But that didn't matter. Let the dead lie still, and the dying find what little peace they had left. The judgment was out of human hands anyway.

I tried not to think about Nick Damiano any more, but it was too soon and I couldn't blot him out yet. Harmless old Nick, the happy whack. Jesus Christ. Seven people—he had slaughtered seven people that day in 1957. And for what? For a lost woman; for a lost love. No wonder he'd gone batty and developed an obsession for skeletons. He had lived with them, seven of them, all those years, heard them clattering and clacking all those thousands of nights. And now, pretty soon, he would be one himself.

Skeleton rattle your mouldy leg.

All men's lovers come to this.

TWENTY MILES FROM PARADISE

WE were still twenty miles from Paradise when the skies opened up on us.

It was 7:30 on a Sunday evening in late October and Kerry and I had spent the afternoon driving around the Sierra Nevada up near Lake Almanor. The sun had been shining when we'd started out from Paradise just before noon, but the sky had begun to cloud up in mid-afternoon and the first rain had begun falling at half-past four. We'd have started back before that, and been in Paradise long since, except for the tire that had got punctured by some litterbug's broken beer bottle and the damn spare that had turned up just as flat. We'd had to wait for a good Samaritan to come along and take us into Almanor, and then wait to ride back out with a Triple-A truck and a new tire. The whole episode had cost us well over two hours and neither of us was in a very good mood. And then the rain had changed from a drizzle to a deluge so heavy the windshield wipers couldn't get rid of the water fast enough. I had to slow to twenty-five or run the risk of losing the car on one of the sharp turns in the two-lane mountain road.

Kerry said, "Oh God, just what we need. Can you see? It's just a blur out there to me."

"Barely."

"We'd better pull over until it lets up."

"No place to go."

"The first place we come to, then."

"Don't worry, we'll be all right."

"Some Sunday," she said irritably. "Some terrific weekend."

I had nothing to say to that. My temper was as short as hers and I did not want us to start bickering; the road and that silver curtain of rain took all my attention. But the truth was, it hadn't been such a bad getaway weekend until this afternoon. On Friday night we'd driven up to Paradise, a resort and retirement community in the Sierra foothills a dozen miles northeast of Chico, and taken a room in a first-class motel. The weather was good, with no early snow and no hint then of rain; it was the off-season so there weren't many other tourists; and we'd been having a pretty nice time eating out, exploring, making love.

Now we were paying for it.

The rain seemed to be coming down harder, if that were possible. It was like trying to drive under and through a seemingly endless waterfall. Close on both sides of the road, pine forest loomed black and indistinct; there wasn't even a turnout where I could pull off. I let our speed slacken to under twenty. At least there was no other traffic: we hadn't seen another car traveling in either direction in the past five minutes.

The night was pitch black except for the shimmer of our headlights against the rain. Or it was until we came around another curve. Kerry said, "Up ahead, look!"

Through the downpour I could make out the reds and blues of a neon sign, the squat shape of a single log and shake-roofed building set back at the edge of a clearing. There were lights in one of the front windows, and more neon that materialized as beer advertisements. The big sign on the roof said liquidly: *Kern's Woodland Tavern and Cafe.*

I eased the car off the highway, onto a deserted gravel parking area that fronted the building. There was nothing behind the place except more trees and an empty access road that vanished in among them. Directly in front was a pair of gas pumps: I stopped the car between them and the entrance to the tavern half, the part that was lighted. The other half, the cafe, had a *Closed* sign in its darkened window.

"The bar's open, at least," Kerry said. "Why don't we go in? I can use something hot to drink."

"Might as well. It's better than sitting here."

We ran to the tavern entrance, a distance of maybe ten feet; but we were both half-drenched by the time we pushed inside. Some hard rain, the kind you get only in the mountains and that might last anywhere from three minutes to thirty.

The tavern was one of those rustic country types, full of roughhewn furniture and deer heads; this one also had a big American flag stretched out across the wall that bisected the building, one made before Alaska and Hawaii were admitted to the Union because it had only forty-eight stars. A three-log fire blazed hotly in a nativestone fireplace. Near the window was a musicians' dais, empty now, and a scattering of maybe a dozen tables. Opposite was the bar, rough-hewn like the furnishings; on the wall behind it were a lot of little burnt-wood plaques that had cute sayings on them like *If You Don't Ask Us for Credit, We Won't Double the Price of Your Drinks.*

There were only two people in the place, both of them men. One, a middle-aged guy wearing a plaid shirt and a tight-fitting woolen hunter's hat, was passed out at one of the tables, his head cradled in both arms. The other man was upright and conscious, standing at the near end of the bar, on the customer side of it. He was a few years older than the drunk, short and wiry and pasty-faced; dressed in shirt and chinos and a loose-fitting barman's apron.

He came forward a few paces, hands on his hips, as Kerry and I entered and I shut the door against the force of the storm.

"Something I can do for you folks?"

"Lord, yes," Kerry said. "We need a drink. Another few minutes and we'd have drowned out there."

"You visitors in these parts?"

"Yes. We're staying in Paradise."

"Bad night to be out driving," the barman said. "Fact is, I was just about to close up and head home. Not many customers on a night like this."

"Close up? You're not going to send us back out in *that?*"

"Well . . ."

"We won't stay long," I said. "Just until the rain lets up enough so I can see where I'm driving."

"We *could* wait in the car," Kerry said, "but the heater's not working." Which was the kind of sneaky lie they teach you in the advertising business; the heater was working fine. "It's nice and warm in here."

The barman shrugged and said without much enthusiasm, "Guess it'll be all right. Supper'll wait a few more minutes."

Kerry smiled at him and went over to the fire. He moved to the door and locked it, just in case some other damn fools showed up out of the storm. I unbuttoned my coat, opened it up like a flasher to the room's warmth.

At the fire Kerry took off the wet paisley scarf she was wearing and fluffed out her thick auburn hair. The firelight made it shine like burnished copper. "I'll have a toddy," she said to the barman.

"Lady?"

"A hot toddy. A strong one."

"Oh. Sure."

I said, "Just a beer for me. Miller Lite."

The wiry guy moved around behind the plank. Outside, the rain was still hammering down with a vengeance; it sounded like a load of pebbles being dumped relentlessly on the tavern's roof. You could hear the wind skirling around in the eaves and rattling the windows, as if it, too, were seeking sanctuary from the storm.

"What was *he* celebrating?" Kerry asked the barman.

"What's that, lady?"

"Your other customer." She nodded at the drunk sprawled over the table.

"Oh, that's Clint Jackson. Good customer. He . . . well, he takes a little too much now and then. Got a drinking problem."

"I'll say he does. What are you going to do with him?"

"Do with him?"

"You're not going to let him sleep there all night, are you?"

"No, no. I'll get him sobered up. Wouldn't let him drive home in the shape he's in now."

"I should hope not."

"He can be a little mean when he's been drinking heavy," the barman said. That was directed at me because I had wandered over toward the drunk's table. The rasp of the man's breathing was audible from nearby, even with the pound of the rain. "Better just let him be."

"I won't disturb him, don't worry."

I turned over to the bar and sat on one of the green-leatherette stools and watched the barman set up Kerry's hot toddy and my beer. He asked me as he worked, "Where you folks from?"

"San Francisco."

"Long time since I been there. Fifteen years."

"It's changed. You wouldn't recognize parts of it."

"I guess not."

"You own this tavern, Mr.—?"

"Kern's my name, Sam Kern. Sure, I own it."

"Nice place. Had it long?"

"Twenty years."

"You live nearby do you?"

"Not far. House back in the woods a ways."

"Must be peaceful, out here in the middle of nowhere."

"Sure," he said. "The wife and I like it fine. Plenty of business in the summer, plenty of time to loaf in the winter."

"You don't stay open during the winter?"

"Nope. Close down the end of this month."

"Nope. Close down the end of this month."

Kerry came over from the fireplace, sat down next to me, took a sip of her hot toddy. And made a face and said, "Ugh. Rum."

"Something wrong, lady?"

"You made it with rum instead of bourbon. I hate rum."

"I did? Must've picked up the wrong bottle. Sorry, I'll mix you up another one."

He did that. When he brought the drink I laid a twenty-dollar bill on the bar. He looked at it and shook his head. "Afraid I can't change that, mister," he said. "Already closed up my register and put every dime in the safe. You wouldn't have anything smaller, would you?"

"No, I wouldn't."

"I've got some singles," Kerry said. "How much is it?"

"Three dollars."

She paid him out of her purse. He rang up the sale and put the singles in the empty cash drawer and shut it again. Pretty soon he moved down to the other end of the bar and began using a bar towel on some glasses.

A couple of minutes passed in silence, except for the noise of the rain on the roof. I glanced over at the drunk. He still had his head buried in his arms; he hadn't moved since we'd come in.

The steady drum of the rain began to diminish finally, and the wind quit howling and rattling the window panes. The wiry guy looked over at the front window, at the wet night beyond. "Letting up," he said. "You folks should be all right on the road now."

I finished the beer in my glass. "Drink up," I said to Kerry. "We'd better get moving."

"What if it's just a momentary lull?"

"I don't think it is. Come on, Mr. Kern wants to close up and go have his supper."

"All right."

She drank the last of her toddy, and when she was on her feet I took her arm and steered her to the door. The wiry guy came out from behind the plank and followed us, so he could lock the door again after we were gone. I let Kerry flip the lock over; as she did I half-turned back toward him.

He said, "Good night, folks, stop in again—" and that was when I hit him.

It was a sucker punch and he was wide open to it; the blow caught him just under the left eye, spun him and knocked him off his feet, sent him skidding on his backside toward the bar. Kerry let out a startled yell that got lost in the clatter of the guy hitting the bar stools; one of them fell over on top of him. He lay crumpled and unmoving against the brass rail, with the stool's cushion hiding part of his face.

Kerry said, "For God's sake, what did you do *that* for?" in horrified tones. "Have you lost your mind?"

I didn't answer her. Instead I went to where the guy lay and knelt down and got the gun out from where it was tucked inside his pants, under the apron. It was a .357 Magnum—a hell of a piece of artillery. Behind me, Kerry gasped when she saw it. I put it into the pocket of my coat without looking at her and felt the artery in the guy's neck to make sure he was still alive: I'd hit him pretty hard, hard enough to numb the first three fingers on my right hand. But he was all right, if you didn't count the blood leaking out of his nose, the bruise that was already forming on his cheek, and the fact that he was out cold.

Straightening again, flexing my sore hand, I crossed to where the drunk was draped over the table. Only he *wasn't* a drunk; when I took the hunter's hat off I could see the lump on the back of his head, the coagulating blood that matted his hair. I felt his neck the way I had the other guy's: his pulse was shallow but regular. But he was in worse shape than the wiry guy—the way that head wound looked, he had at least a concussion. He needed a doctor's attention, and soon.

Kerry was standing a few feet away gawping at me. I said to her, "Get on the phone, call the county sheriff. Tell them we need an ambulance. Tell them to hurry."

"I don't understand, what's going *on*—?"

"This man is the real Sam Kern, or at least somebody who works here," I said. "The one I hit is an impostor—probably either an escaped convict or a recent parolee. Tell the sheriff that, too."

"God," she said, but she didn't argue; she went straight to the phone behind the bar.

I took another look at the wiry guy. He hadn't moved an inch, and the way he was breathing satisfied me he was going to be out for some time. In the pocket of his chinos I found a wallet full of ID that identified it as Sam Kern's; but the photograph on the driver's license was that of the wounded man at the table.

I went out into the rain, got the set of emergency handcuffs I keep in the trunk of the car, took them back inside, and snapped one cuff around the wiry guy's wrist and the other around the brass rail. I was over looking at Sam Kern again when Kerry finished with her telephone call.

"They're sending people out right away," she said.

"Good. This is Kern, all right, and I think he'll be okay; but you can't tell with head injuries. We'd better just leave him where he is."

She wet a cloth and brought it over and laid it across Kern's neck without touching his wound. Her eyes were big and her cheeks had a milky cast; she still looked confused.

"How did you know?" she said.

"That the other guy was an impostor? Half a dozen reasons. You're always trying to play detective; how come *you* didn't spot them?"

"Don't kid around, you. What reasons?"

"All right. One, he told us he was just getting ready to close up and go home, yet there's a big log fire blazing in the fireplace. No tavern owner would stoke up a fire like that just before closing for the night.

"Two, he told us this man here was a regular customer and that he wouldn't let him drive home until he sobered up. But where's his car? It's not out front; the parking area was deserted when we drove in. There's no room for a car around back and there wasn't one on that access road either. Somebody must give the real Kern a ride to and from work.

"Three, the hat the real Kern was wearing. How many men sit in a bar and get drunk with their coat *off* but their hat still *on*? And not only on, but jammed down tight on his head. Had to be some reason for the hat—to hide something like that head wound.

"Four, you asked the other one for a toddy; he didn't know what you meant at first. Then he made it with rum instead of bourbon. Could have been a mistake, but that's not likely for a man who has been serving drinks at the same bar for twenty years; that man *knows* which bottle is which.

"Five, he said he couldn't change my twenty because he'd taken every dime out of the cash register and put it in the safe. And the drawer is empty, I saw it when you paid him. But what kind of businessman empties his cash drawer *before* he locks up for the night, when customers like us might still show up? And how many businessmen clean out their cash drawers completely? All the ones I know leave at least the change in there and most also leave a few singles, so they won't have to bother putting it all back the next day."

Kerry no longer looked confused; now she looked a little subdued.

"You said he's probably an escaped convict or a recent parolee. How could you possibly know that?"

"That's number six," I said. "The color of his skin, babe—it's white, pasty. No man who has lived in these mountains for twenty years, as hot as it gets up here in the summer, could have a complexion like that; the only people who do are shut-ins, hospital patients, and convicts."

"Oh," she said.

"I figure it happened something like this: He arrived here earlier tonight—hitchhiking, probably; which would make him a parolee, or else he'd have picked up his own set of wheels. He found himself alone with Kern and it was a set-up he couldn't resist. Maybe he had that .357 Magnum with him—more likely it belongs to Kern. In any case he used something hard to knock Kern over the head—out on this side of the bar, maybe while Kern was stoking the fire. Then he rifled the till. But he's not too smart, he forgot to lock the front door first.

"Then we showed up. When he saw our headlights through the window he didn't know who we might be. He could have done any of three things. Run and lock the door and pretend the place was closed—but what if we were friends or relatives of Kern's? What if we looked through the window in any event and saw Kern lying on the floor? His second alternative was to let us come in and throw down on us, rob us too and steal our car. But he didn't want to do it that way; it would only buy him more trouble. And he's not a killer, thank Christ, so that alternative was out. His only other choice was to find out if we were strangers—he asked about that right away, remember—and if we were, to run a bluff and get rid of us quick.

"He picked Kern up off the floor, draped him over the table, and shoved that hat down over his head to hide the wound. His own hat, maybe; it had to have been handy. Kern was probably wearing the apron, so all he had to do was yank it off and tie it around himself to cover the gun inside his belt. All of that wouldn't have taken more than thirty seconds—less time than it took us to stop the car, get out, and come inside."

Kerry was silent for a space of time. Then she asked, "You didn't know he had that gun, did you? Before you hit him?"

"Sure I did. It made a bulge under his apron when he moved around. Didn't you notice it?"

"Well," she said, "I . . . um, I guess I did, when we first came in. But I thought . . . I mean, I didn't look again because . . .

"Because why?"

"I thought . . . oh hell, I thought something had aroused him."

"*Aroused* him?"

"I thought he had a damn erection, all right?"

I looked at her. And then I burst out laughing.

"Oh shut up," she said.

I was still chuckling when the sheriff's deputies and a county ambulance got there a few minutes later.

ACE IN THE HOLE

I WAS twenty minutes late to the poker game that Friday night, but the way Eberhardt and the other three looked at me when I came in, you'd have thought I was two hours late and had sprouted tentacles besides. The four of them were grouped around the table in Eberhardt's living room—Eb, Barney Rivera, Jack Logan, and Joe DeFalco—and I could feel their eyes on me as I shrugged out of my overcoat and took the one empty chair. I put twenty dollars on the table and said, "All right, who's banking?"

I said, "Well? Come on, you guys, are we going to play poker or what?"

I said, "For Christ's sake, why do you keep *staring* at me like that?"

"You're on the spot, pal," DeFalco said, and grinned all over his blocky face. He was a reporter for the *Chronicle,* but he didn't look like a reporter; nor, for that matter, did he look Italian. He looked like Pat O'Brien playing Father Jerry in *Angels with Dirty Faces.* People told him things they wouldn't tell anybody else.

"Meaning what?"

"Meaning Eb and Barney have a hot bet on you. Your exalted reputation as a detective is on the line."

"What the hell are you talking about?"

Eberhardt said, "I bet Barney twenty bucks you can make sense out of the Gallatin thing within twenty-four hours."

"What Gallatin thing?"

"The shooting this noon. Jack's baby. Don't tell me you didn't hear about it?"

"As a matter of fact, I didn't."

"You see, Eb?" Barney Rivera said. He was a tubby little Chicano, Barney, with a mop of unruly black hair, big doe eyes, a fondness for peppermints, and a way with women that was as uncanny as it was unlikely. He didn't look like what *he* was, either: chief claims adjuster for the San Francisco branch of Great Western Insurance. "Your partner just won't read the newspapers or listen to news programs. When it comes to current events, he lives with his head in a hole like an ostrich."

I told him which hole he could put his head in. Everybody laughed, including Barney. He's not a bad guy; he just likes to use the needle. But he's got a sense of humor, and he can take it as well as dish it out.

Jack Logan hadn't said anything, so I turned to him. He was in his mid-fifties, Eberhardt's and my age—a quiet, hard-working career cop who had been promoted to lieutenant when Eberhardt retired a couple of years ago. Now that I was looking at him up close, I saw that he seemed a little worn around the edges tonight.

"What's this all about, Jack?"

He sighed. "Frank Gallatin . . . you know who he is, don't you?"

"Westate Trucking?"

"Right. This morning we thought we finally had him nailed on racketeering and extortion charges, maybe even a mob connection. This afternoon we thought we had him nailed on something even better—a one-eight-seven. Tonight we don't have him on either score."

One-eight-seven is police slang for willful homicide, as defined in Section 187 of the California Penal Code. I said, "Why not?"

"Because even though we know damned well he shot an accountant named Lamar Trent a little past noon," Logan said, "we can't prove it. We can't find the gun he used. Nor can we find an incriminating file we know—or at least are pretty sure—Trent had in his possession earlier. Without the file, now that Trent is dead, the D.A. can't indict Gallatin on the racketeering and extortion charges. And without the gun, Gallatin's cockamamie version of the shooting stands up by default."

"How come you're so positive he killed this Trent?"

"I was there when he did it. So was Ben Klein. Not fifty feet away, outside Trent's locked office door. We piled in on Gallatin inside of fifteen seconds; there's no way he could have got the gun out of the office in that length of time, just no way. Only it wasn't anywhere *in* the office when we searched the place. And I mean we did everything but pry up the floorboards and strip the plaster off the walls."

"Just your kind of case, paisan," Eberhardt said happily. "Locked doors, disappearing guns—screwball stuff."

I gave him a look. There were times, like right now, when I was sorry I'd taken him into my agency as a full partner. "Thanks a lot."

"Well, you've worked on this kind of thing before. You're good at it."

"Not good," Barney the Needle said, "just lucky. But this one's a pip. If the rest of us can't figure it, neither can he."

"Hey," I said, "I came here for poker, not abuse."

"So you're not even interested, huh?" DeFalco asked. He was still grinning. But behind the grin and his Father Jerry facade, his journalistic zeal was showing; his interest in all of this was strictly professional.

"Did I say I wasn't interested?"

"Ah," he said. "I thought so."

Rivera said, "Wait until you hear the rest of the story," and rubbed his pudgy hands together in exaggerated anticipation.

"I'm sure I'll hang on every word."

Eberhardt was firing up one of his smelly pipes. "So am I," he said between puffs. "Jack, lay it out for him."

I said, "All right, but can we play cards while I'm listening?"

Nobody objected to that. So we played a few hands of five-card stud, none of which I won, while Logan told the story. It was a pip, all right. And in spite of myself, just as Eberhardt had predicted, I was hooked from the start.

This morning, one of the SFPD's battery of informants had come through with the tip that Lamar Trent was Gallatin's private accountant —a fact that Gallatin had managed to keep an ironbound secret until now. The word was that Gallatin and Trent had had a falling out, either over money or some of the nastier aspects of Gallatin's operation, and that Trent had grown so afraid of his employer he might be willing to sell him out in exchange for police protection and immunity. And what he had to sell was a complete and documented file on Westate Trucking's illegal enterprises, which it was rumored he kept in his office safe.

So as soon as they got the tip, around noon, Logan and Ben Klein had gone over to the Wainright Building, a relic of better days on lower Market, for a talk with Trent. When they came into the lobby, they found both of the ancient and sometimes unreliable elevators in use; instead of waiting they took the stairs up, since Trent's office was only one flight up. They were moving along the empty second-floor hallway when they heard the shot.

"It came from inside Trent's office," Jack said, "there isn't any doubt of that. Then there was some kind of commotion, followed by a yell and a thud like a body hitting the floor. We were already at the door by then. It was locked, but it wasn't much of a lock; Ben kicked it open first try.

"First thing we saw when we barreled inside was a man we later ID'ed as Trent lying face down across his desk. Shot once in the middle of his face, blood all over the remains of his brown bag lunch. Gallatin was down on the floor, holding his head and looking groggy. The window behind him was open—looks out onto a fire escape and down into an alley that intersects with Market. It's a corner office; the other window, the one at right angles that overlooks Market, was jammed shut."

"Let me guess," I said. "Gallatin claims somebody came up or down the fire escape, shot Trent through the open window, knocked him to the floor when he tried to interfere, and then went back up or down."

"That's about it. He says he went there to see Trent on a routine business matter. They were talking while Trent was eating his lunch; the window was open because Trent was a fresh-air nut. Then this phantom with a gun showed up out of nowhere on the fire escape. Gallatin's story is that he didn't get a good look at him, it all happened too fast—the usual crap. But the odds of it having gone down that way are at least a couple of thousand to one.

"In the first place, the Wainright Building has six floors; two of the corner offices on the four floors above Trent's were occupied at the time. None of the people in those two offices saw anybody go up or down the fire escape past their windows. Nobody except Klein, that is, on *his* way to the roof. He didn't find a trace of anyone up there; and no one could have got *off* the roof except by way of the fire escape because the closest building is only four stories high—too far down to jump—and the door to the inside stairwell was locked tight.

"It's not any more likely that this phantom assailant came up from the alley or went down into it afterward. A teamster was unloading his truck down there, not fifty yards away, and he didn't see or hear anybody on the fire escape; and he sure as hell would have because the lower section is weighted and hasn't been oiled in twenty years, if ever: it makes plenty of noise when you swing on it. I know that for a fact because Klein played Tarzan after he came down from the roof. We also checked the teamster out, just to make sure he has no connection with Gallatin. He hasn't; he's a model citizen.

"And if that isn't enough, we had a doctor examine Gallatin. His claim—Gallatin's—is that the assailant whacked him on the side of the head to knock him down, but there's not a mark on him."

"What about a nitrate test to determine if he fired a gun?" I asked.

"Negative. He must have used gloves or something and got rid of them the same way he got rid of the gun."

"Didn't the people in the offices near Trent's see or hear anything?"

"No, because the only two offices close by were empty at the time. The elevators are directly across the hall from Trent's office, and the stairs are next to them, so there aren't any offices on that side. The one adjacent to Trent's belongs to a CPA, who was out to an early lunch; the one next to that is occupied by a mail-order housewares outfit that was closed for the day. Nearest occupied office was halfway to the rear of the building and off another corridor, and the woman holding it down is half deaf."

"You search the two empty offices?"

"Damn right we searched them," Logan said. "Got a pass key from the janitor and combed them as fine as we combed Trent's. All the other offices on that floor, too, just to be safe. Nothing. Not that we expected to find anything; like I told you, Klein and I were in on Gallatin within fifteen seconds after he shot Trent. He just didn't have time to get out of that office and hide the gun somewhere else."

"There's no chance of some clever hiding place in Trent's office that you might have overlooked?"

"None—I'll swear to that. And that's the hell of it. He couldn't have made that damn gun disappear, yet he did. Just as if he'd thrown it down a hole somewhere."

"Maybe he ate it," Barney said.

"Ha ha. Very funny."

"No, I'm serious. I read about a case like that once. Guy used a zip gun, knocked it down into its components after the shooting, and then swallowed the pieces. He was an ex-carnival sideshow performer—one of those dudes with a cast-iron stomach."

"Well, Gallatin's not an ex-carnival sideshow performer, and I'd like to see anybody eat a Beretta in fifteen seconds or fifteen *hours.*"

I asked him, "How do you know it's a Beretta?"

Logan smiled grimly. "Gallatin just happens to have one registered in his name. Same caliber as the bullet that killed Trent."

"Which is?"

"Twenty-five."

"One of those small, flat pocket jobs?"

"Right. Not much of a piece, but deadly enough."

"Any way he could have got rid of it through the open window?"

"No. If he'd chucked it into the alley, we'd have found it. And the teamster unloading his truck would have heard it hit; even a little gun makes plenty of noise when you drop it twenty feet onto pavement."

"How about if Gallatin chucked it straight *across* the alley?" I said. "Through an open window in the facing building, maybe?"

"Nice try, but no dice there, either. The first two floors of that building belong to a men's haberdashery; windows are kept locked at all times, and there were sales personnel and customers on both floors.

Third and fourth floors are offices, most of them occupied and all with their windows shut. It was pretty cold and windy today, remember. I had the empty offices checked anyway: no sign of the Beretta."

He made an exasperated noise and shook his head. "Even as weak as Gallatin's story is, we can't charge him without hard evidence—without the gun. It's his ace in the hole, and he bloody well knows it."

I folded another lousy hand and ruminated a little. At length I said, "You know, Jack, there's one big fat inconsistency in this thing."

"There's more than one," he said.

"No, I mean the shot you heard, the commotion and the yell and the thud. It has a stagey ring to it."

"How do you mean?"

"As if he put it all on just for your benefit."

Jack scowled. "He couldn't have known it was Ben and me out in the hallway."

I said musingly, "Maybe he could. Had he ever seen either of you before today? Had any dealings with either of you?"

"No."

"Was it just you and Ben? Or was anyone else with you?"

"Couple of uniformed officers, as backups. They stayed down in the lobby."

"Well, he could've spotted them, couldn't he, through the window that overlooks Market Street? The four of you coming into the building together?"

"I guess he could have," Logan admitted. "But hell, if he *did* know police officers were on the scene, it doesn't make sense he'd have shot Trent. Gallatin is a lot of things but crazy isn't one of them."

Eberhardt, who was raking in a small pot with a pair of queens, said, "Could be he didn't intend to shoot Trent. Maybe there was a struggle, the gun went off, and Gallatin decided to improvise to cover up."

"Some fast improvisation," I said.

He shrugged. "It's possible."

"I suppose so. But it still doesn't add up right. Why was the door locked?"

Rivera said, "Gallatin wanted privacy when he confronted Trent. He might not have gone there to kill him, but he did go there to get that file; otherwise, why bring the gun with him?"

Logan nodded. "We figure he picked up the same information we got about Trent's willingness to sell him out. He just didn't expect us to get it and come after Trent as fast as we did."

"I still don't like that door being locked," I said. "Or that window conveniently being open."

Barney gave me a sly look; he had the needle out again. "So what's your theory, then? You must have one by now."

"No. Not yet."

"Not even a little one?"

"I'm as stymied as you are."

Eberhardt said, "Give him time, Barney. He can't come up with an answer in fifteen minutes; he's not a goddamn genius." He sounded disappointed that I wasn't.

"I'm beginning to wish I'd stayed home," I said. "Eb, is there any beer?"

"Fridge is full. Help yourself. Maybe it'll help you think."

I went and got a bottle of Bud and when I came back we settled down to some semi-serious poker. Nobody said much about the Gallatin business for the next two and a half hours, but we might as well have been talking about it all along: the events as Jack Logan had described them kept running around inside my head, and I couldn't concentrate on the flow of cards. It all seemed so damned screwy and impossible. And yet, if you looked at it in just the right way . . .

Five-card stud was what we played for the most part—strict traditionalists, that was us; anybody who even suggested a wild-card game would have been tossed out on his ear—and DeFalco was dealing a new hand. My up card was the ace of hearts. I lifted a corner on my hole card: ace of clubs. Wired aces. The best start of a hand I'd had all night. Joe nodded at me and said, "Your bet," and I said, "Open for ten," and pushed a dime into the middle of the table. Then I looked at my down card again, my ace in the hole.

Eberhardt called my dime; he had a king showing. Jack and Barney folded. Joe called with an eight up, and then dealt me a deuce of something and Eb and himself cards that I didn't even notice.

Ace in the hole . . .

I sat there. Then somebody—Barney—poked me with an elbow and said, "Hey, wake up. We're waiting."

"Huh?"

"For you to bet. What are you waiting for?"

"Nothing. I was just thinking."

Eberhardt perked up. "About the Gallatin thing?"

"Yeah. The Gallatin thing."

"You're onto something, right? I know that look. Come on, paisan —spill it."

"Give me a minute, will you?"

I got up and went into the kitchen and opened another bottle of Bud. When I came back with it, the poker game had been temporarily suspended and they were all watching me again, waiting. Time for the Big Dick to perform, I thought sourly. And maybe do a comical pratfall like Clarabelle the Clown. Bah.

I sat down again. "All right," I said, "I've got an idea. Maybe it's way off base, I don't know, but you asked for it. It fits all the facts, anyhow. Just don't anybody make any smart cracks if it fizzles."

Eb said, "Go, boy. Go."

I ignored him. To Logan I said, "The key isn't what Gallatin did with the murder weapon, Jack. It's that shot you and Ben heard."

"What about it?"

"Well, suppose it was a phony. Suppose Gallatin staged it and everything else to make you think that was when Trent was killed, when in reality he'd been dead from two to five minutes—shot *before* the two of you were even in the building."

Frown lines made a puckered V above Jack's nose. "You mean Gallatin fired a second shot out the window?"

"No. He didn't have the gun then. I mean a phony all the way—it *wasn't* a gunshot you heard."

DeFalco said, "How do you fake a gunshot?" He had his notebook out and was scribbling in it.

I didn't answer him directly. Still talking to Logan, I said, "You mentioned that Trent was eating a brown bag lunch when he was killed or just before it. You meant that literally, right?" He nodded. "Okay, then. Where was the paper bag?"

"Wadded up in the wastebasket—" He broke off abruptly, and his frown changed shape.

"Sure," I said. "An old kids' trick. You blow up a paper sack, hold the opening pinched together to keep the air in, and then burst the sack between your hands. From a distance, from behind a closed door, it would sound just like a small-caliber gun going off."

There was silence for a few seconds while they all digested that. Then Rivera said, "Wait a minute. I'll grant you the possibility of a trick like that being worked. But why would Gallatin get so fancy? He's not some amateur playing games. If he killed Trent before Jack and Ben came into the building, why did he hang around? Why didn't he just beat it out of there?"

"Circumstances. And some bad judgment."

"All right, what's your scenario?"

"Try it like this. He arrives at Trent's office while Trent is eating his lunch; he waves his gun around, gets Trent to open his safe and hand over the incriminating file, and then shoots him for whatever reason. Afterward he pokes his head out the office door; the hallway's deserted, nobody seems to have heard the shot. So far, so good; he figures he's in the clear. Now . . ." I paused. "Jack, is there a window at the end of the hallway, overlooking Market?"

"Yeah, there is."

"I thought there might be. Back to the scenario: Gallatin pockets the Beretta, goes out with the file tucked under his arm, and pushes the button for the elevator. While he's waiting for it, he happens to glance through the window; *that's* when he sees you and Ben and the uniformed officers entering the building. Gives him quite a jolt. He's got to figure you're there to see Trent, the man he's just killed. And he's got both the murder weapon and the file in his possession. If he hangs onto them and tries to take them out of the building, he runs the risk of capture—too big a risk. For all he knows, cops are swarming all over the place. He's got to get rid of the evidence, and fast. That's his first priority."

"But where, for God's sake? Not in the hallway; we searched it, just like we searched the offices and everything else on that floor."

"The gun and file weren't on that floor when you searched it. Not anymore."

"Where the hell were they, then? Where are they now?"

"I'll get to that in a minute," I said, and watched the four of them grumble and squirm. A little payback for putting *me* on the spot the way they had. "Let me lay out the rest of it first. Gallatin dumps the gun and the file in a matter of seconds. . . . *Now* what does he do? The smart thing is to play it cool, take the elevator down to the lobby and try to walk out unobserved; but he doesn't see it that way. He's afraid he'll be recognized and detained; that it'll look like he's trying to run away from the scene of the murder. Maybe he hears you and Ben coming up the stairs just then; in any case, he gets a bright idea, and bad judgment takes over. Why not stay right where he is, right on the scene, and divert suspicion from himself by making it look as if somebody else shot Trent? After all, he's already dumped both the gun and the file; as long as you

gationACE IN THE HOLE ♠ 71

don't find either one, he's in the clear. And he doesn't believe you're going to find them.

"So he ducks back into Trent's office, locks the door to give himself a little extra time, opens the window, and then goes into his act. He hasn't had time to think it through or to check who might be down in the alley; the result is that the whole thing comes off weak and stagey. Still, as you said before, without the murder weapon . . ."

"Will you quit dragging it out? What did he do with the gun?"

I let them stew another few seconds while I drank some of my beer. Then I said, "You supplied the answer yourself, Jack: you said he made it disappear as if he'd thrown it down a hole somewhere. Well, that's just what he *did* do. The file, too."

"Hole? What are you talking about?"

"I was in the Wainright Building once, about six months ago. At that time those cranky old elevators didn't always stop flush with the level of each floor, going up or down. If they've been fixed since then, my whole theory goes down a different kind of hole. But if they haven't been fixed, if they still sometimes stop a couple of inches above or below floor level . . ."

Logan sat up straight and stiff, as if somebody had just goosed him. "Well, I'll be damned. They *don't* stop flush, no."

Eberhardt said, "The elevator shaft!"

"Why not?" I said. "One of those flat, .25 caliber Beretta pocket jobs is about an inch and a half wide. Even a thick file of papers probably wouldn't be any wider. It would only take a few seconds, once the elevator doors opened, for Gallatin to spot the opening between the car floor and the shaft, wedge both the gun and the file through it, and then push one of the buttons inside to close the doors again and start the car."

DeFalco was scribbling furiously now. He said without looking up, "So Gallatin *literally* had an ace in the hole all along. I love it."

"Well, I don't," Barney the Needle said. He sounded pissy, but he wasn't; he was still playing Devil's Advocate, a role he enjoys almost as much as that of Grand Seducer. "I don't believe a word of it."

"No? Why not?"

"It's got too many holes in it," Barney said, straight-faced. "On the whole, I mean."

Logan was on his feet. "We'll see about this," he said, and hurried off to use the phone. Three minutes later he was on his way to the Wainright Building downtown.

The rest of us were still hanging around Eberhardt's living room, drinking beer and playing desultory four-handed poker, when Logan telephoned a few minutes before midnight. Gallatin's Beretta had been at the bottom of one of the elevator shafts, all right. Along with the papers from Trent's file and a pair of custom-made doeskin gloves with the initials F. G. inside each one. They had Frankie boy but good.

Murderers, especially the ones who think they're clever, are all damned fools.

So Barney paid off to Eberhardt, with a great show of grumbling reluctance. Eb said, grinning, "I told you, didn't I? I told you the paisano here was a whiz when it comes to this kind of screwball stuff. Three hours, that's all it took him. *Three*, Barney, not twenty-four."

"Luck," Barney the Needle said. "Pure blind luck. He's the luckiest private eye on the face of this earth."

Sure I am. Eberhardt collected on his twenty-buck bet, and won gloating rights in the bargain. Barney won twenty-nine dollars on the poker table, which left him nine bucks up for the evening. Jack Logan won five dollars early on, got to put the blocks to a nasty bastard like Frank Gallatin, and had a large burden lifted from his shoulders. Joe DeFalco won three dollars and got a story that he didn't dare print as straight news—it would have embarrassed Jack and made the SFPD look bad; but he'd find a way to turn it into a feature or something. And what did I get? I got a headache from too much beer, an empty wallet—I won exactly two hands all night and ended seventeen dollars poorer—and the privilege of plying my trade and overworking my brain for no compensation whatsoever.

Mr. Lucky, that's me. . . .

INCIDENT IN A NEIGHBORHOOD TAVERN

WHEN the holdup went down I was sitting at the near end of the Foghorn Tavern's scarred mahogany bar talking to the owner, Matt Candiotti.

It was a little before seven of a midweek evening, lull-time in working-class neighborhood saloons like this one. Blue-collar locals would jam the place from four until about six-thirty, when the last of them headed home for dinner; the hard-core drinkers wouldn't begin filtering back in until about seven-thirty or eight. Right now there were only two customers, and the jukebox and computer hockey games were quiet. The TV over the back bar was on but with the sound turned down to a tolerable level. One of the customers, a porky guy in his fifties, drinking Anchor Steam out of the bottle, was watching the last of the NBC national news. The other customer, an equally porky and middle-aged female barfly, half in the bag on red wine, was trying to convince him to pay attention to her instead of Tom Brokaw.

I had a draft beer in front of me, but that wasn't the reason I was there. I'd come to ask Candiotti, as I had asked two dozen other merchants here in the Outer Mission, if he could offer any leads on the rash of burglaries that were plaguing small businesses in the neighborhood. The police hadn't come up with anything positive after six weeks, so a couple of the victims had gotten up a fund and hired me to see what I could find out. They'd picked me because I had been born and raised in the Outer Mission, I still had friends and shirttail relatives living here, and I understood the neighborhood a good deal better than any other private detective in San Francisco.

But so far I wasn't having any more luck than the SFPD. None of the merchants I'd spoken with today had given me any new ideas. And Candiotti was proving to be no exception. He stood slicing limes into wedges as we talked. They might have been onions the way his long, mournful face was screwed up, like a man trying to hold back tears. His gray-stubbled jowls wobbled every time he shook his head. He reminded me of a tired old hound, friendly and sad, as if life had dealt him a few kicks but not quite enough to rob him of his good nature.

"Wish I could help," he said. "But hell, I don't hear nothing. Must be pros from Hunters Point or the Fillmore, hah?"

Hunters Point and the Fillmore were black sections of the city, which was a pretty good indicator of where his head was at. I said, "Some of the others figure it for local talent."

"Out of this neighborhood, you mean?"

I nodded, drank some of my draft.

"Nah, I doubt it," he said. "Guys that organized, they don't shit where they eat. Too smart, you know?"

"Maybe. Any break-ins or attempted break-ins here?"

"Not so far. I got bars on all the windows, double dead-bolt locks on the storeroom door off the alley. Besides, what's for them to steal besides a few cases of whiskey?"

"You don't keep cash on the premises overnight?"

"Fifty bucks in the till," Candiotti said, "that's all; that's my limit. Everything else goes out of here when I close up, down to the night deposit at the B of A on Mission. My mama didn't raise no airheads." He scraped the lime wedges off his board, into a plastic container, and racked the serrated knife he'd been using. "One thing I did hear," he said. "I heard some of the loot turned up down in San Jose. You know about that?"

"Not much of a lead there. Secondhand dealer named Pitman had a few pieces of stereo equipment stolen from the factory outlet store on Geneva. Said he bought it from a guy at the San Jose flea market, somebody he didn't know, never saw before."

"Yeah, sure," Candiotti said wryly. "What do the cops think?"

"That Pitman bought it off a fence."

"Makes sense. So maybe the boosters are from San Jose, hah?"

"Could be," I said, and that was when the kid walked in.

He brought bad air in with him; I sensed it right away and so did Candiotti. We both glanced at the door when it opened, the way you do, but we didn't look away again once we saw him. He was in his early twenties, dark-skinned, dressed in chinos, a cotton windbreaker, sharp-toed shoes polished to a high gloss. But it was his eyes that put the chill on my neck, the sudden clutch of tension down low in my belly. They were bright, jumpy, on the wild side, and in the dim light of the Foghorn's interior, the pupils were so small they seemed nonexistent. He had one hand in his jacket pocket and I knew it was clamped around a gun even before he took it out and showed it to us.

He came up to the bar a few feet on my left, the gun jabbing the air in front of him. He couldn't hold it steady; it kept jerking up and down, from side to side, as if it had a kind of spasmodic life of its own. Behind me, at the other end of the bar, I heard Anchor Steam suck in his breath, the barfly make a sound like a stifled moan. I eased back a little on the stool, watching the gun and the kid's eyes flick from Candiotti to me to the two customers and back around again. Candiotti didn't move at all, just stood there staring with his hound's face screwed up in that holding-back-tears way.

"All right all right," the kid said. His voice was high pitched, excited, and there was drool at one corner of his mouth. You couldn't get much more stoned than he was and still function. Coke, crack, speed—maybe a combination. The gun that kept flicking this way and that had to be a goddamn Saturday night special. "Listen good, man, everybody listen good. I don't want to kill none of you, man, but I will if I got to, you believe it?"

None of us said anything. None of us moved.

The kid had a folded-up paper sack in one pocket; he dragged it out with his free hand, dropped it, broke quickly at the middle to pick it up without lowering his gaze. When he straightened again there was sweat on his forehead, more drool coming out of his mouth. He threw the sack on the bar.

"Put the money in there Mr. Cyclone Man," he said to Candiotti. "All the money in the register but not the coins; I don't want the fuckin' coins, you hear me?"

Candiotti nodded; reached out slowly, caught up the sack, turned toward the back bar with his shoulders hunched up against his neck. When he punched *No Sale* on the register, the ringing thump of the cash drawer sliding open seemed overloud in the electric hush. For a few seconds the kid watched him scoop bills into the paper sack; then his eyes and the gun skittered my way again. I had looked into the muzzle of a handgun before and it was the same feeling each time: dull fear, helplessness, a kind of naked vulnerability.

"Your wallet on the bar, man, all your cash." The gun barrel and the wild eyes flicked away again, down the length of the plank, before I could move to comply. "You down there, dude, you and fat mama put your money on the bar. All of it, hurry up."

Each of us did as we were told. While I was getting my wallet out I managed to slide my right foot off the stool, onto the brass rail, and to get my right hand pressed tight against the beveled edge of the bar. If I had to make any sudden moves, I would need the leverage.

Candiotti finished loading the sack, turned from the register. There was a grayish cast to his face now—the wet gray color of fear. The kid said to him, "Pick up their money, put it in the sack with the rest. Come on come on come on!"

Candiotti went to the far end of the plank, scooped up the wallets belonging to Anchor Steam and the woman; then he came back my way, added my wallet to the contents of the paper sack, put the sack down carefully in front of the kid.

"Okay," the kid said, "okay all right." He glanced over his shoulder at the street door, as if he'd heard something there; but it stayed closed. He jerked his head around again. In his sweaty agitation the Saturday night special almost slipped free of his fingers; he fumbled a tighter grip on it, and when it didn't go off I let the breath I had been holding come out thin and slow between my teeth. The muscles in my shoulders and back were drawn so tight I was afraid they might cramp.

The kid reached out for the sack, dragged it in against his body. But he made no move to leave with it. Instead he said, "Now we go get the big pile, man."

Candiotti opened his mouth, closed it again. His eyes were almost as big and starey as the kid's.

"Come on Mr. Cyclone Man, the safe, the safe in your office. We goin' back there *now.*"

"No money in that safe," Candiotti said in a thin, scratchy voice. "Nothing valuable."

"Oh man I'll kill you man I'll blow your fuckin' head off! I ain't playin' no games I want that money!"

He took two steps forward, jabbing with the gun up close to Candiotti's gray face. Candiotti backed off a step, brought his hands up, took a tremulous breath.

"All right," he said, "but I got to get the key to the office. It's in the register."

"Hurry up hurry up!"

Candiotti turned back to the register, rang it open, rummaged inside with his left hand. But with his right hand, shielded from the kid by his body, he eased up the top on a large wooden cigar box adjacent. The hand disappeared inside; came out again with metal in it, glinting in the back bar lights. I saw it and I wanted to yell at him, but it wouldn't have done any good, would only have warned the kid . . . and he was already turning with it, bringing it up with both hands now—the damn gun of his own he'd had hidden inside the cigar box. There was no time for me to do anything but shove away from the bar and sideways off the stool just as Candiotti opened fire.

The state he was in, the kid didn't realize what was happening until it was too late for him to react; he never even got a shot off. Candiotti's first slug knocked him halfway around, and one of the three others that followed it opened up his face like a piece of ripe fruit smacked by a hammer. He was dead before his body, driven backward, slammed into the cigarette machine near the door, slid down it to the floor.

The half-drunk woman was yelling in broken shrieks, as if she couldn't get enough air for a sustained scream. When I came up out of my crouch I saw that Anchor Steam had hold of her, clinging to her as much for support as in an effort to calm her down. Candiotti stood flat-footed, his arms down at his sides, the gun out of sight below the bar, staring at the bloody remains of the kid as if he couldn't believe what he was seeing, couldn't believe what he'd done.

Some of the tension in me eased as I went to the door, found the lock on its security gate, fastened it before anybody could come in off the street. The Saturday night special was still clutched in the kid's hand; I bent, pulled it free with my thumb and forefinger, broke the cylinder. It was loaded, all right—five cartridges. I dropped it into my jacket pocket, thought about checking the kid's clothing for identification, didn't do it. It wasn't any of my business, now, who he'd been. And I did not want to touch him or any part of him. There was a queasiness in my stomach, a fluttery weakness behind my knees—the same delayed reaction I always had to violence and death—and touching him would only make it worse.

To keep from looking at the red ruin of the kid's face, I pivoted back to the bar. Candiotti hadn't moved. Anchor Steam had gotten the woman to stop screeching and had coaxed her over to one of the handful of tables near the jukebox; now she was sobbing, "I've got to go home, I'm gonna be sick if I don't go home." But she didn't make any move to get up and neither did Anchor Steam.

I walked over near Candiotti and pushed hard words at him in an undertone. "That was a damn fool thing to do. You could have got us all killed."

"I know," he said. "I know."

"Why'd you do it?"

"I thought . . . hell, you saw the way he was waving that piece of his . . . ."

"Yeah," I said. "Call the police. Nine-eleven."

"Nine-eleven. Okay."

"Put that gun of yours down first. On the bar."

He did that. There was a phone on the back bar; he went away to it in shaky strides. While he was talking to the Emergency operator I picked up his weapon, saw that it was a .32 Charter Arms revolver. I held it in my hand until Candiotti finished with the call, then set it down again as he came back to where I stood.

"They'll have somebody here in five minutes," he said.

I said, "You know that kid?"

"Christ, no."

"Ever see him before? Here or anywhere else?"

"No."

"So how did he know about your safe?"

Candiotti blinked at me. "What?"

"The safe in your office. Street kid like that . . . how'd he know about it?"

"How should I know? What difference does it make?"

"He seemed to think you keep big money in that safe."

"Well, I don't. There's nothing in it."

"That's right, you told me you don't keep more than fifty bucks on the premises overnight. In the till."

"Yeah."

"Then why have you got a safe, if it's empty?"

Candiotti's eyes narrowed. "I used to keep my receipts in it, all right? Before all these burglaries started. Then I figured I'd be smarter to take the money to the bank every night."

"Sure, that explains it," I said. "Still, a kid like that, looking for a big score to feed his habit, he wasn't just after what was in the till and our wallets. No, it was as if he'd gotten wind of a heavy stash—a grand or more."

Nothing from Candiotti.

I watched him for a time. Then I said, "Big risk you took, using that .32 of yours. How come you didn't make your play the first time you went to the register? How come you waited until the kid mentioned your office safe?"

"I didn't like the way he was acting, like he might start shooting any second. I figured it was our only chance. Listen, what're you getting at, hah?"

"Another funny thing," I said, "is the way he called you 'Mr. Cyclone Man.' Now why would a hopped-up kid use a term like that to a bar owner he didn't know?"

"How the hell should I know?"

"Cyclone," I said. "What's a cyclone but a big destructive wind? Only one other thing I can think of."

"Yeah? What's that?"

"A fence. A cyclone fence."

Candiotti made a fidgety movement. Some of the wet gray pallor was beginning to spread across his cheeks again, like a fungus.

I said, "And a fence is somebody who receives and distributes stolen goods. A Mr. Fence Man. But then you know that, don't you, Candiotti? We were talking about that kind of fence before the kid came in . . . how Pitman, down in San Jose, bought some hot stereo equipment off of one. That fence could just as easily be operating here in San Francisco, though. Right here in this neighborhood, in fact. Hell, suppose the stuff taken in all those burglaries never left the neighborhood. Suppose it was brought to a place nearby and stored until it could be trucked out to other cities—a tavern storeroom, for instance. Might even be some of it is *still* in that storeroom. And the money he got for the rest he'd keep locked up in his safe, right? Who'd figure it? Except maybe a poor junkie who picked up a whisper on the street somewhere—"

Candiotti made a sudden grab for the .32, caught it and backed up a step with it leveled at my chest. "You smart son of a bitch," he said. "I ought to kill you too."

"In front of witnesses? With the police due any minute?"

He glanced over at the two customers. The woman was still sobbing, lost in a bleak outpouring of self-pity; but Anchor Steam was staring our way, and from the expression on his face he'd heard every word of my exchange with Candiotti.

"There's still enough time for me to get clear," Candiotti said grimly. He was talking to himself, not to me. Sweat had plastered his lank hair to his forehead; the revolver was not quite steady in his hand. "Lock you up in my office, you and those two back there . . ."

"I don't think so," I said.

"Goddamn you, you think I won't use this gun again?"

"I *know* you won't use it. I emptied out the last two cartridges while you were on the phone."

I took the two shells out of my left-hand jacket pocket and held them up where he could see them. At the same time I got the kid's Saturday night special out of the other pocket, held it loosely pointed in his direction. "You want to put your piece down now, Candiotti? You're not going anywhere, not for a long time."

He put it down—dropped it clattering onto the bartop. And as he did his sad hound's face screwed up again, only this time he didn't even try to keep the wetness from leaking out of his eyes. He was leaning against the bar, crying like the woman, submerged in his own outpouring of self-pity, when the cops showed up.

SOMETHING WRONG

THE instant I unlocked the door and walked into my flat, I knew something was wrong.

I stopped a couple of paces through the door, with the hairs pulling at the nape of my neck. Kerry had entered ahead of me and she was halfway across the room before she realized I wasn't following. She turned, saw me standing rigid, and said immediately, "What's the matter?"

I didn't answer. I kept searching the room with my eyes: the old mismatched furniture, the shelves containing my collection of pulp magazines, the bay window beyond which a thick San Francisco fog crawled sinuously across the night. There were no signs of disturbance. Nor was there anything unusual to hear. And yet the feeling of wrongness remained sharp and urgent. When you've been a detective as long as I have, you develop a kind of protective sixth sense and you learn to trust it.

Somebody had gotten in here while Kerry and I were out to dinner and a movie in North Beach.

Somebody who was still here now?

Kerry came back toward me, saying again, "What's the matter?"

"Go out into the hall."

"What for?"

"Just do it."

We'd been together long enough and she knew me well enough not to argue. Frowning now, worry-eyed, she moved past me and out into the hall.

I shut the door after her and turned back to face the room. Nothing out of place in here . . . or was there? Something didn't seem quite right, but I couldn't identify it—couldn't focus on anything right now except the possibility of the intruder still being on the premises.

This was one of the few times I regretted my fundamental distaste for guns; I owned one, a .38 S&W Bodyguard, but I kept it clipped under the dash in the car. Strictly for emergencies. Yeah—like now. I picked up a heavy alabaster bookend, not much of a weapon but the only one handy, and went across to the half-closed bedroom door.

Nobody in there; I opened the closet and looked under the bed to make sure. No evidence of invasion or forced entry, either—not that anyone could get in through the bedroom window, or any of the other windows, without using a tall ladder. The bathroom was also empty and undisturbed. So were the kitchen and the rear porch. The back door, accessible by a set of outside stairs from an alley off Laguna Street, was still secured by its spring lock and chain lock.

Back in the bedroom, I opened the middle dresser drawer. The leather case in which I keep my few items of jewelry and a small amount of spare cash was still in place under my clean shirts. The valuables inside were likewise untouched.

But that reassured me only a little. The feeling of wrongness, of a violation of my private space, would not go away. As unlikely as it seemed, somebody had gotten in during our absence. I was as sure of it as you can be of something unproven.

I recrossed the front room, opened the door. Kerry was standing in front of it, fidgeting. "Just in time," she said. "I was about to start making some noise. What is it? Burglars?"

"Something like that."

I got down on one knee to examine the two locks on the front door. One dead-bolt, one push-button on the knob. When I was done I asked Kerry, "When we left earlier, did I use my key to lock the dead-bolt? You remember?"

"I think you did. You always do, don't you?"

"Almost always, unless I'm distracted. I wasn't distracted tonight. But the dead-bolt wasn't on when we got back just now." That was the first thing that had made me feel the wrongness—the key turning but the lock not being in place.

"What about the push-button?"

"I'm sure that was locked."

"You think somebody picked it and the dead-bolt?"

"I wish it was that simple. The answer is no."

A professional burglar can get past the best dead-bolt made, but not even a locksmith with a set of precision picks can do it without leaving marks. There were none on the dead-bolt, none on the push-button. Nobody could possibly have come in this way, unless he had a key.

I asked Kerry if she'd lost or misplaced her key recently; she hadn't. Mine hadn't been out of my possession, either. And ours were the only two keys to the flat. Not even the landlord had one: I had lived here for more than twenty years and had had the locks changed more than once at my own expense.

Kerry asked, "Is anything missing?"

"Doesn't seem to be. Nothing disturbed, no sign of forced entry. But I can't shake the feeling someone was in here."

"For what reason, if not to steal something?"

"I can't even guess."

"How could somebody get in, with everything locked up tight?"

"No guess there either."

We prowled the flat together, room to room and back again. There was absolutely nothing missing or disarranged. I checked the locks on the windows and on the back door; all were secure and had not been tampered with as far as I could tell. I did find a half-inch sliver of metal on the floor of the utility porch, the same sort of brass as the chain lock. But it hadn't come from the lock because I checked to make sure. It could have been splintered off just about anything made of brass; could have lain there for days.

We were in the front room again when Kerry said, with an edge of exasperation in her voice, "You must be mistaken. A false alarm."

"I'm not mistaken."

"Even great detectives have paranoid flashes now and then."

"This isn't funny, Kerry."

"Did I say it was?" She sighed elaborately, the way she does when her patience is being tried. "I'm going to make some coffee," she said. "You want a cup?"

"All right."

She went into the kitchen. I stayed in the middle of the room and kept looking around—turning my eyes and my body both in slow quadrants. Couch, end tables, coffee table, leather recliner Kerry had given me on my last birthday, shelves full of bright-spined pulps, old secretary desk. All just as we'd left it. Yet *something* wasn't as it should be. I made another slow circuit: couch, end tables, coffee tables, recliner, bookshelves, desk. And a third circuit: couch, tables, recliner—

Recliner.

The chair's footrest was pushed in, out of sight.

It was a small thing, but that didn't make it any less wrong. The chair is a good one, comfortable, but the footrest has never worked quite right. To get it folded all the way back under on its metal hinges, you have to give it a kick; and when you sit down again later, you have to struggle to work it free so you can recline. So I don't bother anymore to boot it all the way under. I *always* leave the footrest part way out, with its metal hinges showing.

Why would an intruder bother to kick it under? Only one conceivable reason: he thought it was supposed to be that way and wanted the chair to look completely natural. But why would he be messing around my recliner in the first place. . . ?

"Jesus," I said aloud, and again the hair pulled along my neck. I went to the recliner, gingerly eased the seat cushion out so I could see under it.

What I was looking at then was a bomb.

Two sticks of dynamite wired together with a detonator plate on top, set into a slit in the fabric so that it was resting on the chair's inner springs. The weight of a person settling onto the cushion would depress the plate and set off the dynamite—

"Good God!"

Kerry was standing behind me, staring open-mouthed at the thing in the chair. I hadn't even heard her come in.

"Not a burglar after all," I said angrily. "Somebody who came in to leave something. This."

"I . . . don't hear any ticking," she said.

"It's a pressure-activated bomb, not a time bomb. Nothing to worry about as long as we stay away from it."

"But who . . . why . . . ?"

I caught her arm and steered her into the bedroom, where I keep my phone. I rang up the Hall of Justice, got through to an inspector I knew named Jordan, and explained the situation. He said he'd be right over with the bomb squad.

When I hung up, Kerry said in a shaky voice, "I just don't understand. All the doors and windows were locked—they're *still* locked. How did whoever it was get in and back out again?"

I had no answer for her then. But by the time the police arrived, I had done some hard thinking and a little more checking and I did have an answer—the only possible explanation. And along with it, I had the who and the why.

"His name is Howard Lynch," I said to Jordan. He and Kerry and I were in the hallway, waiting for the bomb squad to finish up inside. "Owns a hardware store out on Clement. He hired me about a month ago to find his wife; said she'd run off with another man. She had, too, but nobody could blame her. I found out later Lynch had been abusing her for years."

"So why would he want to kill you?"

"He must blame me for his wife's death. I found her, all right, but when I told her Lynch was my employer she panicked and took off in her boyfriend's car. She didn't get far—a truck stopped her three blocks away."

"Pretty story."

"That's the kind of business we're in, Mack."

"Don't I know it. Did Lynch threaten you?"

"No. He's the kind who nurses his hatred in private."

"Then what makes you so sure he's the one who planted the bomb?"

"He showed up here one night a couple of weeks after the accident. Said it was to give me a check for my services—I probably shouldn't have, but I'd sent him a bill—and to tell me there were no hard feelings. I knew about the abuse by then, but he seemed contrite about it, said he was in therapy . . . hell, I bought it all and felt sorry enough for him to let him in. He wasn't here long, just long enough to ask to use the bathroom and sneak a quick look at the back door."

Kerry said, "I don't see why the bomber has to be somebody who was here before tonight."

"That's the only way it makes senses. To begin with, he had to've gotten in tonight through one of the doors, front or back. The windows are all secure and there's nothing but empty space below them. There're no marks of any kind on the front door locks, no way he could've gotten a key, and he would've had a hard time even getting into the building because of the security lock on the main entrance downstairs. That leaves the alley staircase and the back door."

"But that one was—is—double-locked too."

"Right. But the lock on the door is a push-button, the kind anybody can pick with a credit card or the like. There's a tiny fresh scratch on the bolt."

"You can't pick a chain lock with a credit card," Jordan said.

"No, but once the spring lock is free, the door will open a few inches —wide enough to reach through with a pair of bolt cutters and snip the chain. That explains the brass sliver I found on the porch floor. Easy work for a man who owns a hardware store, and so is the rest of it: When he was here the first time he noted the type of chain lock back there, and among the other things he brought with him tonight was an exact duplicate of that lock. After he was inside, he unscrewed the old chain-lock plates from the door and jamb and installed the new ones, using the same holes— a job that wouldn't have taken more than a few minutes. Then he reset the spring lock, put the new chain on, and took the pieces of the old lock away with him when he was done planting the bomb."

"If he relocked the door," Jordan said, "how did he get out of the flat?"

"Walked out through the front door. Opened the dead-bolt, opened the door, reset the push-button on the knob, and closed the door behind him. Simple as that."

Kerry said, "It would have worked, too, if you hadn't realized the dead-bolt was off when we got back and felt something was wrong." She shivered a little. "If you'd sat down in that chair . . ."

"Don't even think about it," I said.

HERE COMES SANTA CLAUS

KERRY sprang her little surprise on me the week before Christmas. And the worst thing about it was, I was no longer fat. The forty-pound bowlful of jelly that had once hung over my belt was long gone.

"That doesn't matter," she said. "You can wear a pillow."

"Why me?" I said.

"They made me entertainment chairperson, for one thing. And for another, you're the biggest and jolliest man I know."

"Ho, ho, ho," I said sourly.

"It's for a good cause. Lots of good causes—needy children, the homeless, three other charities. Where's your Christmas spirit?"

"I don't have any. Why don't you ask Eberhardt?"

"Are you serious? *Eberhardt?*"

"Somebody else, then. Anybody else."

"You," she said.

"Uh-uh. No. I love you madly and I'll do just about anything for you, but not this. This is where I draw the line."

"Oh, come on, quit acting like a scrooge."

"I *am* a scrooge. Bah, humbug."

"You like kids, you know you do—"

"I don't like kids. Where did you get that idea?"

"I've seen you with kids, that's where."

"An act, just an act."

"So put it on again for the Benefit. Five o'clock until nine, four hours out of your life to help the less fortunate. Is that too much to ask?"

"In this case, yes."

She looked at me. Didn't say anything, just looked at me.

"*No,*" I said. "There's no way I'm going to wear a Santa Claus suit and dandle little kiddies on my knee. You hear me? Absolutely no way!"

"Ho, ho, ho," I said.

The little girl perched on my knee looked up at me out of big round eyes. It was the same sort of big roundeyed stare Kerry had given me the previous week.

"Are you really Santa Claus?" she asked.

"Yes indeedy. And who would you be?"

"Melissa."

"That's a pretty name. How old are you, Melissa?"

"Six and a half."

"Six and a half. Well, well. Tell old Santa what it is you want for Christmas."

"A dolly."

"What sort of dolly?"

"A big one."

"Just a big one? No special kind?"

"Yes. A dolly that you put water in her mouth and she wee-wees on herself."

I sighed. "Ho, ho, ho," I said.

The Gala Family Christmas Charity Benefit was being held in the Lowell High School gymnasium, out near Golden Gate Park. Half a dozen San Francisco businesses were sponsoring it, including Bates and Carpenter, the ad agency where Kerry works as a senior copywriter, so it was a pretty elaborate affair. The decoration committee had dressed the gym up to look like a cross between Santa's Village and the Dickens Christmas Fair. There was a huge gaudy tree, lots of red-and-green bunting and seasonal decorations, big clusters of holly and mistletoe, even fake snow; and the staff members were costumed as elves and other creatures imaginary and real. Carols and traditional favorites poured out of loudspeakers. Booths positioned along the walls dispensed food—meat pies, plum pudding, gingerbread, and other sweets—and a variety of handmade toys and crafts, all donated. For the adults, there were a couple of city-sanctioned games of chance and a bar supplying wassail and other Christmassy drinks.

For the kiddies, there was me.

I sat on a thronelike chair on a raised dais at one end, encased in false whiskers and wig and paunch, red suit and cap, black boots and belt. All around me were cotton snowdrifts, a toy bag overflowing with gaily wrapped packages, a shiny papier-mâché version of Santa's sleigh with some cardboard reindeer. A couple of young women dressed as elves were there, too, to act as my helpers. Their smiles were as phony as my whiskers and paunch; they were only slightly less miserable than I was. For snaking out to one side and halfway across the packed enclosure was a line of little children the Pied Piper of Hamlin would have envied, some with their parents, most without, and all eager to clamber up onto old St. Nick's lap and share with him their innermost desires.

Inside the Santa suit, I was sweating—and not just because it was warm in there. I imagined that every adult eye was on me, that snickers were lurking in every adult throat. This was ridiculous, of course, the more so because none of the two hundred or so adults in attendance knew Santa's true identity. I had made Kerry swear an oath that she wouldn't tell anybody, especially not my partner, Eberhardt, who would never let me hear the end of it if he knew. No more than half a dozen of those present knew me anyway, this being a somewhat ritzy crowd; and of those who did know me, three were members of the private security staff.

Still, I felt exposed and vulnerable and acutely uncomfortable. I felt the way you would if you suddenly found yourself naked on a crowded city street. And I kept thinking: What if one of the newspaper photographers recognizes me and decides to take my picture? What if Eberhardt finds out? Or Barney Rivera or Joe DeFalco or one of my other so-called friends?

Another kid was on his way toward my lap. I smiled automatically and sneaked a look at my watch. My God! It seemed as though I'd been here at least two hours, but only forty-five minutes had passed since the opening ceremonies. More than three hours left to go. Close to two hundred minutes. Nearly twelve thousand seconds . . .

The new kid climbed onto my knee. While he was doing that, one of those near the front of the line, overcome at the prospect of his own imminent audience with the Nabob of the North Pole, began to make a series of all-too-familiar sounds. Another kid said, "Oh, gross, he's gonna throw up!" Fortunately, however, the sick one's mother was with him; she managed to hustle him out of there in time, to the strains of "Walking in a Winter Wonderland."

I thought: What if he'd been sitting on my lap instead of standing in line?

I thought: Kerry, I'll get you for this, Kerry.

I listened to the new kid's demands, and thought about all the other little hopeful piping voices I would have to listen to, and sweated and smiled and tried not to squirm. If I squirmed, people *would* start to snicker—the kids as well as the adults. They'd think Santa had to go potty and was trying not to wee-wee on himself.

This one had cider-colored hair. He said, "You're not Santa Claus."

"Sure I am. Don't I look like Santa?"

"No. Your face isn't red and you don't have a nose like a cherry."

"What's your name, sonny?"

"Ronnie. You're not fat, either."

"Sure I'm fat. Ho, ho, ho."

"No, you're not."

"What do you want for Christmas, Ronnie?"

"I won't tell you. You're a fake. I don't need you to give me toys. I can buy my own toys."

"Good for you."

"I don't believe in Santa Claus anyway," he said. He was about nine, and in addition to being belligerent, he had mean little eyes. He was probably going to grow up to be an axe murderer. Either that, or a politician.

"If you don't want to talk to Santa," I said, feigning patience, "then how about getting off Santa's lap and letting one of the other boys and girls come up—"

"No." Without warning he punched me in the stomach. Hard. "Hah!" he said. "A pillow. I *knew* your gut was just a pillow."

"Get off Santa's lap, Ronnie."

"No."

I leaned down close to him so only he could hear when I said, "Get off Santa's lap or Santa will take off his pillow and stuff it down your rotten little throat."

We locked gazes for about five seconds. Then, taking his time, Ronnie got down off my lap. And stuck his tongue out at me and said, "Asshole." And went scampering away into the crowd.

I put on yet another false smile behind my false beard. Said grimly to one of the elves, "Next."

While I was listening to an eight-year-old with braces and a homicidal gleam in his eye tell me he wanted "a tank that has this neat missile in it and you shoot the missile and it blows everything up when it lands," Kerry appeared with a cup in her hand. She motioned for me to join her at the far side of the dais, behind Santa's sleigh. I got rid of the budding warmonger, told the nearest elf I was taking a short break, stood up creakily and with as much dignity as I could muster, and made my way through the cotton snowdrifts to where Kerry stood.

She looked far better in her costume than I did in mine; in fact, she looked so innocent and fetching I forgot for a moment that I was angry with her. She was dressed as an angel—all in white, with a coat-hanger halo wrapped in tinfoil. If real angels looked like her, I couldn't wait to get to heaven.

She handed me the cup. It was full of some sort of punch with a funny-looking skinny brown thing floating on top. "I thought you could use a little Christmas cheer," she said.

"I can use a lot of Christmas cheer. Is this stuff spiked?"

"Of course not. Since when do you drink hard liquor?"

"Since I sat down on that throne over there."

"Oh, now, it can't be that bad."

"No? Let's see. A five-year-old screamed so loud in my left ear that I'm still partially deaf. A fat kid stepped on my foot and nearly broke a toe. Another kid accidentally kneed me in the crotch and nearly broke something else. Not three minutes ago, a mugger-in-training named Ronnie punched me in the stomach and called me an asshole. And those are just the lowlights."

"Poor baby."

". . .That didn't sound very sincere."

"The fact is," she said, "most of the kids love you. I overheard a couple of them telling their parents what a nice old Santa you are."

"Yeah." I tried some of the punch. It wasn't too bad, considering the suspicious brown thing floating in it. Must be a deformed clove, I decided; the only other alternative—something that had come out of the back end of a mouse—was unthinkable. "How much more of this does the nice old Santa have to endure?"

"Two and a half hours."

"God! I'll never make it."

"Don't be such a curmudgeon," she said. "It's two days before Christmas, we're taking in lots of money for the needy, and everybody's having a grand time except you. Well, you and Mrs. Simmons."

"Who's Mrs. Simmons?"

"Randolph Simmons's wife. You know, the corporate attorney. She lost her wallet somehow—all her credit cards and two hundred dollars in cash."

"That's too bad. Tell her I'll replace the two hundred if she'll agree to trade places with me right now."

Kerry gave me her sometimes-you're-exasperating look. "Just hang in there, Santa," she said and started away.

"Don't use that phrase around the kid named Ronnie," I called after her. "It's liable to give him ideas."

I had been back on the throne less than ten seconds when who should reappear but the little thug himself. Ronnie wasn't alone this time; he had a bushy-mustached, gray-suited, scowling man with him. The two of them clumped up onto the dais, shouldered past an elf with a cherubic little girl in hand, and confronted me.

The mustached guy said in a low, angry voice, "What the hell's the idea threatening my kid?"

Fine, dandy. This was all I needed—an irate father.

"Answer me, pal. What's the idea telling Ronnie you'd shove a pillow down his throat?"

"He punched me in the stomach."

"So? That don't give you the right to threaten him. Hell, *I* ought to punch you in the stomach."

"Do it, Dad," Ronnie said, "punch the old fake."

Nearby, the cherub started to cry. Loudly.

We all looked at her. Ronnie's dad said, "What'd you do? Threaten her too?"

"Wanna see Santa! It's my turn, it's my turn!"

The elf said, "Don't worry, honey, you'll get your turn."

Ronnie's dad said, "Apologize to my kid and we'll let it go."

Ronnie said, "Nah, sock him one!"

I said, "Mind telling me your name?"

It was Ronnie's dad I spoke to. He looked blank for two or three seconds, after which he said, "Huh?"

"Your name. What is it?"

"What do you want to know for?"

"You look familiar. Very familiar, in fact. I think maybe we've met before."

He stiffened. Then he took a good long wary look at me, as if trying to see past my whiskers. Then he blinked, and all of a sudden his righteous indignation vanished and was replaced by a nervousness that bordered on the furtive. He wet his lips, backed off a step.

"Come on, Dad," the little thug said, "punch his lights out."

His dad told him to shut up. To me he said, "Let's just forget the whole thing, okay?" and then he turned in a hurry and dragged a protesting Ronnie down off the dais and back into the crowd.

I stared after them. And there was a little click in my mind and I was seeing a photograph of Ronnie's dad as a younger man without the big bushy mustache—and with a name and number across his chest.

Ronnie's dad and I knew each other, all right. I had once had a hand in having him arrested and sent to San Quentin on a grand larceny rap.

Ronnie's dad was Markey Waters, a professional pickpocket and jack-of-all-thievery who in his entire life had never gone anywhere or done anything to benefit anyone except Markey Waters. So what was he doing at the Gala Family Christmas Charity Benefit?

She lost her wallet somehow—all her credit cards and two hundred dollars in cash.

Right.

Practicing his trade, of course.

I should have stayed on the dais. I should have sent one of the elves to notify Security, while I perched on the throne and continued to act as a listening post for the kiddies.

But I didn't. Like a damned fool, I decided to handle the matter myself. Like a damned fool, I went charging off into the throng with the cherub's cries of "Wanna see Santa, *my* turn to see Santa!" rising to a crescendo behind me.

The milling crush of celebrants had closed around Markey Waters and his son and I could no longer see them. But they had been heading at an angle toward the far eastside entrance, so that was the direction I took. The rubber boots I wore were a size too small and pinched my feet, forcing me to walk in a kind of mincing step; and as if that wasn't bad enough, the boots were new and made squeaking sounds like a pair of rusty hinges. I also had to do some jostling to get through and around little knots of people, and some of the looks my maneuvers elicited were not of the peace-on-earth, goodwill-to-men variety. One elegantly dressed guy said, "Watch the hands, Claus," which might have been funny if I were not in such a dark and stormy frame of mind.

I was almost to the line of food booths along the east wall when I spotted Waters again, stopped near the second-to-last booth. One of his hands was clutching Ronnie's wrist and the other was plucking at an obese woman in a red-and-green, diagonally striped dress that made her look like a gigantic candy cane. Markey had evidently collided with her in his haste and caused her to spill a cup of punch on herself; she was loudly berating him for being a clumsy oaf, and refusing to let go of a big handful of his jacket until she'd had her say.

I minced and squeaked through another cluster of adults, all of whom were singing in accompaniment to the song now playing over the loud-speakers. The song, of all damn things, was "Here Comes Santa Claus."

Waters may not have heard the song, but its message got through to him just the same. He saw me bearing down on him from thirty feet away and understood immediately what my intentions were. His expression turned panicky; he tried to tear loose from the obese woman's grip. She hung on with all the tenacity of a bulldog.

I was ten feet from getting *my* bulldog hands on him when he proceeded to transform the Gala Family Christmas Charity Benefit from fun and frolic into chaos.

He let go of Ronnie's wrist, shouted, "Run, kid!" and then with his free hand he sucker-punched the obese woman on the uppermost of her chins. She not only released his jacket, she backpedaled into a lurching swoon that upset three other merrymakers and sent all four of them to the floor in a wild tangle of arms and legs. Voices rose in sudden alarm; somebody screamed like a fire siren going off. Bodies scattered out of harm's way. And Markey Waters went racing toward freedom.

I gave chase, dodging and juking and squeaking. I wouldn't have caught him except that while he was looking back over his shoulder to see how close I was, he tripped over something—his own feet maybe—and down he went in a sprawl. I reached him just as he scrambled up again. I laid both hands on him and growled, "This is as far as you go, Waters," whereupon he kicked me in the shin and yanked free.

I yelled, he staggered off, I limped after him. Shouts and shrieks echoed through the gym; so did the thunder of running feet and thudding bodies as more of the party animals stampeded. A woman came rushing out from inside the farthest of the food booths, got in Markey's path, and caused him to veer sideways to keep from plowing into her. That in turn allowed me to catch up to him in front of the booth. I clapped a hand on his shoulder this time, spun him around—and he smacked me in the chops with something warm and soggy that had been sitting on the booth's serving counter.

A meat pie.

He hit me in the face with a *pie.*

That was the last indignity in a night of indignities. Playing Santa Claus was bad enough; playing Lou Costello to a thief's Bud Abbott was intolerable. I roared; I pawed at my eyes and scraped off beef gravy and false whiskers and white wig; I lunged and caught Waters again before he could escape; I wrapped my arms around him. It was my intention to twist him around and get him into a crippling hammerlock, but he was stronger than he looked. So instead we performed a kind of crazy, lurching bear-hug dance for a few seconds. That came to an end—predictably —when we banged into one of the booth supports and the whole front framework collapsed in a welter of wood and bunting and pie and paper plates and plastic utensils, with us in the middle of it all.

Markey squirmed out from underneath me, feebly, and tried to crawl away through the wreckage. I disentangled myself from some of the bunting, lunged at his legs, hung on when he tried to kick loose. And then crawled on top of him, flipped him over on his back, fended off a couple of ineffectual blows, and did some effectual things to his head until he stopped struggling and decided to become unconscious.

I sat astraddle him, panting and puffing and wiping gravy out of my eyes and nose. The tumult, I realized then, had subsided somewhat behind me. I could hear the loudspeakers again—the song playing now was "Rudolph, the Red-Nosed Reindeer"—and I could hear voices lifted tentatively nearby. Just before a newspaper photographer came hurrying up and snapped a picture of me and my catch, just before a horrified Kerry and a couple of tardy security guards arrived, I heard two voices in particular speaking in awed tones.

"My God," one of them said, "what *happened?*"

"I dunno," the other one said. "But it sure looks like Santa Claus went berserk."

There were three of us in the football coach's office at the rear of the gym: Markey Waters and me and one of the security guards. It was fifteen minutes later and we were waiting for the arrival of San Francisco's finest. Waters was dejected and resigned, the guard was pretending not to be amused, and I was in a foul humor thanks to a combination of acute embarrassment, some bruises and contusions, and the fact that I had no choice but to keep on wearing the gravy-stained remnants of the Santa Claus suit. It was what I'd come here in; my own clothes were in Kerry's apartment.

On the desk between Waters and me was a diamond-and-sapphire brooch, a fancy platinum cigarette case, and a gold money clip containing three crisp fifty-dollar bills. We had found all three items nestled companionably inside Markey's jacket pocket. I prodded the brooch with a finger, which prompted the guard to say, "Nice haul. The brooch alone must be worth a couple of grand."

I didn't say anything. Neither did Markey.

The owner of the gold clip and the three fifties had reported them missing to Security just before Waters and I staged our minor riot; the owners of the brooch and cigarette case hadn't made themselves known yet, which was something of a tribute to Markey's light-fingered talents —talents that would soon land him back in the slammer on another grand larceny rap.

He had had his chin resting on his chest; now he raised it and looked at me. "My kid," he said, as if he'd just remembered he had one. "He get away?"

"No. One of the other guards nabbed him out front."

"Just as well. Where is he?"

"Being held close by. He's okay."

Markey let out a heavy breath. "I shouldn't of brought him along," he said.

"So why did you?"

"It's Christmas and the papers said this shindig was for kids, too. Ronnie and me don't get out together much since his mother ran out on us two years ago."

"Uh-huh," I said. "And besides, you figured it would be easier to make your scores if you had a kid along as camouflage."

He shrugged. "You, though—I sure didn't figure on somebody like you being here. What in hell's a private dick doing dressed up in a Santa Claus suit?"

"I've been asking myself that question all night."

"I mean, how can you figure a thing like that?" Markey said. "Ronnie comes running up, he says it's not really Santa up there and the guy pretending to be Santa threatened him, said he'd shove a pillow down the kid's throat. What am I supposed to do? I'd done a good night's work, I wanted to get out of here while the getting was good, but I couldn't let some jerk get away with threatening my kid, could I? I mean, I'm a father, too, right?" He let out another heavy breath. "I wish I wasn't a father," he said.

I said, "What about the wallet, Markey?"

"Huh?"

"The wallet and the two hundred in cash that was in it."

"Huh?"

"This stuff here isn't all you swiped tonight. You also got a wallet belonging to a Mrs. Randolph Simmons. It wasn't on you and neither was the two hundred. What'd you do with them?"

"I never scored a wallet," he said. "Not tonight."

"Markey . . ."

"I swear it. The other stuff, sure, you got me on that. But I'm telling you, I didn't score a wallet tonight."

I scowled at him. But his denial had the ring of truth; he had no reason to lie about the wallet. Well, then? Had Mrs. Simmons lost it after all? If that was the case, then I'd gone chasing after Waters for no good reason except that he was a convicted felon. I felt the embarrassment warming my face again. What if he *hadn't* dipped anybody tonight? I'd have looked like an even bigger fool than I did right now. . . .

Something tickled my memory and set me to pursuing a different and more productive line of thought. Oh, hell—of course. I'd been right in the first place; Mrs. Randolph Simmons's wallet had been stolen, not lost. And I knew now who had done the stealing.

But the knowledge didn't make me feel any better. If anything, it made me feel worse.

"Empty your pockets," I said.

"What for?"

"Because I told you to, that's what for."

"I don't have to do what you tell me."

"If you don't, I'll empty them for you."

"I want a lawyer," he said.

"You're too young to need a lawyer. Now empty your pockets before I smack you one."

Ronnie glared at me. I glared back at him. "If you smack me," he said, "it's police brutality." Nine years old going on forty.

"I'm not the police, remember? This is your last chance, kid: empty the pockets or else."

"Ahhh," he said, but he emptied the pockets.

He didn't have Mrs. Randolph Simmons's wallet, but he did have her two hundred dollars. Two hundred and four dollars to be exact. *I don't need you to give me toys. I can buy my own toys.* Sure. Two hundred and four bucks can buy a lot of toys, not to mention a lot of grief.

"What'd you do with the wallet, Ronnie?"

"What wallet?"

"Dumped it somewhere nearby, right?"

"I dunno what you're talking about."

"No? Then where'd you get the money?"

"I found it."

"Uh-huh. In Mrs. Randolph Simmons's purse."

"Who's she?"

"Your old man put you up to it, or was it your own idea?"

He favored me with a cocky little grin. "I'm smart," he said. "I'm gonna be just like my dad when I grow up."

"Yeah," I said sadly. "A chip off the old block if ever there was one."

Midnight.

Kerry and I were sitting on the couch in her living room. I sat with my head tipped back and my eyes closed; I had a thundering headache and a brain clogged with gloom. It had been a long, long night, full of all sorts of humiliations; and the sight of a nine-year-old kid, even a thuggish nine-year-old kid, being carted off to the Youth Authority at the same time his father was being carted off to the Hall of Justice was a pretty unfestive one.

I hadn't seen the last of the humiliations, either. Tonight's fiasco would get plenty of tongue-in-cheek treatment in the morning papers, complete with photographs—half a dozen reporters and photographers had arrived at the gym in tandem with the police and so there was no way Eberhardt and my other friends could help but find out. I was in for weeks of sly and merciless ribbing.

Kerry must have intuited my headache because she moved over close beside me and began to massage my temples. She's good at massage; some of the pain began to ease almost immediately. None of the gloom, though. You can't massage away gloom.

After a while she said, "I guess you blame me."

"Why should I blame you?"

"Well, if I hadn't talked you into playing Santa . . ."

"You didn't talk me into anything; I did it because I wanted to help you and the Benefit. No, I blame myself for what happened. I should have handled Markey Waters better. If I had, the Benefit wouldn't have come to such a bad end and you'd have made a lot more money for the charities."

"We made quite a bit as it is," Kerry said. "And you caught a professional thief and saved four good citizens from losing valuable personal property."

"And put a kid in the Youth Authority for Christmas."

"You're not responsible for that. His father is."

"Sure, I know. But it doesn't make me feel any better."

She was silent for a time. At the end of which she leaned down and kissed me, warmly.

I opened my eyes. "What was that for?"

"For being who and what you are. You grump and grumble and act the curmudgeon, but that's just a facade. Underneath you're a nice caring man with a big heart."

"Yeah. Me and St. Nick."

"Exactly." She looked at her watch. "It is now officially the twenty-fourth—Christmas Eve. How would you like one of your presents a little early?"

"Depends on which one."

"Oh, I think you'll like it." She stood up. "I'll go get it ready for you. Give me five minutes."

I gave her three minutes, which—miraculously enough—was all the time it took for my pall of gloom to lift. Then I got to my feet and went down the hall.

"Ready or not," I said as I opened the bedroom door, "here comes Santa Claus!"

STAKEOUT

FOUR o'clock in the morning. And I was sitting huddled and ass-numb in my car in a freezing rainstorm, waiting for a guy I had never seen in person to get out of a nice warm bed and drive off in his Mercedes, thus enabling me to follow him so I could find out where he lived.

Thrilling work if you can get it. The kind that makes any self-respecting detective wonder why he didn't become a plumber instead.

Rain hammered against the car's metal surfaces, sluiced so thickly down the windshield that it transformed the glass into an opaque screen; all I could see were smeary blobs of light that marked the street lamps along this block of 47th Avenue. Wind buffeted the car in forty-mile-an-hour gusts off the ocean nearby. Condensation had formed again on the driver's door window, even though I had rolled it down half an inch; I rubbed some of the mist away and took another bleary-eyed look across the street.

This was one of San Francisco's older middle-class residential neighborhoods, desirable—as long as you didn't mind fog-belt living—because Sutro Heights Park was just a block away and you were also within walking distance of Ocean Beach, the Cliff House, and Land's End. Most of the houses had been built in the thirties and stood shoulder-to-shoulder with their neighbors, but they seemed to have more individuality than the bland row houses dominating the avenues farther inland; out here, California Spanish was the dominant style. Asians had bought up much of the city's west side housing in recent years, but fewer of those close to the ocean than anywhere else. A lot of homes in pockets such as this were still owned by older-generation, blue-collar San Franciscans.

The house I had under surveillance, number 9279, was one of the Spanish stucco jobs, painted white with a red tile roof. Yucca palms, one large and three small, dominated its tiny front yard. The three-year-old Mercedes with the Washington state license plates was still parked, illegally, across the driveway. Above it, the house's front windows remained dark. If anybody was up yet I couldn't tell it from where I was sitting.

I shifted position for the hundredth time, wincing as my stiffened joints protested with creaks and twinges. I had been here four and a half hours now, with nothing to do except to sit and wait and try not to fall asleep; to listen to the rain and the rattle and stutter of my thoughts. I was weary and irritable and I wanted some hot coffee and my own warm bed. It would be well past dawn, I thought bleakly, before I got either one.

Stakeouts . . . God, how I hated them. The passive waiting, the boredom, the slow, slow passage of dead time. How many did this make over the past thirty-odd years? How many empty, wasted, lost hours? Too damn many, whatever the actual figure. The physical discomfort was also becoming less tolerable, especially on nights like this, when not even a heavy overcoat and gloves kept the chill from penetrating bone-deep. I had lived fifty-eight years; fifty-eight is too old to sit all-night stakeouts on the best of cases, much less on a lousy split-fee skip-trace.

I was starting to hate Randolph Hixley, too, sight unseen. He was the owner of the Mercedes across the street and my reason for being here. To his various and sundry employers, past and no doubt present, he was a highly paid free-lance computer consultant. To his ex-wife and two kids, he was a probable deadbeat who currently owed some $24,000 in back alimony and child support. To me and Puget Sound Investigations of Seattle, he was what should have been a small but adequate fee for routine work. Instead, he had developed into a minor pain in the ass. Mine.

Hixley had quit Seattle for parts unknown some four months ago, shortly after his wife divorced him for what she referred to as "sexual misconduct," and had yet to make a single alimony or child support payment. For reasons of her own, the wife had let the first two barren months go by without doing anything about it. On the occasion of the third due date, she had received a brief letter from Hixley informing her in tear-jerk language that he was so despondent over the breakup of their marriage he hadn't worked since leaving Seattle and was on the verge of becoming one of the homeless. He had every intention of fulfilling his obligations, though, the letter said; he would send money as soon as he got back on his feet. So would she bear with him for a while and please not sic the law on him? The letter was postmarked San Francisco, but with no return address.

The ex-wife, who was no dummy, smelled a rat. But because she still harbored some feelings for him, she had gone to Puget Sound Investigations rather than to the authorities, the object being to locate Hixley and determine if he really was broke and despondent. If so, then she would show the poor dear compassion and understanding. If not, then she would obtain a judgment against the son-of-a-bitch and force him to pay up or get thrown in the slammer.

Puget Sound had taken the job, done some preliminary work, and then called a San Francisco detective—me—and farmed out the tough part for half the fee. That kind of cooperative thing is done all the time when the client isn't wealthy enough and the fee isn't large enough for the primary agency to send one of its own operatives to another state. No private detective likes to split fees, particularly when he's the one doing most of the work, but ours is sometimes a back-scratching business. Puget Sound had done a favor for me once; now it was my turn.

Skip-tracing can be easy or it can be difficult, depending on the individual you're trying to find. At first I figured Randolph Hixley, broke or not, might be one of the difficult ones. He had no known relatives or friends in the Bay Area. He had stopped using his credit cards after the divorce, and had not applied for new ones, which meant that if he was working and had money, he was paying his bills in cash. In Seattle, he'd provided consultancy services to a variety of different companies, large and small, doing most of the work at home by computer link. If he'd hired out to one or more outfits in the Bay Area, Puget Sound had not been able to turn up a lead as to which they might be, so I probably wouldn't be able to either. There is no easy way to track down that information, not without some kind of insider pull with the IRS.

And yet despite all of that, I got lucky right away—so lucky I revised my thinking and decided, prematurely and falsely, that Hixley was going to be one of the easy traces after all. The third call I made was to a contact in the San Francisco City Clerk's office, and it netted me the information that the 1987 Mercedes 560 SL registered in Hixley's name had received two parking tickets on successive Thursday mornings, the most recent of which was the previous week. The tickets were for identical violations: illegal parking across a private driveway and illegal parking during posted street-cleaning hours. Both citations had been issued between seven and seven-thirty A.M. And in both instances, the address was the same: 9279 47th Avenue.

I looked up the address in my copy of the reverse city directory. 9279 47th Avenue was a private house occupied by one Anne Carswell, a commercial artist, and two other Carswells, Bonnie and Margo, whose ages were given as eighteen and nineteen, respectively, and who I presumed were her daughters. The Carswells didn't own the house; they had been renting it for a little over two years.

Since there had been no change of registration on the Mercedes—I checked on that with the DMV—I assumed that the car still belonged to Randolph Hixley. And I figured things this way: Hixley, who was no more broke and despondent than I was, had met and established a relationship with Anne Carswell, and taken to spending Wednesday nights at her house. Why only Wednesdays? For all I knew, once a week was as much passion as Randy and Anne could muster up. Or it could be the two daughters slept elsewhere that night. In any case, Wednesday was Hixley's night to howl.

So the next Wednesday evening I drove out there, looking for his Mercedes. No Mercedes. I made my last check at midnight, went home to bed, got up at six A.M., and drove back to 47th Avenue for another look. Still no Mercedes.

Well, I thought, they skipped a week. Or for some reason they'd altered their routine. I went back on Thursday night. And Friday night and Saturday night. I made spot checks during the day. On one occasion I saw a tall, willowy redhead in her late thirties—Anne Carswell, no doubt—driving out of the garage. On another occasion I saw the two daughters, one blond, one brunette, both attractive, having a conversation with a couple of sly college types. But that was all I saw. Still no Mercedes, still no Randolph Hixley.

I considered bracing one of the Carswell women on a ruse, trying to find out that way where Hixley was living. But I didn't do it. He might have put them wise to his background and the money he owed, and asked them to keep mum if anyone ever approached them. Or I might slip somehow in my questioning and make her suspicious enough to call Hixley. I did not want to take the chance of warning him off.

Last Wednesday had been another bust. So had early Thursday—I drove out there at five A.M. that time. And so had the rest of the week. I was wasting time and gas and sleep, but it was the only lead I had. All the other skip-trace avenues I'd explored had led me nowhere near my elusive quarry.

Patience and perseverance are a detective's best assets; hang in there long enough and as often as not you find what you're looking for.

Tonight I'd finally found Hixley and his Mercedes, back at the Carswell house after a two-week absence.

The car hadn't been there the first two times I drove by, but when I made what would have been my last pass, at twenty of twelve, there it was, once again illegally parked across the driveway. Maybe he didn't give a damn about parking tickets because he had no intention of paying them. Or maybe he disliked walking fifty feet or so, which was how far away the nearest legal curb space was. Or, hell, maybe he was just an arrogant bastard who thumbed his nose at the law any time it inconvenienced him. Whatever his reason for blocking Anne Carswell's driveway, it was his big mistake.

The only choice I had, spotting his car so late, was to stake it out and wait for him to show. I would have liked to go home and catch a couple of hours sleep, but for all I knew he wouldn't spend the entire night this time. If I left and came back and he was gone, I'd have to go through this whole rigmarole yet again.

So I parked and settled in. The lights in the Carswell house had gone off at twelve-fifteen and hadn't come back on since. It had rained off and on all evening, but the first hard rain started a little past one. The storm had steadily worsened until, now, it was a full-fledged howling, ripping blow. And still I sat and still I waited. . . .

A blurred set of headlights came boring up 47th toward Geary, the first car to pass in close to an hour. When it went swishing by I held my watch up close to my eyes: 4:07. Suppose he stays in there until eight or nine? I thought. Four or five more hours of this and I'd be too stiff to move. It was meatlocker cold in the car. I couldn't start the engine and put the heater on because the exhaust, if not the idle, would call attention to my presence. I'd wrapped my legs and feet in the car blanket, which provided some relief; even so, I could no longer feel my toes when I tried to wiggle them.

The hard drumming beat of the rain seemed to be easing a little. Not the wind, though; a pair of back-to-back gusts shook the car, as if it were a toy in the hands of a destructive child. I shifted position again, pulled the blanket more tightly around my ankles.

A light went on in the Carswell house.

I scrubbed mist off the driver's door window, peered through the wet glass. The big front window was alight over there, behind drawn curtains. That was a good sign: People don't usually put their living room lights on at four A.M. unless somebody plans to be leaving soon.

Five minutes passed while I sat chafing my gloved hands together and moving my feet up and down to improve circulation. Then another light went on—the front porch light this time. And a few seconds after that, the door opened and somebody came out onto the stoop.

It wasn't Randolph Hixley; it was a young blond woman wearing a trenchcoat over what looked to be a lacy nightgown. One of the Carswell daughters. She stood still for a moment, looking out over the empty street. Then she drew the trenchcoat collar up around her throat and ran down the stairs and over to Hixley's Mercedes.

For a few seconds she stood hunched on the sidewalk on the passenger side, apparently unlocking the front door with a set of keys. She pulled the door open, as if making sure it was unlocked, then slammed it shut again. She turned and ran back up the stairs and vanished into the house.

I thought: Now what was that all about?

The porch light stayed on. So did the light in the front room. Another three minutes dribbled away. The rain slackened a little more, so that it was no longer sheeting; the wind continued to wail and moan. And then things got even stranger over there.

First the porch light went off. Then the door opened and somebody exited onto the stoop, followed a few seconds later by a cluster of shadow-shapes moving in an awkward, confused fashion. I couldn't identify them or tell what they were doing while they were all grouped on the porch; the tallest yucca palm cast too much shadow and I was too far away. But when they started down the stairs, there was just enough extension of light from the front window to individuate the shapes for me.

There were four of them, by God—three in an uneven line on the same step, the fourth backing down in front of them as though guiding the way. Three women, one man. The man—several inches taller, wearing an overcoat and hat, head lolling forward as if he were drunk or unconscious—was being supported by two of the women.

They all managed to make it down the slippery stairs without any of them suffering a misstep. When they reached the sidewalk, the one who had been guiding ran ahead to the Mercedes and dragged the front passenger door open. In the faint outspill from the dome light, I watched the other two women, with the third one's help, push and prod the man inside. Once they had the door shut again, they didn't waste any time catching their breaths. Two of them went running back to the house; the third hurried around to the driver's door, bent to unlock it. She was the only one of the three, I realized then, who was fully dressed: raincoat, rainhat, slacks, boots. When she slid in under the wheel I had a dome-lit glimpse of reddish hair and a white, late-thirties face under the rainhat. Anne Carswell.

She fired up the Mercedes, let the engine warm for all of five seconds, switched on the headlights, and eased away from the curb at a crawl, the way you'd drive over a surface of broken glass. The two daughters were already back inside the house, with the door shut behind them. I had long since unwrapped the blanket from around my legs; I didn't hesitate in starting my car. Or in trying to start it: The engine was cold and it took three whiffing tries before it caught and held. If Anne Carswell had been driving fast, I might have lost her. As it was, with her creeping along, she was only halfway along the next block behind me when I swung out into a tight U-turn.

I ran dark through the rain until she completed a slow turn west on Point Lobos and passed out of sight. Then I put on my lights and accelerated across Geary to the Point Lobos intersection. I got there in time to pick up the Mercedes' taillights as it went through the flashing yellow traffic signal at 48th Avenue. I let it travel another fifty yards downhill before I turned onto Point Lobos in pursuit.

Five seconds later, Anne Carswell had another surprise for me.

I expected her to continue down past the Cliff House and around onto the Great Highway; there is no other through direction once you pass 48th. But she seemed not to be leaving the general area after all. The Mercedes' brake lights came on and she slow-turned into the Merrie Way parking area above the ruins of the old Sutro Baths. The combination lot and overlook had only the one entrance/exit; it was surrounded on its other three sides by cliffs and clusters of wind-shaped cypress trees and a rocky nature trail that led out beyond the ruins to Land's End.

Without slowing, I drove on past. She was crawling straight down the center of the unpaved, potholed lot, toward the trees at the far end. Except for the Mercedes, the rain-drenched expanse appeared deserted.

Below Merrie Way, on the other side of Point Lobos, there is a newer, paved parking area carved out of Sutro Heights park for sightseers and patrons of Louis' Restaurant opposite and the Cliff House bars and eateries farther down. It, too, was deserted at this hour. From the overlook above, you can't see this curving downhill section of Point Lobos; I swung across into the paved lot, cut my lights, looped around to where I had a clear view of the Merrie Way entrance. Then I parked, shut off the engine, and waited.

For a few seconds I could see a haze of slowly moving light up there, but not the Mercedes itself. Then the light winked out and there was nothing to see except wind-whipped rain and dark. Five minutes went by. Still nothing to see. She must have parked, I thought—but to do what?

Six minutes, seven. At seven and a half, a shape materialized out of the gloom above the entrance—somebody on foot, walking fast, bent against the lashing wind. Anne Carswell. She was moving at an uphill angle out of the overlook, climbing to 48th Avenue.

When she reached the sidewalk, a car came through the flashing yellow at the intersection and its headlight beams swept over her; she turned away from them, as if to make sure her face wasn't seen. The car swished down past where I was, disappeared beyond the Cliff House. I watched Anne Carswell cross Point Lobos and hurry into 48th at the upper edge of the park.

Going home, I thought. Abandoned Hixley and his Mercedes on the overlook and now she's hoofing it back to her daughters.

What the hell?

I started the car and drove up to 48th and turned there. Anne Carswell was now on the opposite side of the street, near where Geary dead-ends at the park; when my lights caught her she turned her head away as she had a couple of minutes ago. I drove two blocks, circled around onto 47th, came back a block and then parked and shut down again within fifty yards of the Carswell house. Its porch light was back on, which indicated that the daughters were anticipating her imminent return. Two minutes later she came fast-walking out of Geary onto 47th. One minute after that, she climbed the stairs to her house and let herself in. The porch light went out immediately, followed fifteen seconds later by the light in the front room.

I got the car moving again and made my way back down to the Merrie Way overlook.

The Mercedes was still the only vehicle on the lot, parked at an angle just beyond the long terraced staircase that leads down the cliffside to the pitlike bottom of the ruins. I pulled in alongside, snuffed my lights. Before I got out, I armed myself with the flashlight I keep clipped under the dash.

Icy wind and rain slashed at me as I crossed to the Mercedes. Even above the racket made by the storm, I could hear the barking of sea lions on the offshore rocks beyond the Cliff House. Surf boiled frothing over those rocks, up along the cliffs and among the concrete foundations that are all that's left of the old bathhouse. Nasty night, and a nasty business here to go with it. I was sure of that now.

I put the flashlight up against the Mercedes' passenger window, flicked it on briefly. He was in there, all right; she'd shoved him over so that he lay half sprawled under the wheel, his head tipped back against the driver's door. The passenger door was unlocked. I opened it and got in and shut the door again to extinguish the dome light. I put the flash beam on his face, shielding it with my hand.

Randolph Hixley, no doubt of that; the photograph Puget Sound Investigations had sent me was a good one. No doubt, either, that he was dead. I checked for a pulse, just to make sure. Then I moved the light over him, slowly, to see if I could find out what had killed him.

There weren't any discernible wounds or bruises or other marks on his body; no holes or tears or bloodstains on his damp clothing. Poison? Not that, either. Most any deadly poison produces convulsions, vomiting, rictus; his facial muscles were smooth and when I sniffed at his mouth I smelled nothing except Listerine.

Natural causes, then? Heart attack, stroke, aneurysm? Sure, maybe. But if he'd died of natural causes, why would Anne Carswell and her daughters have gone to all the trouble of moving his body and car down here? Why not just call Emergency Services?

On impulse I probed Hixley's clothing and found his wallet. It was empty—no cash, no credit cards, nothing except some old photos. Odd. He'd quit using credit cards after his divorce; he should have been carrying at least a few dollars. I took a close look at his hands and wrists. He was wearing a watch, a fairly new and fairly expensive one. No rings or other jewelry but there was a white mark on his otherwise tanned left pinkie, as if a ring had been recently removed.

They rolled him, I thought. All the cash in his wallet and a ring off his finger. Not the watch because it isn't made of gold or platinum and you can't get much for a watch, anyway, these days.

But why? Why would they kill a man for a few hundred bucks? Or rob a dead man and then try to dump the body? In either case, the actions of those three women made no damn sense. . . .

Or did they?

I was beginning to get a notion.

I backed out of the Mercedes and went to sit and think in my own car. I remembered some things, and added them together with some other things, and did a little speculating, and the notion wasn't a notion anymore—it was the answer.

Hell, I thought then, I'm getting old. Old and slow on the uptake.
I should have seen this part of it as soon as they brought the body out.
And I should have tumbled to the other part a week ago, if not sooner.

I sat there for another minute, feeling my age and a little sorry for
myself because it was going to be quite a while yet before I got any sleep.
Then, dutifully, I hauled up my mobile phone and called in the law.

They arrested the three women a few minutes past seven A.M. at the
house on 47th Avenue. I was present for identification purposes. Anne
Carswell put up a blustery protest of innocence until the inspector in
charge, a veteran named Ginzberg, tossed the words "foul play" into the
conversation; then the two girls broke down simultaneously and soon
there were loud squawks of denial from all three: "We didn't hurt him!
He had a heart attack, he died of a heart attack!" The girls, it turned out,
were not named Carswell and were not Anne Carswell's daughters. The
blonde was Bonnie Harper; the brunette was Margo LaFond. They were
both former runaways from southern California.

The charges against the trio included failure to report a death,
unlawful removal of a corpse, and felony theft. But the main charge was
something else entirely.

The main charge was operating a house of prostitution.

Later that day, after I had gone home for a few hours' sleep, I laid the
whole thing out for my partner, Eberhardt.

"I should have known they were hookers and Hixley was a
customer," I said. "There were enough signs. His wife divorced him for
'sexual misconduct'; that was one. Another was how unalike those three
women were—different hair colors, which isn't typical in a mother and
her daughters. Then there were those sly young guys I saw with the two
girls. They weren't boyfriends, they were customers too."

"Hixley really did die of a heart attack?" Eberhardt asked.

"Yeah. Carswell couldn't risk notifying Emergency Services; she
didn't know much about Hixley and she was afraid somebody would
come around asking questions. She had a nice discreet operation going
there, with a small but high-paying clientele, and she didn't want a dead
man to rock the boat. So she and the girls dressed the corpse and hustled
it out of there. First, though, they emptied Hixley's wallet and she
stripped a valuable garnet ring off his pinkie. She figured it was safe to do

that; if anybody questioned the empty wallet and missing ring, it would look like the body had been rolled on the Merrie Way overlook, after he'd driven in there himself and had his fatal heart attack. As far as she knew, there was nothing to tie Hixley to her and her girls—no direct link, anyhow. He hadn't told her about the two parking tickets."

"Uh-huh. And he was in bed with all three of them when he croaked?"

"So they said. Right in the middle of a round of fun and games. That was what he paid them for each of the times he went there—seven hundred and fifty bucks for all three, all night."

"Jeez, three women at one time." Eberhardt paused, thinking about it. Then he shook his head. "*How?*" he said.

I shrugged. "Where there's a will, there's a way."

"Kinky sex—I never did understand it. I guess I'm old fashioned."

"Me too. But Hixley's brand is pretty tame, really, compared to some of the things that go on nowadays."

"Seems like the whole damn world gets a little kinkier every day," Eberhardt said. "A little crazier every day, too. You know what I mean?"

"Yeah," I said, "I know what you mean."

SOULS BURNING

HOTEL Majestic, Sixth Street, downtown San Francisco. A hell of an address—a hell of a place for an ex-con not long out of Folsom to set up housekeeping. Sixth Street, south of Market—South of the Slot, it used to be called—is the heart of the city's Skid Road and has been for more than half a century.

Eddie Quinlan. A name and a voice out of the past, neither of which I'd recognized when he called that morning. Close to seven years since I had seen or spoken to him, six years since I'd even thought of him. Eddie Quinlan. Edgewalker, shadow-man with no real substance or purpose, drifting along the narrow catwalk that separates conventional society from the underworld. Information seller, gofer, small-time bagman, doer of any insignificant job, legitimate or otherwise, that would help keep him in food and shelter, liquor and cigarettes. The kind of man you looked at but never really saw: a modern-day Yehudi, the little man who wasn't there. Eddie Quinlan. Nobody, loser—fall guy. Drug bust in the Tenderloin one night six and a half years ago; one dealer setting up another, and Eddie Quinlan, small-time bagman, caught in the middle; hard-assed judge, five years in Folsom, goodbye Eddie Quinlan. And the drug dealers? They walked, of course. Both of them.

And now Eddie was out, had been out for six months. And after six months of freedom, he'd called me. Would I come to his room at the Hotel Majestic tonight around eight? He'd tell me why when he saw me. It was real important—would I come? All right, Eddie. But I couldn't figure it. I had bought information from him in the old days, bits and pieces for five or ten dollars; maybe he had something to sell now. Only I wasn't looking for anything and I hadn't put the word out, so why pick me to call?

If you're smart you don't park your car on the street at night South of the Slot. I put mine in the Fifth and Mission Garage at 7:45 and walked over to Sixth. It had rained most of the day and the streets were still wet, but now the sky was cold and clear. The kind of night that is as hard as black glass, so that light seems to bounce off the dark instead of shining through it; lights and their colors so bright and sharp reflecting off the night and the wet surfaces that the glare is like splinters against your eyes.

Friday night, and Sixth Street was teeming. Sidewalks jammed—old men, young men, bag ladies, painted ladies, blacks, whites, Asians, addicts, pushers, muttering mental cases, drunks leaning against walls in tight little clusters while they shared paper-bagged bottles of sweet wine and cans of malt liquor; men and women in filthy rags, in smart new outfits topped off with sunglasses, carrying ghetto blasters and red-and-white canes, some of the canes in the hands of individuals who could see as well as I could, carrying a hidden array of guns and knives and other lethal instruments. Cheap hotels, greasy spoons, seedy taverns, and liquor stores complete with barred windows and cynical proprietors that stayed open well past midnight. Laughter, shouts, curses, threats; bickering and dickering. The stenches of urine and vomit and unwashed bodies and rotgut liquor, and over those like an umbrella, the subtle effluvium of despair. Predators and prey, half hidden in shadow, half revealed in the bright, sharp dazzle of fluorescent lights and bloody neon.

It was a mean street, Sixth, one of the meanest, and I walked it warily. I may be fifty-eight but I'm a big man and I walk hard too; and I look like what I am. Two winos tried to panhandle me and a fat hooker in an orange wig tried to sell me a piece of her tired body, but no one gave me any trouble.

The Majestic was five stories of old wood and plaster and dirty brick, just off Howard Street. In front of its narrow entrance, a crack dealer and one of his customers were haggling over the price of a baggie of rock cocaine; neither of them paid any attention to me as I moved past them. Drug deals go down in the open here, day and night. It's not that the cops don't care, or that they don't patrol Sixth regularly; it's just that the dealers outnumber them ten to one. On Skid Road any crime less severe than aggravated assault is strictly low priority.

Small, barren lobby: no furniture of any kind. The smell of ammonia hung in the air like swamp gas. Behind the cubbyhole desk was an old man with dead eyes that would never see anything they didn't want to see. I said, "Eddie Quinlan," and he said, "Two-oh-two" without moving his lips. There was an elevator but it had an *Out of Order* sign on it; dust speckled the sign. I went up the adjacent stairs.

The disinfectant smell permeated the second floor hallway as well. Room 202 was just off the stairs, fronting on Sixth; one of the metal 2s on the door had lost a screw and was hanging upside down. I used my knuckles just below it. Scraping noise inside, and a voice said, "Yeah?"

I identified myself. A lock clicked, a chain rattled, the door wobbled open, and for the first time in nearly seven years I was looking at Eddie Quinlan.

He hadn't changed much. Little guy, about five-eight, and past forty now. Thin, nondescript features, pale eyes, hair the color of sand. The hair was thinner and the lines in his face were longer and deeper, almost like incisions where they bracketed his nose. Otherwise he was the same Eddie Quinlan.

"Hey," he said, "thanks for coming. I mean it, thanks."

"Sure, Eddie."

"Come on in."

The room made me think of a box—the inside of a huge rotting packing crate. Four bare walls with the scaly remnants of paper on them like psoriatic skin, bare uncarpeted floor, unshaded bulb hanging from the center of a bare ceiling. The bulb was dark; what light there was came from a low-wattage reading lamp and a wash of red-and-green neon from the hotel's sign that spilled in through a single window. Old iron-framed bed, unpainted nightstand, scarred dresser, straight-backed chair next to the bed and in front of the window, alcove with a sink and toilet and no door, closet that wouldn't be much larger than a coffin.

"Not much, is it," Eddie said.

I didn't say anything.

He shut the hall door, locked it. "Only place to sit is that chair there. Unless you want to sit on the bed? Sheets are clean. I try to keep things clean as I can."

"Chair's fine."

I went across to it; Eddie put himself on the bed. A room with a view, he'd said on the phone. Some view. Sitting here you could look down past Howard and up across Mission—almost two full blocks of the worst street in the city. It was so close you could hear the beat of its pulse, the ugly sounds of its living and its dying.

"So why did you ask me here, Eddie? If it's information for sale, I'm not buying right now."

"No, no, nothing like that. I ain't in the business any more."

"Is that right?"

"Prison taught me a lesson. I got rehabilitated." There was no sarcasm or irony in the words; he said them matter-of-factly.

"I'm glad to hear it."

"I been a good citizen ever since I got out. No lie. I haven't had a drink, ain't even been in a bar."

"What are you doing for money?"

"I got a job," he said. "Shipping department at a wholesale sporting goods outfit on Brannan. It don't pay much but it's honest work."

I nodded. "What is it you want, Eddie?"

"Somebody I can talk to, somebody who'll understand—that's all I want. You always treated me decent. Most of 'em, no matter who they were, they treated me like I wasn't even human. Like I was a turd or something."

"Understand what?"

"About what's happening down there."

"Where? Sixth Street?"

"Look at it," he said. He reached over and tapped the window; stared through it. "Look at the people . . . there, you see that guy in the wheelchair and the one pushing him? Across the street there?"

I leaned closer to the glass. The man in the wheelchair wore a military camouflage jacket, had a heavy wool blanket across his lap; the black man manipulating him along the crowded sidewalk was thick-bodied, with a shiny bald head. "I see them."

"White guy's name is Baxter," Eddie said. "Grenade blew up under him in 'Nam and now he's a paraplegic. Lives right here in the Majestic, on this floor down at the end. Deals crack and smack out of his room. Elroy, the black dude, is his bodyguard and roommate. Mean, both of 'em. Couple of months ago, Elroy killed a guy over on Minna that tried to stiff them. Busted his head with a brick. You believe it?"

"I believe it."

"And they ain't the worst on the street. Not the worst."

"I believe that too."

"Before I went to prison I lived and worked with people like that and I never saw what they were. I mean I just never saw it. Now I do, I see it clear—every day walking back and forth to work, every night from up here. It makes you sick after a while, the things you see when you see 'em clear."

"Why don't you move?"

"Where to? I can't afford no place better than this."

"No better room, maybe, but why not another neighborhood? You don't have to live on Sixth Street."

"Wouldn't be much better, any other neighborhood I could buy into. They're all over the city now, the ones like Baxter and Elroy. Used to be it was just Skid Road and the Tenderloin and the ghettos. Now they're everywhere, more and more every day. You know?"

"I know."

"Why? It don't have to be this way, does it?"

Hard times, bad times: alienation, poverty, corruption, too much government, not enough government, lack of social services, lack of caring, drugs like a cancer destroying society. Simplistic explanations that were no explanations at all and as dehumanizing as the ills they described. I was tired of hearing them and I didn't want to repeat them, to Eddie Quinlan or anybody else. So I said nothing.

He shook his head. "Souls burning everywhere you go," he said, and it was as if the words hurt his mouth coming out.

Souls burning. "You find religion at Folsom, Eddie?"

"Religion? I don't know, maybe a little. Chaplain we had there, I talked to him sometimes. He used to say that about the hardtimers, that their souls were burning and there wasn't nothing he could do to put out the fire. They were doomed, he said, and they'd doom others to burn with 'em."

I had nothing to say to that either. In the small silence a voice from outside said distinctly, "Dirty bastard, what you doin' with my pipe?" It was cold in there, with the hard bright night pressing against the window. Next to the door was a rusty steam radiator but it was cold too; the heat would not be on more than a few hours a day, even in the dead of winter, in the Hotel Majestic.

"That's the way it is in the city," Eddie said. "Souls burning. All day long, all night long, souls on fire."

"Don't let it get to you."

"Don't it get to *you*?"

". . . Yes. Sometimes."

He bobbed his head up and down. "You want to do something, you know? You want to try to fix it somehow, put out the fires. There has to be a way."

"I can't tell you what it is," I said.

He said, "If we all just did *something*. It ain't too late. You don't think it's too late?"

"No."

"Me neither. There's still hope."

"Hope, faith, blind optimism—sure."

"You got to believe," he said, nodding. "That's all, you just got to believe."

Angry voices rose suddenly from outside; a woman screamed, thin and brittle. Eddie came off the bed, hauled up the window sash. Chill damp air and street noises came pouring in: shouts, cries, horns honking, cars whispering on the wet pavement, a Muni bus clattering along Mission; more shrieks. He leaned out, peering downward.

"Look," he said, "look."

I stretched forward and looked. On the sidewalk below, a hooker in a leopard-skin coat was running wildly toward Howard; she was the one doing the yelling. Chasing behind her, tight black skirt hiked up over the tops of net stockings and hairy thighs, was a hideously rouged transvestite waving a pocket knife. A group of winos began laughing and chanting "Rape! Rape!" as the hooker and the transvestite ran zigzagging out of sight on Howard.

Eddie pulled his head back in. The flickery neon wash made his face seem surreal, like a hallucinogenic vision. "That's the way it is," he said sadly. "Night after night, day after day."

With the window open, the cold was intense; it penetrated my clothing and crawled on my skin. I'd had enough of it, and of this room and Eddie Quinlan and Sixth Street.

"Eddie, just what is it you want from me?"

"I already told you. Talk to somebody who understands how it is down there."

"Is that the only reason you asked me here?"

"Ain't it enough?"

"For you, maybe." I got to my feet. "I'll be going now."

He didn't argue. "Sure, you go ahead."

"Nothing else you want to say?"

"Nothing else." He walked to the door with me, unlocked it, and then put out his hand. "Thanks for coming. I appreciate it, I really do."

"Yeah. Good luck, Eddie."

"You too," he said. "Keep the faith."

I went out into the hall, and the door shut gently and the lock clicked behind me.

Downstairs, out of the Majestic, along the mean street and back to the garage where I'd left my car. And all the way I kept thinking: There's something else, something more he wanted from me . . . and I gave it to him by going there and listening to him. But what? What did he really want?

I found out later that night. It was all over the TV—special bulletins and then the eleven o'clock news.

Twenty minutes after I left him, Eddie Quinlan stood at the window of his room-with-a-view, and in less than a minute, using a high-powered semiautomatic rifle he'd taken from the sporting goods outfit where he worked, he shot down fourteen people on the street below. Nine dead, five wounded, one of the wounded in critical condition and not expected to live. Six of the victims were known drug dealers; all of the others also had arrest records, for crimes ranging from prostitution to burglary. Two of the dead were Baxter, the paraplegic ex-Vietnam vet, and his bodyguard, Elroy.

By the time the cops showed up, Sixth Street was empty except for the dead and the dying. No more targets. And up in his room, Eddie Quinlan had sat on the bed and put the rifle's muzzle in his mouth and used his big toe to pull the trigger.

My first reaction was to blame myself. But how could I have known or even guessed? Eddie Quinlan. Nobody, loser, shadow-man without substance or purpose. How could anyone have figured him for a thing like that?

Somebody I can talk to, somebody who'll understand—that's all I want.

No. What he'd wanted was somebody to help him justify to himself what he was about to do. Somebody to record his verbal suicide note. Somebody he could trust to pass it on afterward, tell it right and true to the world.

You want to do something, you know? You want to try to fix it somehow, put out the fires. There has to be a way.

Nine dead, five wounded, one of the wounded in critical condition and not expected to live. Not that way.

Souls burning. All day long, all night long, souls on fire.

The soul that had burned tonight was Eddie Quinlan's.

BEDEVILED

"YOUNG man," Mrs. Abbott said to me, "do you believe in ghosts?"

The "young man" surprised me almost as much as the question. But then, when you're eighty, fifty-eight looks pretty damn young. "Ghosts?"

"Crossovers. Visitors from the Other Side."

"Well, let's say I'm skeptical."

"I've always been skeptical myself. But I just can't help wondering if it might be Carl who is deviling me."

"Carl?"

"My late husband. Carl's ghost, you see."

Beside me on the sofa, Addie Crenshaw sighed and rolled her eyes in my direction. Then she smiled tolerantly across at Mrs. Abbott in her Boston rocker. "Nonsense," she said. "Carl has been gone ten years, Margaret. Why would his ghost come back *now*?"

"Well, it could be he's angry with me."

"Angry?"

"I'm not sure I did all I could for him when he was ill. He may blame me for his death; he always did have a tendency to hold a grudge. And surely the dead know when the living's time is near. Suppose he has crossed over to give me a sample of what our reunion on the Other Side will be like?"

There was a small silence.

Mrs. Crenshaw, who was Margaret Abbott's neighbor, friend, watchdog, and benefactor, and who was also my client, shifted her long, lean body and said patiently, "Margaret, ghosts can't ring the telephone in the middle of the night. Or break windows. Or dig up rose bushes."

"Perhaps if they're motivated enough . . ."

"Not under any circumstances. They can't put poison in cat food, either. You know they can't do *that*."

"Poor Harold," Mrs. Abbott said. "Carl wasn't fond of cats, you know. In fact, he used to throw rocks at them."

"It wasn't Carl. You and I both know perfectly well who is responsible."

"We do?"

"Of course we do. The Petersons."

"Who, dear?"

"The Petersons. Those real estate people."

"Oh, I don't think so. Why would they poison Harold?"

"Because they're vermin. They're greedy swine."

"Addie, don't be silly. People can't be vermin or swine."

"Can't they?" Mrs. Crenshaw said. "Can't they just?"

I put my cup and saucer down on the coffee table, just hard enough to rattle one against the other, and cleared my throat. The three of us had been sitting here for ten minutes, in the old-fashioned living room of Margaret Abbott's Parkside home, drinking coffee and dancing around the issue that had brought us together. All the dancing was making me uncomfortable; it was time for me to take a firm grip on the proceedings.

"Ladies," I said, "suppose we concern ourselves with facts, not speculation. That'll make my job a whole lot easier."

"I've already told you the facts," Mrs. Crenshaw said. "Margaret and I both have."

"Let's go over them again anyway. I want to make sure I have everything clear in my mind. This late-night harassment started two weeks ago, is that right? On a Saturday night?"

"Saturday morning, actually," Mrs. Abbott said. "It was just three A.M. when the phone rang. I know because I looked at my bedside clock." She was tiny and frail and she couldn't get around very well without a walker, and Mrs. Crenshaw had warned me that she was inclined to be "a little dotty," but there was nothing wrong with her memory. "I thought someone must have died. That is usually why the telephone rings at such an hour."

"But no one was on the line."

"Well, someone was breathing."

"But whoever it was didn't say anything."

"No. I said hello several times and he hung up."

"The other three calls came at the same hour?"

"Approximately, yes. Four mornings in a row."

"And he didn't say a word until the last one."

"Two words. I heard them clearly."

" 'Drop dead.' "

"It sounds silly but it wasn't. It was very disturbing."

"I'm sure it was. Can you remember anything distinctive about the voice?"

"Well, it was a man's voice. I'm certain of that."

"But you didn't recognize it."

"No. It was muffled, as if it were coming from . . . well, from the Other Side."

Mrs. Crenshaw started to say something, but I got words out first. "Then the calls stopped and two days later somebody broke the back porch window. Late at night again."

"With a rock," Mrs. Abbott said, nodding. "Charley came and fixed it."

"Charley. That would be your nephew, Charley Doyle."

"Yes. Fixing windows is his business. He's a glazier."

"And after that, someone spray-painted the back and side walls of the house."

"Filthy words," Mrs. Abbott said, "dozens of them. It was a terrible mess. Addie and Leonard . . . Leonard is Addie's brother, you know."

"Yes, ma'am."

"They cleaned it up. It took them an entire day. Then my rose bushes . . . oh, I cried when I saw what had been done to them. I loved my roses. Pink floribundas and dark red and orange teas." She wagged her white head sadly. "He didn't like roses any more than he did cats."

"Who didn't?"

"Carl. My late husband. And he sometimes had a foul mouth. He knew all those words that were painted on the house."

"Margaret," Mrs. Crenshaw said firmly, "it wasn't Carl. There is no such thing as a ghost, there simply isn't."

"Well, all right. But I do wonder, Addie. I really do."

"About the poison incident," I said. "That was the most recent thing, two nights ago?"

"Poor Harold almost died," Mrs. Abbott said. "If Addie and Leonard hadn't rushed him to the vet, he would have."

"Arsenic," Mrs. Crenshaw said. "That's what the vet said it was. Arsenic in Harold's food bowl."

"Which is kept inside or outside the house?"

"Oh, inside," Mrs. Abbott said. "On the back porch. Harold isn't allowed outside. Not the way people drive their cars nowadays."

"So whoever put the poison in the cat's bowl had to get inside the house to do it."

"Breaking and entering," Mrs. Crenshaw said. "That was the final straw."

"Were there any signs of forced entry?"

"Leonard and I couldn't find any."

Mrs. Abbott said abruptly, "Oh, there he is now. He must have heard us talking about him."

I looked where she was looking, behind me. There was nobody there. "Leonard?"

"No, Harold. Harold, dear, come and meet the nice gentleman Addie brought to help us."

The cat that came sauntering around the sofa was a rotund and middle-aged orange tabby, with a great swaying paunch that brushed the carpet as he moved. He plunked himself down five feet from where I was, paying no attention to any of us, and began to lick his shoulder. For a cat that had been sick as a dog two days ago, he looked pretty fit.

"Mrs. Abbott," I said, "who has a key to this house?"

She blinked at me behind her glasses. "Key?"

"Besides you and Mrs. Crenshaw, I mean."

"Why, Charley has one, of course."

"Any other member of your family?"

"Charley is my only living relative."

"Is there anyone else who . . . *uff*!"

An orange blur came flying through the air and a pair of meaty forepaws almost destroyed what was left of my manly pride. The pain made me writhe a little but the movement didn't dislodge Harold; he had all four claws anchored to various portions of my lap. I thought an evil thought that had to do with retribution, but it died in shame when he commenced a noisy purring. Like a fool I put forth a tentative hand and petted him. He tolerated that for all of five seconds; then he bit me on the soft webbing between my thumb and forefinger. Then he jumped down and streaked wildly out of the room.

"He likes you," Mrs. Abbott said.

I looked at her.

"Oh, he does," she said. "It's just his way with strangers. When Harold nips you it's a sign of affection."

I looked down at my hand. The sign of affection was bleeding.

It was one of those cases, all right. I'd sensed it as soon as Addie Crenshaw walked into my office that morning, and I'd known it for sure two minutes after she started talking. City bureaucracy, real estate squabbles, nocturnal prowlings, poisoned cats, a half-dotty old lady—off-the-wall stuff, with seriocomic overtones. The police weren't keen on investigating the more recent developments and I didn't blame them. Neither was I. So I said no.

But Addie Crenshaw was not someone who listened to no when she wanted to hear yes. She pleaded, she cajoled, she gave me the kind of sad, anxious, worried, reproving looks matronly women in their fifties cultivate to an art form—the kind calculated to make you feel heartless and ashamed of yourself and to melt your resistance faster than fire melts wax. I hung in there for a while, fighting to preserve my better judgment . . . until she started to cry. Then I went all soft-hearted and soft-headed and gave in.

According to Mrs. Crenshaw, Margaret Abbott's woes had begun three months ago, when Allan and Doris Peterson and the city of San Francisco contrived to steal Mrs. Abbott's house and property. The word "steal" was hers, not mine. It seemed the Petersons, who owned a real estate firm in the Outer Richmond district, had bought the Abbott property at a city-held auction where it was being sold for nonpayment of property taxes dating back to the death of Mrs. Abbott's husband in 1981. She wouldn't vacate the premises, so they'd sought to have her legally evicted. Sheriff's deputies refused to carry out the eviction notice, however, after a Sheriff's Department administrator went out to talk to her and came to the conclusion that she was the innocent victim of circumstances and cold-hearted bureaucracy.

Margaret Abbott's husband had always handled the couple's finances; she was an old-fashioned sheltered housewife who knew nothing at all about such matters as property taxes. She hadn't heeded notices of delinquency mailed to her by the city tax collector because she didn't understand what they were. When the tax collector received no response from her, he ordered her property put up for auction without first making an effort to contact her personally. House and property were subsequently sold to the Petersons for $186,000, less than half of what they were worth on the current real estate market. Mrs. Abbott hadn't even been told that an auction was being held.

Armed with this information, the Sheriff's Department administrator went to the mayor and to the local newspapers on her behalf. The mayor got the Board of Supervisors to approve city funds to reimburse the Petersons, so as to allow Mrs. Abbott to keep her home. But the Petersons refused to accept the reimbursement; they wanted the property and the fat killing they'd make when they sold it. They hired an attorney, which prompted Mrs. Crenshaw to step in and enlist the help of lawyers from Legal Aid for the Elderly. A stay of the eviction order was obtained and the matter was put before a Superior Court judge, who ruled in favor of Margaret Abbott. She was not only entitled to her property, he decided, but to a tax waiver from the city because she lived on a fixed income. The Petersons might have tried to take the case to a higher court, except for the fact that negative media attention was harming their business. So, Mrs. Crenshaw said, "They crawled back into the woodwork. But not for long, if you ask me."

It was Addie Crenshaw's contention that the Petersons had commenced the nocturnal "reign of terror" against Mrs. Abbott out of "just plain vindictive meanness. And maybe because they think that if they drive Margaret crazy or straight into her grave, they can get their greedy claws on her property after all." How could they hope to do that? I'd asked. She didn't know, she said, but if there was a way, "Those two slimeballs have found it out."

That explanation didn't make much sense to me. But based on what I'd been told so far, I couldn't think of a better one. Margaret Abbott lived on a quiet street in a quiet residential neighborhood; she seldom left the house anymore, got on fine with her neighbors and her nephew, hadn't an enemy in the world nor any money or valuables other than her house and property that anybody could be after. If not the Petersons, then who would want to bedevil a harmless old woman? And why?

Well, I could probably rule out Harold the psychotic cat and the ghost of Mrs. Abbott's late husband. If old Carl's shade really was lurking around here somewhere, Addie Crenshaw would just have to get herself another soft-headed detective. I don't do ghosts. I definitely do not do ghosts.

Mrs. Crenshaw and I left Margaret Abbott in her Boston rocker and went to have a look around the premises, starting with the rear porch.

A close-up examination of the back door revealed no marks on the locking plate or any other indication of forced entry. But the lock itself was of the push-button variety: anybody with half an ounce of ingenuity could pop it open in ten seconds flat. The cat's three bowls—water, dried food, wet food—were over next to the washer and dryer, ten feet from the door. Easy enough for someone to slip in here late at night and dose one of the bowls with arsenic.

Outside, then, into the rear yard. It was a cold autumn day, clear and windy—the kind of day that makes you think of football games and the good smell of burning leaves and how much you looked forward to All Hallows Eve when you were a kid. The wind had laid a coating of dead leaves over a small patch of lawn and flower beds that were otherwise neatly tended; Mrs. Crenshaw had told me her brother, Leonard, took care of Mrs. Abbott's yardwork. The yard itself was enclosed by fences, no gate in any of them and with neighboring houses on two sides; but beyond the back fence, which was low and easily climbable, was a kids' playground. I walked across the lawn, around on the north side of the house, and found another trespasser's delight: a brick path that was open all the way to the street.

I went down the path a ways, looking at the side wall of the house. Mrs. Crenshaw and her brother had done a good job of eradicating the words that had been spray-painted there, except for the shadow of a *bullsh* that was half hidden behind a hedge.

In the adjacent yard on that side, a man in a sweatshirt had been raking leaves fallen from a pair of white birches. He'd stopped when he saw Mrs. Crenshaw and me, and now he came over to the fence. He was about fifty, thin, balding, long-jawed. He nodded to me, said to Mrs. Crenshaw, "How's Margaret holding up, Addie?"

"Fair, the poor thing. Now she thinks it might be ghosts."

"Ghosts?"

"Her late husband come back to torment her."

"Uh-oh. Sounds like she's ready for the loony bin."

"Not yet she isn't. Not if this man"—she patted my arm—"and I have anything to say about it. He's a detective and he is going to put a stop to what's been going on."

"Detective?"

"Private investigator. I hired him."

"What can a private eye do that the police can't?"

"I told you, Ev. Put a stop to what's been going on."

Mrs. Crenshaw introduced us. The thin guy's name was Everett Mihalik.

He asked me, "So how you gonna do it? You got some plan in mind?"

People always want to know how a detective works. They think there is some special methodology that sets private cops apart from public cops and even farther apart from those in other public-service professions.

Another byproduct of the mystique created by Hammett and Chandler and nurtured—and badly distorted—by films and TV.

I told Mihalik the truth. "No, I don't have a plan. Just hard work and perseverance and I hope a little luck." And of course it disappointed him, as I'd known it would.

"Well, you ask me," he said, "it's kids. Street punks."

"What reason would they have?"

"They need a reason nowadays?"

"Any particular kids you have in mind?"

"Nah. But this neighborhood's not like it used to be. Full of minorities now, kids looking for trouble. They hang out at Ocean Beach and the zoo."

"Uh-huh." I asked Mrs. Crenshaw, "There been any other cases of malicious mischief around here recently?"

"Not that I heard about."

"So Margaret's the first," Mihalik said. "They start with one person, then they move on to somebody else. Me, for instance. Or you, Addie." He shook his head. "I'm telling you, it's those goddamn punks hang out at Ocean Beach and the zoo."

Maybe, I thought. But I didn't believe it. The things that had been done to Margaret Abbott didn't follow the patterns of simple malicious mischief, didn't feel random to me. They felt calculated to a specific purpose. Find that purpose and I'd find the person or persons responsible.

Addie Crenshaw lived half a block to the west, just off Ulloa. This was a former blue-collar Caucasian neighborhood, built in the thirties on what had once been a windswept stretch of sand dunes. The parcels were small, the houses of mixed architectural styles and detached from one another, unlike the ugly shoulder-to-shoulder row houses farther inland. Built cheap and bought cheap fifty years ago, but now worth small fortunes thanks to San Francisco's overinflated real estate market and a steady influx of Asian families, both American- and foreign-born, with money to spend and a desire for a piece of the city. Original owners like Margaret Abbott, and people who had lived here for decades like Addie Crenshaw, were now the exceptions rather than the norm.

The Crenshaw house was of stucco and similar in type and size, if not in color, to the one owned by Mrs. Abbott. It was painted a garish brown with orange-yellow trim, which made me think of a gigantic and artfully sculpted grilled-cheese sandwich. The garage door was up and a slope-shouldered man in a Giants baseball cap was doing something at a workbench inside. Mrs. Crenshaw ushered me in that way.

The slope-shouldered man was Leonard Crenshaw. A few years older than his sister and on the dour side, he had evidently lived here for a number of years, though the house belonged to Mrs. Crenshaw; Leonard had moved in after her husband died, she'd told me, to help out with chores and to keep her company. If he had a job or profession, she hadn't confided what it was.

"Don't mind telling you," he said to me, "I think Addie made a mistake hiring you."

"Why is that, Mr. Crenshaw?"

"Always sticking her nose in other people's business. Been like that her whole life. Nosy and bossy."

"Better than putting my head in the sand like an ostrich," Mrs. Crenshaw said. She didn't seem upset or annoyed by her brother's comments. I had the impression this was an old sibling disagreement, one that went back a lot of years through a lot of different incidents.

"Can't just live her life and let others live theirs," Leonard said. "It's Charley Doyle should be taking care of his aunt and her problems, spending his money on a fancy detective."

Fancy detective, I thought. Leonard, if you only knew.

"Charley Doyle can barely take care of himself," Mrs. Crenshaw said. "He has two brain cells and one of those works only about half the time. All he cares about is gambling and liquor and cheap women."

"A heavy gambler, is he?" I asked.

"Oh, I don't think so. He's too lazy and too stupid. Besides, he plays poker with Ev Mihalik and Ev is so tight he squeaks."

Leonard said, "You know what's going to happen to you, Addie, talking about people behind their backs that way? You'll spend eternity hanging by your tongue, that's what."

"Oh, put a sock in it, Leonard."

"Telling tales about people, hiring detectives. Next thing you know, *our* phone'll start ringing in the middle of the night, somebody'll bust one of *our* windows."

"Nonsense."

"Is it? Stir things up, you're bound to make 'em worse. For everybody. You mark my words."

Mrs. Crenshaw and I went upstairs and she provided me with work and home addresses for Charley Doyle and the address of the real estate agency owned by the Petersons. "Don't mind Leonard," she said then. "He's not as much of a curmudgeon as he pretends to be. This crazy business with Margaret has him almost as upset as it has me."

"I try not to be judgmental, Mrs. Crenshaw."

"So do I," she said. "Now you go give those Petersons hell, you hear? A taste of their own medicine, the dirty swine."

The impressive-sounding Peterson Realty Company, Inc. was in fact a storefront hole-in-the-wall on Balboa near Forty-sixth, within hailing distance of the Great Highway and Ocean Beach.

Coming to this part of the city always gave me pangs of nostalgia. It was where Playland-at-the-Beach used to be, and Playland—a ten-acre amusement park in the grand old style—had been where I'd spent a good portion of my youth. Funhouses, shooting galleries, games of chance, the Big Dipper roller coaster swooping down out of the misty dark, laughing girls with windcolor in their cheeks and sparkle in their eyes . . . and all of it wrapped in thick ocean fogs that added an element of mystery to the general excitement. All gone now; closed nearly twenty years ago and then allowed to sit abandoned for several more before it was torn down; nothing left of it except bright ghost-images in the memories of gray-beards like me. Condo and rental apartment buildings occupied the space these days: Beachfront Luxury Living, Spectacular Views. Yeah, sure. Luxuriously cold gray weather and spectacular weekend views of Ocean Beach and its parking areas jammed with rowdy teenagers and beer-guzzling adult children.

It made me sad, thinking about it. Getting old. Sure sign of it when you started lamenting the dead past, glorifying it as if it were some kind of flawless Valhalla when you knew damned well it hadn't been. Maybe so, maybe so—but nobody could convince me Beachfront Luxury Living condos were better than Playland and the Big Dipper, or that some of the dead past wasn't a hell of a lot better than most of the half-dead present.

There were two desks inside the Peterson Realty Company offices, each of them occupied. The man was dark, forty, dressed to the nines, with a smiley demeanor and earnest eyes that locked onto yours and hung on as if they couldn't bear to let go. The woman was a few years younger, ash-blonde, just as smiley but not quite as determinedly earnest or slick. Allan and Doris Peterson. Nice attractive couple, all right. Just the kind you'd expect to find in the front row at a city-held tax auction.

They were friendly and effusive until I told them who I was and that I was investigating the harassment of Margaret Abbott. No more smiles then; unveiling of the true colors. Allan Peterson said, with more than a little nastiness, "That Crenshaw woman hired you, I suppose. Damn her; she's out to get us."

"I don't think so, Mr. Peterson. All she wants is to get to the bottom of the trouble."

"Well, my God," Doris Peterson said, "why come to us about that? We don't have anything to do with it. What earthly good would it do us to harass the old woman? We've already lost her property, thanks to that bleeding-heart judge."

"I'm not here to accuse you of anything," I said. "I just want to ask you a few questions."

"We don't have anything to say to you. We don't know anything, we don't want to know anything."

"And furthermore, you don't give a damn. Right?"

"You said that, I didn't. Anyway, why should we?"

Peterson said, "If you or that Crenshaw woman try to imply that we're involved, or even that we're in any way exploiters of the chronologically gifted, we'll sue. I mean that—we'll sue."

"Exploiters of the what?" I said.

"You heard me. The chronologically gifted."

Christ, I thought. Old people hadn't been old people—or elderly people—for some time, but I hadn't realized that they were no longer even senior citizens. Now they were "the chronologically gifted"—the most asinine example of newspeak I had yet encountered. The ungifted ad agency types who coined such euphemisms ought to be excessed, transitioned, offered voluntary severance, or provided with immediate career-change opportunities. Or better yet, subjected to permanent chronological interruption.

So much for the Petersons. A waste of time coming here; all it had accomplished was to confirm Addie Crenshaw's low opinion of them. I would be happy if it turned out they had something to do with the nocturnal prowling, but hell, where was their motive? Assholes, yes; childishly vindictive bedevilers, no. And unfortunately there is no law against being an asshole in today's society. If there was, five percent of the population would be in jail and another ten percent would be on the cusp.

♠

Charley Doyle's place of employment was a glass-service outfit in Daly City. But it was already shut down for the weekend when I got there; glaziers, like plumbers and other union tradesmen, work four- or four-and-a-half-day weeks. So I drove back into San Francisco via Mission Street, to the run-down apartment building in Visitacion Valley where Doyle resided. He wasn't there either. The second neighbor I talked to said he hung out in a tavern called Fat Leland's, on Geneva Avenue, and that was where I finally ran him down.

He was sitting in a booth with half a dozen bottles of beer and a hefty, big-chested blonde who reminded me of a woman my partner, Eberhardt, mistakenly came close to marrying a few years ago. They were all over each other, rubbing and groping and swapping beer-and-cigarette-flavored saliva. They didn't like it when I sat down across from them; and Doyle liked it even less when I told him who I was and why I was there.

"I don't know nothing about it," he said. He was a big guy with a beer belly and dim little eyes. Two brain cells, Addie Crenshaw had said. Right. "What you want to bother me for?"

"I thought you might have an idea of who's behind the trouble."

"Not me. Old Lady Crenshaw thinks it's them real estate people that tried to steal my aunt's house. Why don't you go talk to them?"

"I already did. They deny any involvement."

"Lying bastards," he said.

"Maybe. You been out to see your aunt lately?"

"Not since I fixed her busted window. Why?"

"Well, you're her only relative. She could use some moral support."

"She's got the Crenshaws to take care of her. She don't need me hanging around."

"No, I guess she doesn't at that. Tell me, do you stand to inherit her entire estate?"

"Huh?"

"Do you get her house and property when she dies?"

His dim little eyes got brighter. "Yeah, that's right. So what? You think it's me doing that stuff to her?"

"I'm just asking questions, Mr. Doyle."

"Yeah, well, I don't like your questions. You can't pin it on me. Last Saturday night, when them rose bushes of hers was dug up, I was in Reno with a couple of buddies. And last Wednesday, when that damn cat got poisoned, me and Mildred here was together the whole night at her place." He nudged the blonde with a dirty elbow. "Wasn't we, kid?"

Mildred giggled, belched, said, "Whoops, excuse me," and giggled again. Then she frowned and said, "What'd you ask me, honey?"

"Wednesday night," Doyle said. "We was together all night, wasn't we? At your place?"

"Sure," Mildred said, "all night." Another giggle. "You're a real man, Charley, that's what you are."

I left the two of them pawing and drooling on each other—one of those perfect matches you hear about but seldom encounter in the flesh. Cupid triumphant. Four brain cells joined against the world.

Even though it was too late in the day to get much background checking done, I drove down to my office on O'Farrell and put in a couple of calls to start the wheels turning. Credit information and possible arrest records on the Petersons and Charley Doyle, for openers. I had nothing else to go on, and you never know what a routine check might turn up.

At five-thirty I quit the office and drove home to Pacific Heights. Poker game tonight at Eberhardt's; beer and pizza and smelly pipe smoke and lousy jokes. I was looking forward to it. Kerry says all-male poker games are "bonding rituals with their roots in ancient pagan society." I love her anyway.

While I was changing clothes I wondered if maybe, after the game, I ought to run an all-night stakeout on Margaret Abbott's home. It had been two days since the last incident; if the pattern held, another was due any time. But I talked myself out of it. I hate stakeouts, particularly all-night stakeouts. And with two easy ways to get onto her property, front and back, I could cover only one of the possibilities at a time from my car. Of course I could run the stakeout from inside her house, but that wouldn't do much good if the perp stayed outside. Besides, I was not quite ready to spend one or more nights on Mrs. Abbott's couch, and I doubted that she was ready for it either.

So I went to the poker game with a clear conscience, and won eleven dollars and forty cents, most of it on a straight flush to Eberhardt's kings full, and drove back home at midnight and had a pretty good night's sleep. Until the telephone bell jarred me awake at seven-fifteen on Saturday morning. Addie Crenshaw was on the other end.

"He broke into Margaret's house again last night," she said.

"Damn!" I sat up and shook the sleep cobwebs out of my head. "What'd he do this time?"

"Walked right into her bedroom, bold as brass."

"He didn't harm her?"

"No. Just scared her."

"So she's all right?"

"Better than most women her age would be."

"Did she get a good look at him?"

"No. Wouldn't have even if all the lights had been on."

"Why not?"

"He was wearing a sheet."

"He was . . . what?"

"A sheet," Mrs. Crenshaw said grimly, "wearing a white sheet and making noises like a ghost."

When I got to the Abbott house forty-five minutes later I found a reception committee of three on the front porch: Addie and Leonard Crenshaw and Everett Mihalik, talking animatedly among themselves. Leonard was saying as I came up the walk ". . . should have called the police instead. They're the ones who should be investigating this."

"What can they do?" his sister said. "There aren't any signs of breaking and entering this time either. Nothing damaged, nothing stolen. Just Margaret's word that a man in a sheet was there in the first place. They'd probably say she imagined the whole thing."

"Well, maybe she did," Mihalik said. "I mean, all that nonsense about her dead husband coming back to haunt her . . ."

"Ev, she didn't say it was a ghost she saw. She said it was a man dressed up in a sheet pretending to be a ghost. There's a big difference."

"She still could've imagined it."

Mrs. Crenshaw appealed to me. "It happened, I'm sure it did. She may be a bit dotty, but she's not senile."

I nodded. "Is she up to talking about it?"

"I told her you were coming. She's waiting."

"Guess you don't need me," Mihalik said. A gust of icy wind swept over the porch and he rubbed at a red-stained hand, then winced, and said, "Brr, it's cold out here. Come on, Leonard, I've got a pot of fresh coffee made."

"No thanks," Leonard said, "I got work to do." He gave me a brief disapproving look and then said pointedly to his sister, "Just remember, Addie—chickens always come home to roost."

Mrs. Crenshaw and I went into the house. Margaret Abbott was sitting in her Boston rocker, a shawl over her lap and Harold, the orange tabby, sprawled out asleep on the shawl. She looked tired, and the rouge she'd applied to her cheeks was like bloody splotches on too-white parchment. Still, she seemed to be in good spirits. And she showed no reluctance at discussing her latest ordeal.

"It's really rather amusing," she said, "now that I look back on it. A grown man wearing a sheet and moaning and groaning like Casper with a tummy ache."

"You're sure it was a man?"

"Oh yes. Definitely a man."

"You didn't recognize his voice?"

"Well, he didn't speak. Just moaned and groaned."

"Did you say anything to him?"

"I believe I asked what he thought he was doing in my bedroom. Yes, and I said that he had better not have hurt Harold."

"Harold?"

"It was Harold crying that woke me, you see."

"Not the man entering your bedroom?"

"No. Harold crying. Yowling, actually, as if he'd been hurt. Usually he sleeps on the bed with me, and I think he must have heard the man come into the house and gone to investigate. You know how cats are."

"Yes, ma'am."

"The intruder must have stepped on him or kicked him," Mrs. Abbott said, "to make him yowl like that. Poor Harold, he's been through so much. Haven't you, dear?" She stroked the cat, who started to purr lustily.

"Then what happened?" I asked. "After you woke up."

"Well, I saw a flickery sort of light in the hallway. At first I couldn't imagine what it was."

"Flashlight," Mrs. Crenshaw said.

"Yes. It came closer, right into the doorway. Then it switched off and the intruder walked right up to the foot of my bed and began moaning and groaning and jumping around." She smiled wanly. "Really, it was rather funny."

"How long did he keep up his act?"

"Not long. Just until I spoke to him."

"Then he ran out?"

"Still moaning and groaning, yes. I suppose he wanted me to think he was the ghost of my late husband. As if I wouldn't know a man from a spirit. Or Carl, in or out of a sheet."

I sat quiet for a little time, thinking, remembering some things. I was pretty sure then that I knew the why behind this whole screwy business. I was also pretty sure I knew the who. One more question, of Mrs. Crenshaw this time, and I would go find out for sure.

Everett Mihalik was doing some repair work on his front stoop: down on one knee, using a trowel and a tray of wet cement. But as soon as he saw me approaching he put the trowel down and got to his feet.

"How'd it go with Margaret?" he asked.

"Just fine. Mind answering a couple of questions, Mr. Mihalik?"

"Sure, if I can."

"When I got here this morning, you were on Mrs. Abbott's porch. Had you been inside the house?"

"No. Wasn't any need for me to go in."

"When was the last time you were inside her house?"

"I don't remember exactly. A while."

"More than a few days?"

"A lot longer than that. Why?"

"Do you own a cat?"

"A cat?" Now he was frowning. "What does a cat have to do with anything?"

"Quite a bit. You don't own one, do you?"

"No."

"Then how did you get that bite on your hand?"

"My—?" He looked at his left hand, at the iodine-daubed bite mark just above the thumb. I'd noticed it earlier, when he'd winced while rubbing his reddened hand, but the significance of it hadn't registered until I'd talked with Mrs. Abbott.

"Fresh bite," I said. "Can't be more than a few hours old." I held out my own bitten hand for him to see. "Fresher than mine, and it's only about twenty hours old. Similar marks, too. Looks like they were done by the same cat—Mrs. Abbott's cat, Harold."

Mihalik licked his lips and said nothing.

"Harold is an indoor cat, never allowed outside. And he likes to nip strangers when they aren't expecting it. Somebody comes into his house in the middle of the night, he'd not only go to investigate, he'd be even more inclined to take himself a little nip—especially if the intruder happened to try to pat him to keep him quiet. Mrs. Abbott was woken up last night by Harold yowling; she thought it was because the intruder stepped on him or kicked him, but that wasn't it at all. It was the intruder swatting him after being bitten that made him yell."

"You can't prove it was Harold bit me," Mihalik said. "It was another cat, a neighborhood stray. . . ."

"Harold," I said, "and the police lab people *can* prove it. Test the bites on my hand and yours, test Harold's teeth and saliva . . . they can prove it, all right."

He shook his head, but not as if he were denying my words. As if he were trying to deny the fact that he was caught. "You think I'm the one been doing all that stuff to Margaret?"

"I know you are. Dressing up in that sheet last night, pretending to be a ghost, was a stupid idea in more ways than one. Only one person besides Addie Crenshaw and me knew of Mrs. Abbott's fancy about her dead husband's ghost. You, Mihalik. Mrs. Crenshaw mentioned it when we talked to you yesterday afternoon. She didn't mention it to anybody else, not even her brother; she told me so just a few minutes ago."

Another headshake. "What reason would I have for hassling an old lady like Margaret?"

"The obvious one—money. A cut of the proceeds from the sale of her property after she was dead or declared incompetent."

"That don't make sense. I'm not a relative of hers. . . ."

"No, but Charley Doyle is. And you and Charley are buddies; Mrs. Crenshaw told me you play poker together regularly. Charley's not very bright and just as greedy as you are. Your brainchild, wasn't it, Mihalik? Inspired by that auction fiasco. Hey, Charley, why wait until your aunt dies of natural causes; that might take years. Give her a heart attack or drive her into an institution, get control of her property right away. Then sell it to the Petersons or some other real estate speculator for a nice quick profit. And you earn your cut by doing all the dirty work while Charley sets up alibis to keep himself in the clear."

Mihalik stood tensed now, as if he were thinking about jumping me or maybe just trying to run. But he didn't do either one. After a few seconds he went all loose and saggy, as though somebody had cut his strings; he took a stumbling step backward and sank down on the stairs and put his head in his hands.

"I never done anything wrong before in my life," he said. "Never. But the bills been piling up, it's so goddamn hard to live these days, and they been talking about laying people off where I work and I was afraid I'd lose my house . . . ah, God, I don't know. I don't know." He lifted his head and gave me a moist, beseeching look. "I never meant that

Margaret should die. You got to believe that. Just force her out of there so Charley could take over the house, that's all. I like her, I never meant to hurt her."

Three brain cells to Charley Doyle's two. Half-wits and knaves, fools and assholes—more of each than ever before, proliferating like weeds in what had once been a pristine garden. It's a hell of a world we live in, I thought. A hell of a mess we're making of the garden.

I went to see Mrs. Abbott again later that day, after Everett Mihalik and Charley Doyle had been arrested and I'd finished making my statement at the Hall of Justice. Addie and Leonard Crenshaw were both there. All three were still a little shaken at the betrayal of a neighbor and a relative, but relief was the dominant emotion. Even Leonard was less dour than usual.

A celebration was called for, Mrs. Crenshaw said, and so we had one: coffee and apple strudel. Harold joined in too. Mrs. Abbott had some "special kitty treats" for him and she insisted that I give him one; he was, after all, something of a hero in his own right. So I got down on one knee and gave him one.

In gratitude and affection, he bit me. Different hand, same place.

ONE NIGHT AT DOLORES PARK

DOLORES Park used to be the hub of one of the better residential neighborhoods in San Francisco: acres of tall palms and steeply rolling lawns in the Western Mission, a gentrifying area up until a few years ago. Well-off Yuppies, lured by scenic views and an easy commute to downtown, bought and renovated many of the old Victorians that rim the park. Singles and couples, straights and gays, moved into duplexes that sold for $300,000 and apartments that rented for upwards of a grand a month. WASPs, Latinos, Asian Americans . . . an eclectic mix that lived pretty much in harmony and were dedicated to preserving as much of the urban good life as was left these days.

Then the drug dealers moved in.

Marijuana sellers at first, aiming their wares at students at nearby Mission High School. The vanguard's success brought in a scruffier variety and their equally scruffy customers. As many as forty dealers allegedly had been doing business in Dolores Park on recent weekends, according to published reports. The cops couldn't do much; marijuana selling and buying is a low-priority crime in the city. But the lack of control, the wide-open open-air market, brought in fresh troops: heroin and crack dealers. And where you've got hard drugs, you also have high stakes and violence. Eight shootings and two homicides in and around Dolores Park so far this year. The firebombing of the home of a young couple who tried to form an activist group to fight the dealers. Muggings, burglaries, intimidation of residents. The result was bitterly predictable: frightened people moving out, real estate values dropping, and as the dealers widened their territory to include Mission Playground down on 19th Street, the entire neighborhood beginning to decline. The police had stepped up patrols, were making arrests, but it was too little too late: they didn't have the manpower or the funds, and there was so damned much of the same thing happening elsewhere in the city. . . .

"It's like Armageddon," one veteran cop was quoted as saying. "And the forces of evil are winning."

They were winning tonight, no question of that. It was a warm October night and I had been staked out on the west side of the park, nosed downhill near the intersection of Church and 19th, since a few minutes before six o'clock. Until it got dark I had counted seven drug transactions within the limited range of my vision—and no police presence other than a couple of cruising patrol cars. Once darkness closed down, the park had emptied fast. Now, at nine-ten, the lawns and paths appeared deserted. But I wouldn't have wanted to walk around over there, as early as it was. If there were men lurking in the shadows —and there probably were—they were dealers armed to the teeth and/or desperate junkies hunting prey. Only damned fools wandered through Dolores Park after nightfall.

Drugs, drug dealers, and the rape of a fine old neighborhood had nothing to do with why I was here; all of those things were a depressing by-product. I was here to serve a subpoena on a man named Thurmond, as a favor to a lawyer I knew. Thurmond was being sought for testimony in a huge stock fraud case. He didn't want to testify because he was afraid of being indicted himself, and he had been hiding out as a result. It had taken me three days to find out he was holed up with an old college buddy. The college buddy owned the blue-and-white Stick Victorian two doors down Church Street from where I was sitting. He was home—I'd seen him arrive, and there were lights on now behind the curtained bay windows—but there was still no sign of Thurmond. I was bored as well as depressed, and irritated, and frustrated. If Thurmond gave me any trouble when he finally put in an appearance, he was going to be sorry for it.

That was what I was thinking when I saw the woman.

She came down 19th, alone, walking fast and hard. The stride and the drawn-back set of her body said she was angry about something. There was a streetlight on the corner, and when she passed under it I could see that she was thirtyish, dark-haired, slender. Wearing a light sweater over a blouse and slacks. She waited for a car to roll by—it didn't slow—and then crossed the street toward the park.

Not smart, lady, I thought. Even if she was a junkie looking to make a connection, it wasn't smart. I had been slouched down on my spine; I sat up straighter, to get a better squint at where she was headed. Not into the park, at least. Away from me on the sidewalk, downhill toward Cumberland. Moving at the same hard, angry pace.

I had a fleeting impulse to chase after her, tell her to get her tail off the street. Latent paternal instinct. Hell, if she wanted to risk her life, that was her prerogative; the world is full of what the newspeakers call "cerebrally challenged individuals." It was none of my business what happened to her—

Yes, it was.

Right then it became my business.

A line of trees and shrubs flanked the sidewalk where she was, with a separating strip of lawn about twenty yards wide. The tall figure of a man came jerkily out of the tree-shadow as she passed. There was enough starlight and other light for me to make out something extended in one hand and that his face was covered except for the eyes and mouth. Gun and ski mask. Mugger.

I hit the door handle with my left hand, jammed my right up under the dash and yanked loose the .38 I keep clipped there. He was ten yards from her and closing as I came out of the car; she'd heard him and was turning toward him. He lunged forward, clawing for her purse.

There were no cars on the street. I charged across at an angle, yelling at the top of my voice, the only words that can have an effect in a situation like this: "Hold it, police officer!" Not this time. His head swiveled in my direction, swiveled back to the woman as she pulled away from him. She made a keening noise and turned to run.

He shot her.

No compunction: Just threw the gun up and fired point blank.

She went down, skidding on her side, as I cut between two parked cars onto the sidewalk. Rage made me pull up and I would have fired at him except that he pumped a round at me first. I saw the muzzle flash, heard the whine of the bullet and the low, flat crack of the gun, and in reflex I dodged sideways onto the lawn. Mistake, because the grass was slippery and my feet went out from under me. I stayed down, squirming around on my belly so I could bring the .38 into firing position. But he wasn't going to stick around for a shootout; he was already running splayfooted toward the trees. He disappeared into them before I could get lined up for a shot.

I'd banged my knee in the fall; it sent out twinges as I hauled myself erect, ran toward the woman. She was still down but not hurt as badly as I'd feared: sitting up on one hip now, holding her left arm cradled in against her breast. She heard me, looked up with fright shining on the pale oval of her face. I said quickly, "It's all right, I'm a detective, he's gone now," and shoved the .38 into my jacket pocket. There was no sign of the mugger. The park was empty as far as I could see, no movement anywhere in the warm dark.

She said, "He shot me," in a dazed voice.

"Where? Where are you hurt?"

"My arm . . ."

"Shoulder area?"

"No, above the elbow."

"Can you move the arm?"

"I don't . . . yes, I can move it."

Not too bad then. "Can you stand up, walk?"

"If you help me . . ."

I put an arm around her waist, lifted her. The blood was visible then, gleaming wetly on the sleeve of her sweater.

"My purse," she said.

It was lying on the sidewalk nearby. I let go of her long enough to pick it up. When I gave it to her she clutched it tightly: something solid and familiar to hang onto.

The street was still empty; so were the sidewalks on both sides. Somebody was standing behind a lighted window in one of the buildings across Church, peering through a set of drapes. No one else seemed to have heard the shots, or to want to know what had happened if they did. Just the woman and me out here at the edge of the light. And the predators—one predator, anyway—hiding somewhere in the dark.

Her name was Andrea Hull, she said, and she lived a few doors up 19th Street. I took her home, walking with my arm around her and her body braced against mine as if we were a pair of lovers. Get her off the street as quickly as possible, to where she would feel safe. I could report the shooting from there. You have to go through the motions even when there's not much chance of results.

Her building was a one-story, stucco-faced duplex. As we started up the front stoop, she drew a shuddering breath and said, "God, he could have killed me," as if the realization had just struck her. "I could be dead right now."

I had nothing to say to that.

"Peter was right, damn him," she said.

"Peter?"

"My husband. He keeps telling me not to go out walking alone at night and I keep not listening. I'm so smart, I am. Nothing ever happened, I thought nothing ever would. . . ."

"You learned a lesson," I said. "Don't hurt yourself anymore than you already are."

"I hate it when he's right." We were in the vestibule now. She said, "It's the door on the left," and fumbled in her purse. "Where the hell did I put the damn keys?"

"Your husband's not home?"

"No. He's the reason I went out."

I found the keys for her, unlocked the door. Narrow hallway, a huge lighted room opening off of it. The room had been enlarged by knocking out a wall or two. There was furniture in it but it wasn't a living room; most of it, with the aid of tall windows and a couple of skylights, had been turned into an artist's studio. A cluttered one full of paintings and sculptures and the tools to create them. An unclean one populated by a tribe of dust mice.

I took a better look at its owner as we entered the studio. Older than I'd first thought, at least thirty-five, maybe forty. A sharp featured brunette with bright, wise eyes and pale lips. The wound in her arm was still bleeding, the red splotch grown to the size of a small pancake.

"Are you in much pain?" I asked her.

"No. It's mostly numb."

"You'd better get out of that sweater. Put some peroxide on the wound if you have it, then wrap a wet towel around it. That should do until the paramedics get here. Where's your phone?"

"Over by the windows."

"You go ahead. I'll call the police."

". . . I thought *you* were a policeman."

"Not quite. Private investigator."

"What were you doing down by the park?"

"Waiting to serve a subpoena."

"Lord," she said. Then she asked, "Do you have to report what happened? They'll never catch the man, you know they won't."

"Maybe not, but yes, I have to report it. You want attention for that arm, don't you?"

"All right," she said. "Actually, I suppose the publicity will do me some good." She went away through a doorway at the rear.

I made the call. The cop I spoke to asked half a dozen pertinent questions, then told me to stay put, paramedics and a team of inspectors would be out shortly. Half hour, maybe less, for the paramedics, I thought as I hung up. Longer for the inspectors. This wasn't an A-priority shooting. Perp long gone, victim not seriously wounded, situation under control. We'd just have to wait our turn.

I took a turn around the studio. The paintings were everywhere, finished and unfinished: covering the walls, propped in corners and on a pair of easels, stacked on the floor. They were all abstracts: bold lines and interlocking and overlapping squares, wedges, triangles in primary colors. Not to my taste, but they appeared to have been done by a talented artist. You couldn't say the same for the forty or so bronze, clay, and metal sculptures. All of those struck me as amateurish, lopsided things that had no identity or meaning, like the stuff kids make free-form in grade school.

"Do you like them? My paintings?"

I turned. Andrea Hull had come back into the room, wearing a sleeveless blouse now, a thick towel wrapped around her arm.

"Still bleeding?" I asked her.

"Not so badly now. *Do* you like my paintings?"

"I don't know much about art but they seem very good."

"They are. Geometric abstraction. Not as good as Mondrian or Glarner or Burgoyne Diller, perhaps. Or Hoffman, of course. But not derivative, either. I have my own unique vision."

She might have been speaking a foreign language. I said, "Uh-huh," and let it go at that.

"I've had several showings, been praised by some of the most eminent critics in the art world. I'm starting to make a serious name for myself —finally, after years of struggle. Just last month one of my best works, 'Tension and Emotion,' sold for fifteen thousand dollars."

"That's a lot of money."

"Yes, but my work will bring much more someday."

No false modesty in her. Hell, no modesty of any kind. "Are the sculptures yours too?"

She made a snorting noise. "Good God, no. My husband's. Peter thinks he's a brilliant sculptor but he's not—he's not even mediocre. Self-delusion is just one of his faults."

"Sounds like you don't get along very well."

"Sometimes we do. And sometimes he makes me so damn mad I could scream. Tonight, for instance. Calling me from some bar downtown, drunk, bragging about a woman he'd picked up. He *knows* that drives me crazy."

"Uh-huh."

"Oh, not the business with the woman. Another one of his lies, probably. It's the drinking and the taunting that gets to me—his jealousy. He's so damned jealous I swear his skin is developing a green tint."

"Of your success, you mean?"

"That's right."

"Why do you stay married to him, if he has that effect on you?"

"Habit," she said. "There's not much love left, but I do still care for him. God knows why. And of course he stays because now there's money, with plenty more in the offing . . . oh! Damn!" She'd made the mistake of trying to gesture with her wounded arm. "Where're those paramedics?"

"They'll be here pretty quick."

"I need a drink. Or don't you think I should have one?"

"I wouldn't. They'll give you something for the pain."

"Well, they'd better hurry up. How about you? Do you want a drink?"

"No thanks."

"Suit yourself. Go ahead and sit down if you want. I'm too restless."

"I've been doing nothing but sitting most of the evening."

"I'm going to pace," she said. "I have to walk, keep moving, when I'm upset. I used to go into the park, walk for an hour or more, but with all the drug problems . . . and now a person isn't even safe on the sidewalk—"

There was a rattling at the front door. Andrea Hull turned, scowling, in that direction. I heard the door open, bang closed; a male voice called, "Andrea?"

"In here, Peter."

The man who came duck-waddling in from the hall was a couple of inches over six feet, fair-haired and pale except for red-blotched cheeks and forehead. Weak-chinned and nervous-eyed. He blinked at her, blinked at me, blinked at her again with his mouth falling open.

"My God, Andrea, what happened to you? That towel . . . there's blood on it. . . ."

"I was mugged a few minutes ago. He shot me."

"*Shot* you? Who . . . ?"

"I told you, a mugger. I'm lucky to be alive."

"The wound . . . it's not serious . . ."

"No." She winced. "What's *keeping* those paramedics?"

He went to her, tried to wrap an arm around her shoulders. She pushed him away. "The man who did it," he said, "did you get a good look at him?"

"No. He was masked. This man chased him off."

Hull remembered me, turned and waddled over to where I was.

"Thank God you were nearby," he said. He breathed on me, reaching for my hand. I let him have it but not for long. "But I don't think I've seen you before. Do you live in the neighborhood?"

"He's a private investigator," Andrea Hull said. "He was serving a subpoena on somebody. His name is Orenzi."

"No it isn't," I said. I told them what it was, not that either of them cared.

"I can never get Italian names right," she said.

Her husband shifted his attention her way again. "Where did it happen? Down by the park, I'll bet. You went out walking by the park again."

"Don't start in, Peter, I'm in no mood for it."

"Didn't I warn you something like this might happen? A hundred times I've warned you but you just won't listen."

"I said don't start in. If you hadn't called drunk from that bar, got me upset, I wouldn't have gone out. It's as much your fault as it is mine."

"*My* fault? Oh sure, blame me. Twist everything around so you don't have to take responsibility."

Her arm was hurting her and the pain made her vicious. She bared her teeth at him. "What are you doing home, anyway? Where's the bimbo you claimed you picked up?"

"I brushed her off. I kept thinking about what I said on the phone, what a jerk I was being. I wanted to apologize—"

"Sure, right. You were drunk, now you're sober; if there was any brushing off, she's the one who did it."

"Andrea . . ."

"What's the matter with your face? She give you some kind of rash?"

"My face? There's nothing wrong with my face. . . ."

"It looks like a rash. I hope it isn't contagious."

"Damn you, Andrea—"

I'd had enough of this. The bickering, the hatred, the deception—everything about the two of them and their not-so-private little war. I said sharply, "All right, both of you shut up. I'm tired of listening to you."

They gawked at me, the woman in disbelief. "How dare you. You can't talk to me like that in my own home—"

"I can and I will. Keep your mouth closed and your ears open for five minutes and you'll learn something. Your husband and I will do the talking."

Hull said, "I don't have anything to say to you."

"Sure you do, Peter. You can start by telling me what you did with the gun."

"Gun? I don't—what gun?"

"The one you shot your wife with."

Him: hissing intake of breath.

Her: strangled bleating noise.

"That's right. No mugger, just you trying to take advantage of what's happened to the park and the neighborhood, make it look like a street killing."

Him: "That's a lie, a damn lie!"

Her, to me in a ground-glass voice: "Peter? How can you know it was Peter? It was dark, the man wore a mask. . . ."

"For openers, you told me he was drunk when he called you earlier. He wasn't, he was faking it. Nobody can sober up completely in an hour, not when he's standing here now without the faintest smell of alcohol on his breath. He wasn't downtown, either; he was somewhere close by. The call was designed to upset you so you'd do what you usually do when you're upset—go out for a walk by the park.

"It may have been dark, but I still got a pretty good look at the shooter coming and going. Tall—and Peter's tall. Walked and ran splayfooted, like a duck—and that's how Peter walks. Then there are those blotches on his face. It's not a rash; look at the marks closely, Mrs. Hull. He's got the kind of skin that takes and retains imprints from fabric, right? Wakes up in the morning with pillow and blanket marks on his face? The ones he's got now are exactly the kind the ribbing on a ski mask would leave."

"You son of a bitch," she said to him. "You dirty rotten son of a—!"

She went for him with nails flashing. I got in her way, grabbed hold of her; her injured arm stopped her from struggling with me. Then he tried to make a run for it. I let go of her and chased him and caught him at the front door. When he tried to kick me I knocked him on his skinny tail.

And with perfect timing, the doorbell rang. It wasn't just the paramedics, either; the law had also arrived.

Peter Hull was an idiot. He had the gun, a .32 revolver, *and* the ski mask in the trunk of his car.

She pressed charges, of course. She would have cut his throat with a dull knife if they'd let her have one. She told him so, complete with expletives.

The Hulls and their private war were finished.

Down in Dolores Park—and in the other neighborhoods in the city, and in cities throughout the country—the other war, the big one, goes on. Armageddon? Maybe. And maybe the forces of evil are winning. Not in the long run, though. In the long run the forces of good will triumph. Always have, always will.

If I didn't believe that, I couldn't work at my job. Neither could anybody else in law enforcement.

No matter how bad things seem, we can't ever stop believing it.

HOME IS THE PLACE WHERE

IT was one of those little crossroads places you still find occasionally in the California backcountry. Relics of another era; old dying things, with precious little time left before they crumble into dust. Weathered wooden store building, gas pumps, a detached service garage that also housed restrooms, some warped little tourist cabins clustered close behind; a couple of junk-car husks and a stand of dusty shade trees. This one was down in the central part of the state, southeast of San Juan Bautista, on the way to the Pinnacles National Monument. The name on the pocked metal sign on the store roof was *Benson's Oasis*. There were four cabins and the shade trees were cottonwoods.

No other cars sat on the apron in front when I pulled in at a few minutes past two. Nor were there any vehicles back by the cabins. The only spot to hide one was in the detached garage—and it was shut up tight. Maybe something in that, maybe not.

Heat hammered at me when I got out, thick and deep-summer dry. In the distance, haze blurred the shapes of the brown hills of the Diablo Range. It was flat here, and dust-blown, and quiet. The feeling you had was of isolation, emptiness, and displacement in time. For me, it was a pleasant feeling, not at all unsettling. I like the past; I like it a hell of a lot better than I like the present or the prospects for the future.

It was even hotter inside the store. No air-conditioning, just an old-fashioned ceiling fan that stirred the air in a way that made me think of a ladle stirring bouillon. Under the fan flies floated in random lethargic circles, as if they'd been drugged. The old man behind the counter at the rear had the same drugged, listless aspect. He was perched on a stool, studying a book of some kind that was open on the countertop. A bell had tinkled to announce my arrival but at first he didn't look up. He turned a page as I crossed the room; it made a dry rustling sound. The page was black, with what looked to be photographs and paper items affixed to it. A scrapbook.

When I reached him he shut the book. It had a brown simulated leather cover, the word *Memories* embossed on it in gilt. The gilt had flaked and faded and the ersatz leather was cracked: the book was almost as old as he was. Over seventy, I judged. Thin, stoop-shouldered, white hair as fine as rabbit fur. Heavily seamed face. Bent left arm that was also knobbed and crooked at the wrist, as if it had been badly broken once and hadn't healed well.

"What can I do for you?" he asked.

"You're the owner? Everett Benson?"

"I am."

"I'm looking for your son, Mr. Benson."

No reaction.

"Have you seen him, heard from him, in the past two days?"

Still nothing for several seconds. Then, "I have no son."

"Stephen," I said. "Stephen Arthur Benson."

"No."

"He's in trouble. Serious trouble."

Face like a chunk of eroded limestone, eyes like cloudy agates imbedded in it. "I have no son," he said again.

I took out one of my business cards, tried to give it to him. He wouldn't take it. Finally I laid it on the counter in front of him. "Stephen was in jail in San Francisco," I said, "on a charge of selling amphetamines and crack cocaine. Did you know that?"

Silence.

"He talked the woman he was living with into going to a bondsman and bailing him out. The bail was low and she had just enough collateral to swing it. His trial date was yesterday. Two nights ago he stole a hundred dollars from the woman, and her car, and jumped bail."

More silence.

"The bondsman hired me to find him and bring him back," I said. "I think he came here. You're his only living relative, and he needs more money than he's got to keep on running. He could steal it but it would be easier and safer to get it from you."

Benson pushed off his stool, picked up the scrapbook, laid it on a shelf behind him. Several regular hardback books lined the rest of the shelf, all of them old and well-read; in the weak light I couldn't make out any of the titles.

"Aiding and abetting a fugitive is a felony," I said to his back, "even if the fugitive is your own son. You don't want to get yourself in trouble with the law, do you?"

He said again, without turning, "I have no son."

For the moment I'd taken the argument as far as it would go. I left him and went out into the midday glare. And straight over to the closed-up service garage.

There were two windows along the near side, both dusty and speckled with ground-in dirt, but I could see clearly enough through the first. Sufficient daylight penetrated the gloom so I could identify the two vehicles parked in there. One was a dented, rusted, thirty-year-old Ford pickup that no doubt belonged to the old man. The other was a newish red Mitsubishi. I didn't have to see the license plate to know that the Mitsubishi belonged to Stephen Arthur Benson's girlfriend.

Cars drifted past on the highway; they made the only sound in the stillness. Behind the store, where the cabins were, nothing moved except for shimmers of heat. I went to my car, sleeving away sweat, and un-clipped the short-barrelled .38 revolver from under the dash and slid it into the pocket of my suit jacket. Maybe I'd need the gun and maybe I wouldn't, but I felt better armed. Stephen Benson was a convicted felon and something of a hardcase, and for all I knew he was armed himself. He hadn't had a weapon two nights ago, according to the girlfriend, but he might have picked one up somewhere in the interim. From his father, for instance.

The stand of cottonwoods grew along the far side of the parking area. I moved over into them, made my way behind the two cabins on the south side. Both had blank rear walls and uncurtained side windows; I took my time approaching each. Their interiors were sparsely furnished, and empty of people and personal belongings.

The direct route to the other two cabins was across open ground. I didn't like the idea of that, so I went the long way—back through the trees, across in front of the store, around on the far side of the garage. It was an unnecessary precaution, as it turned out. The farthest of the northside cabins was also empty; the near one showed plenty of signs of occupancy—clothing, books, photographs, a hotplate, a small refrigerator —but there wasn't anybody in it. This was where the old man lived, I thought. The clothing was the type he would wear and the books were similar to the ones in the store.

Nothing to do now but to go back inside and brace him again. When I entered the store he was on his stool, eating a Milky Way in little nibbling bites. He had loose false teeth and on each bite they clicked like beads on a string.

"Where is he, Mr. Benson?"

No response. The cloudy agate eyes regarded me with the same lack of expression as before.

"I saw the car in the garage," I said. "It's the one Stephen stole from the woman in San Francisco, no mistake. Either he's still in this area or you gave him money and another car and he's on the road again. Which is it?"

He clicked and chewed; he didn't speak.

"All right then. You don't want to do this the easy way, we'll have to do it the hard way. I'll call the county police and have them come out here and look at the stolen car; then they'll charge you with aiding and abetting and with harboring stolen property. And your son will still get picked up and sent back to San Francisco to stand trial. It's only a matter of time."

Benson finished the candy bar; I couldn't tell if he was thinking over what I'd said, but I decided I'd give him a few more minutes in case he was. In the stillness, a refrigeration unit made a broken chattery hum. The heat-drugged flies droned and circled. A car drew up out front and a grumpy-looking citizen came in and bought two cans of soda pop and a bag of potato chips. "Hot as Hades out there," he said. Neither Benson nor I answered him.

When he was gone I said to the old man, "Last chance. Where's Stephen?" He didn't respond, so I said, "I've got a car phone. I'll use that to call the sheriff," and turned and started out.

He let me get halfway to the door before he said, "You win, mister," in a dull, empty voice. "Not much point in keeping quiet about it. Like you said, it's only a matter of time."

I came back to the counter. "Now you're being smart. Where is he?"

"I'll take you to him."

"Just tell me where I can find him."

"No. I'll take you there."

Might be better at that, I thought, if Stephen's close by. Easier, less chance for trouble, with the old man along. I nodded, and Benson came out from behind the counter and crossed to where a sign hung in the window; he reversed the sign so that the word *Closed* faced outward. Then we went out and he locked up.

I asked him, "How far do we have to go?"

"Not far."

"I'll drive, you tell me where."

We got into the car. He directed me east on the county road that intersected the main highway. We rode in silence for about a mile.

Benson sat stiff-backed, his hands gripping his knees, eyes straight ahead. In the hard daylight the knobbed bone on his left wrist looked as big as a plum.

Abruptly he said, " 'Home is the place where.' "

". . . How's that again?"

" 'Home is the place where, when you have to go there, they have to take you in.' "

I shrugged because the words didn't mean anything to me.

"Lines from a poem by Robert Frost," he said. " 'The Death of the Hired Man,' I think. You read Frost?"

"No."

"I like him. Makes sense to me, more than a lot of them."

I remembered the well-read books on the store shelf and in the cabin. A rural storekeeper who read poetry and admired Robert Frost. Well, why not? People don't fit into easy little stereotypes. In my profession, you learn not to lose sight of that fact.

Home is the place where, when you have to go there, they have to take you in. The words ran around inside my head like song lyrics. No, like a chant or an invocation—all subtle rhythm and gathering power. They made sense to me, too, on more than one level. Now I knew something more about Everett Benson, and something more about the nature of his relationship with his son.

Another couple of silent miles through sun-struck farmland. Alfalfa and wine grapes, mostly. A private farm road came up on the right; Benson told me to turn there. It had once been a good road, unpaved but well graded, but that had been a long time ago. Now there were deep grooves in it, and weeds and tall brown grass between the ruts. Not used much these days. It led along the shoulder of a sere hill, then up to the crest; from there I could see where it ended.

Benson's Oasis was a dying place, with not much time left. The farm down below was already dead—years dead. It had been built alongside a shallow creek where willows and cottonwoods grew, in the tuck where two hillocks came together: farmhouse, barn, two chicken coops, a shedlike outbuilding. Skeletons now, all of them, broken and half-hidden by high grass and shrubs and tangles of wild berry vines. Climbing primroses covered part of the house from foundation to roof, bright pink in the sunlight, like a gaudy fungus.

"Your property?" I asked him.

"Built it all with my own hands," he said. "After the war—Second World War—when land was cheap hereabouts. Raised chickens, alfalfa, apples. You can see there's still part of the orchard left."

There were a dozen or so apple trees, stretching away behind the barn. Gnarled, bent, twisted, but still producing fruit. Rotting fruit now.

"Moved out eight years ago, when my wife died," Benson said. "Couldn't bear to live here any more without Betty. Couldn't bear to sell the place, either." He paused, drew a heavy breath, let it out slowly. "Don't come out here much anymore. Just a couple of times a year to visit her grave."

There were no other cars in sight, but I could make out where one had angled off the roadway and mashed down an irregular swath of the summer-dead grass, not long ago. I followed the same route when we reached the farmyard. The swath stopped ten yards from what was left of the farmhouse's front porch. So did I.

I had my window rolled down but there was nothing to hear except birds and insects. The air was swollen with the smells of heat and dry grass and decaying apples.

I said, "Is he inside the house?"

"Around back."

"Where around back?"

"There's a beat-down path. Just follow that."

"You don't want to come along?"

"No need. I'll stay here."

I gave him a long look. There was no tension in him, no guile; not much emotion of any kind, it seemed. He just sat there, hands on knees, eyes front—the same posture he'd held throughout the short trip from the crossroads.

I thought about insisting he come with me, but something kept me from doing it. I got out, taking the keys from the ignition. Before I shut the door I drew the .38; then I leaned back in to look at Benson, holding the gun down low so he couldn't see it.

"You won't blow the horn or anything like that, will you?"

"No," he said, "I won't."

"Just wait quiet."

"Yes."

The beaten-down path was off to the right. I walked it slowly through the tangled vegetation, listening, watching my backtrail. Nothing made noise and nothing happened. The fermenting-apples smell grew stronger as I came around the house to the rear; bees swarmed back there, making a muted sawmill sound. Near where the orchard began, the path veered off toward the creek, toward a big weeping willow that grew on the bank.

And under the willow was where it ended: at the grave of Benson's wife, marked by a marble headstone etched with the words *Beloved Elizabeth—Rest in Eternal Peace.*

But hers was not the only grave there. Next to it was a second one, a new one, the earth so freshly turned some of the clods on top were still moist. That one bore no marker of any kind.

I went back to the car, not quite running. Benson was out of it now, standing a few feet away looking at the house and the climbing primroses. He turned when he heard me coming, faced me squarely as I neared him.

"Now you know," he said without emotion and without irony. "I didn't lie to you, mister. I have no son."

"Why didn't you tell me he was dead?"

"Wanted you to see it for yourself. His grave."

"How did he die?"

"I shot him," the old man said. "Last night, about ten o'clock."

"You shot him?"

"With my old Iver Johnson. Two rounds through the heart."

"Why? What happened?"

"He brought me trouble, just like before."

"You can state it plainer than that."

A little silence. Then, "He was bad, Stephen was. Mean and bad clear through. Always was, even as a boy. Stealing things, breaking up property, hurting other boys. Hurting his mother." Benson held up his crooked left arm. "Hurting me too."

"Stephen did that to you?"

"When he was eighteen. Broke my arm in three places. Two operations and it still wouldn't heal right."

"What made him do it?"

"I wouldn't give him the money he wanted. So he beat up on me to get it. I told him before he ran off, don't ever come back, you're not welcome in my house anymore. And he didn't come back, not in more than a dozen years. Not until last night, at the Oasis."

"He wanted money again, is that it? Tried to hurt you again when you wouldn't give it to him?"

"Punched me in the belly," Benson said. "Still hurts when I move sudden. So I went and got the Iver Johnson. He laughed when I pointed it at him and told him to get out. 'Won't shoot me, old man,' he said. 'Your own son. You won't shoot me.' "

"What did he do? Try to take the gun away from you?"

Benson nodded. "Didn't leave me any choice but to shoot him. Twice through the heart. Then I brought him out here and buried him next to his mother."

"Why did you do that?"

"I told you before. 'Home is the place where.' I had to take him in, didn't I? For the last time?"

The smell of the rotting apples seemed stronger now. And the heat was intense and the skeletal buildings and fungoid primroses were ugly. I didn't want to be here any longer—not another minute in this place.

"Get back in the car, Mr. Benson."

"Where we going?"

"Just get back in the car. Please."

He did what I told him. I backed the car around and drove up the hill and over it without glancing in the rear view mirror. Neither of us said anything until I swung off the county road, onto the apron in front of Benson's Oasis, and braked to a stop.

Then he asked, "You going to call the sheriff now?" Matter-of-factly; not as if he cared.

"No," I said.

"How come?"

"Stephen's dead and buried. I don't see any reason not to leave him right where he is."

"But I killed him. Shot him down like a dog."

Old and dying like his crossroads store, with precious little time left. Where was the sense—or the justice—in forcing him to die somewhere else? But all I said was, "You did what you had to do. I'll be going now. I've got another long drive ahead of me."

He put his hand on the door latch, paused with it there. "What'll you say to the man who hired you, the bail bondsman?"

What would I say to Abe Melikian? The truth—some of it, at least. Stephen Arthur Benson is dead and in the ground and what's left of his family is poor; the bail money's gone, Abe, and there's no way you can get any of it back; write it off your taxes and forget about it. He trusted me and my judgment and he wouldn't press for details, particularly not when I waived the balance of my fee.

"You let me worry about that," I said, and Benson shrugged and lifted himself out of the car. He seemed to want to say something else; instead he turned, walked to the store. There was nothing more to say. Neither thank-yous nor goodbyes were appropriate and we both knew it.

I watched him unlock the door, switch the window sign from *Closed* to *Open* before he disappeared into the dimness within. Then I drove out onto the highway and headed north. To San Francisco. To my office and my flat and Kerry.

Home is the place where.

BOMB SCARE

HE was a hypertensive little man with overlarge ears and buck teeth—Brer Rabbit dressed up in a threadbare brown suit and sunglasses. In his left hand he carried a briefcase with a broken catch; it was held closed by a frayed strap that looked as though it might pop loose at any second. And inside the briefcase—

"A bomb," he kept announcing in a shrill voice. "I've got a remote-controlled bomb in here. Do what I tell you, don't come near me, or I'll blow us all up."

Nobody in the branch office of the San Francisco Trust Bank was anywhere near him. Lawrence Metaxa, the manager, and the other bank employees were frozen behind the row of tellers' cages. The four customers, me included, stood in a cluster out front. None of us was doing anything except waiting tensely for the little rabbit to quit hopping around and get down to business.

It took him another few seconds. Then, with his free hand, he dragged a cloth sack from his coat and threw it at one of the tellers. "Put all the money in there. Stay away from the silent alarm or I'll set off the bomb, I mean it."

Metaxa assured him in a shaky voice that they would do whatever he asked.

"Hurry up, then." The rabbit waved his empty right hand in the air, jerkily, as if he were directing some sort of mad symphony. "Hurry up, hurry up!"

The tellers got busy. While they hurriedly emptied cash drawers, the little man produced a second cloth sack and moved in my direction. The other customers shrank back. I stayed where I was, so he pitched the sack to me.

"Put your wallet in there," he said in a voice like glass cracking. "All your valuables. Then get everybody else's."

I said, "I don't think so."

"What? What?" He hopped on one foot, then the other, making the briefcase dance. "What's the matter with you? Do what I told you!"

When he'd first come in and started yelling about his bomb, I'd thought that I couldn't have picked a worse time to take care of my bank deposits. Now I was thinking that I couldn't have picked a better time. I took a measured step toward him. Somebody behind me gasped. I took another step.

"Stay back!" the little guy shouted. "I'll push the button, I'll blow us up—"

I said, "No, you won't," and rushed him and yanked the briefcase out of his hand.

More gasps, a cry, the sounds of customers and employees scrambling for cover. But nothing happened, except that the little guy tried to run away. I caught him by the collar and dragged him back. His struggles were brief and half-hearted; he'd gambled and lost and he knew when he was licked.

Scared faces peered over counters and around corners. I held the briefcase up so they could all see it. "No bomb in here, folks. You can relax now, it's all over."

It took a couple of minutes to restore order, during which time I marched the little man around to Metaxa's desk and pushed him into a chair. He sat slumped, twitching and muttering. "Lost my job, so many debts . . . must've been crazy to do a thing like this—I'm sorry, I'm sorry . . . ." Poor little rabbit. He wasn't half as sorry now as he was going to be later.

I opened the case while Metaxa called the police. The only thing inside was a city telephone directory for weight.

When Metaxa hung up he said to me, "You took a crazy risk, grabbing the briefcase like that. If he really had had a bomb in there. . ."

"I knew he didn't."

"*Knew* he didn't? How could you?"

"I'm a detective, remember? Three reasons. One: Bombs are delicate mechanisms and people who build them are cautious by necessity. They don't put explosives in a cheap case with a busted catch and just a frayed strap holding it together, not unless they're suicidal. Two: He claimed it was remote-controlled. But the hand he kept waving was empty and all he had in the other one was the case. Where was the remote control? In one of his pockets, where he couldn't get at it easily? No. A real bomber would've had it out in plain sight to back up his threat."

"Still," Metaxa said, "you *could've* been wrong on both counts. Neither is an absolute certainty."

"No, but the third reason is as close to one as you can get."

"Yes?"

"It takes more than just skill to make a bomb. It takes nerve, coolness, patience, and a very steady hand. Look at our friend here. He doesn't have any of those attributes; he's the chronically nervous type, as jumpy as six cats. He could no more manufacture an explosive device than you or I could fly. If he'd ever tried, he'd have blown himself up in two minutes flat."

WORRIED MOTHER JOB

IT was a worried mother job, the kind you get every now and then when you run a one-man, downscale agency like mine. A son or daughter gets into a hassle that can't or won't be taken to the police, the mother starts to fret, and one morning there she is perched on my client's chair, giving me the sort of look only a mother can work up: sad, anxious, frightened, pleading, and re-proving, all at the same time. A look calculated to make a man not only feel sympathetic but conjure up nostalgic images of his own dear old mom; a look calculated to get results.

Her name was Rose Youngblood. She was a widow in her early fif-ties, lived in Hayward, and sold real estate for a living—not a particularly good living if the real estate she sold was in Hayward. Her problem child was a twenty-seven-year-old son, Brian, who lived alone in a flat here in the city and worked as a freelance computer consultant. "He's brilliant at his work and he makes very good money." He'd never been in any trouble before, she said, never given her a moment's worry until now: now somebody had assaulted him and she was convinced that his life was in jeopardy.

For reasons of his own he refused to tell her who was after him or why. She wouldn't have known anything was wrong, she said, if she hadn't come to the city on business last week and gone to his flat for a surprise visit. A friend of her son's, Gary Myers, had answered the door and told her Brian was ill and tried to keep her out. She'd found her son on the couch, naked to the waist, his ribs taped and bruises all over his sides and lower back. "Whoever beat him up must've hit him a dozen times—he couldn't control his bladder for two days afterward." He told her he'd been mugged, but his story didn't jibe with Gary Myers' version when she got Myers alone, and finally she'd prodded Brian into admitting that the beating had been the result of a "personal misunderstanding." That was as much explaining as he was willing to do. He said he'd take care of the problem, there wouldn't be any more violent episodes, but he'd sounded scared—and strange, almost frantic. She knew her son, they'd always been close, and she'd never seen him this shaken or frightened.

By the time I'd heard this much I knew I didn't want anything to do with it. She hadn't consulted Brian before coming to me, she might well have maternally exaggerated both the violence and his state of mind, and in any event an unexplained "personal misunderstanding" is something a private investigator is well-advised to stay out of. This sort of job was on a par with wandering into a back alley in a bad neighborhood at midnight: If you had a choice, why would you do it?

So I should've said no then and there. I started to, in fact, but obliquely instead of straight out; she seemed like a nice lady, genuinely proud of her son, seriously concerned for his safety, and I wanted to let her down easy. Big mistake. She showed me the Look, and I squirmed under it and felt some of my resolve slipping, and the next thing I knew we were into an interview-lengthening q. & a.

"Well . . . could the trouble be over a woman?" I asked.

She frowned at the question, ran nervous fingers through her tight-curled hair. The hair was dark brown, without a strand of gray—a dye job but a good one. She was an attractive woman, if a little too Suburban Mom for my taste. "I don't see how that's possible," she said.

"You said Brian's not married. Divorced? Separated?"

"Neither. He and a girl named Ginny Lawson were engaged last year, but she broke it off a month before the wedding."

"For what reason?"

"Brian said she got cold feet. The commitment and everything. But it seemed awfully sudden and out of character to me."

"Maybe she found someone else."

"That's possible. I don't know."

"How did Brian handle the breakup?"

"Not very well at first. He really loved that girl."

"Was he angry?"

"Yes. Frankly so was I."

"But he did accept her decision, didn't keep after her to reconsider?"

"Of course he accepted it. Brian isn't the type to cling to unrealistic goals; he's very practical."

"Is he seeing anyone now?"

"Not seriously, no. He isn't ready for another commitment."

"Any one woman he dates more than others?"

"No, I don't think so. He hasn't mentioned anyone."

"Tell me about his activities, what he does for recreation."

"Well, I don't know that he goes out much at all. He spends most of his time at his computers. Not just working—the Internet, playing chess, that sort of thing."

I said gently, "Vices, Mrs. Youngblood?"

"He doesn't have any. Really."

"Never any problems with liquor or drugs?"

"Absolutely not. I'd know if he was into anything like that."

Sure you would, I thought. "This friend you mentioned, Gary Myers. Are they close?"

"Fairly close, I think. They live near each other. Gary's a decent sort, polite, but a little . . . well, he doesn't have much personality. Nerdy, you know?" She added quickly, "Not at all like Brian."

"What is it they have in common? Computers?"

"Yes. Gary works as an accountant for an electronics firm in Redwood City. Kelleher Electronics."

"Is Brian close to anyone else? Anyone who might have an idea of what led to the beating?"

"Well, there's Paul Janssen. He's from Hayward too—he and Brian went to school together. They've played computer chess for years."

Except for a few more minor details—Paul Janssen managed a computer store in North Beach, Ginny Lawson lived in Sausalito and was employed at a Wells Fargo branch over there—that was everything she had to tell me. Nothing much in any of it; nothing at all to make me want to change my mind about taking the case. Earnestly and apologetically I said, "I have to be honest with you, Mrs. Youngblood, I really don't see that there's much I can do—"

Before I could get the rest of it out she gave me the Look again, and some verbal firepower to go with it. "Please, won't you at least talk to Brian? Another man, an authority figure . . . he might confide in you. I don't know who else to turn to—he's my only child, his father has been gone ten years. Just talk to him, that's all I ask. Please?"

No, I thought. And looked the Look in the eye and said, "All right, Mrs. Youngblood. I'll do that much, I'll talk to him."

P.T. Barnum would have loved me. Yes he would.

Brian Youngblood lived on the downhill side of Diamond Heights, across from the Douglass Playground. The address wasn't all that far from my office on O'Farrell, so I took a chance and drove over there unannounced. According to his mother Brian did most of his work at home and could usually be found there; and it's always easier to gain an audience with a stranger when you're already camped on his doorstep.

The building was a refurbished Stick Victorian that had been sliced into a pair of good-sized flats, one above the other. Brian had the upper, which meant that the view from his windows of the southern curve of the city, the bay, and the East Bay would be pretty impressive. Doing well for himself, all right. You couldn't rent a flat like this, in a neighborhood like this, for less than $2500 a month.

The two entrances were side by side on the high stoop; the one on the right had his name, B. Youngblood, on the mailbox. I leaned on the bell. Pretty soon the intercom clicked and made noises like a hen laying an egg and a staticky voice said, "Yes?"

"Brian Youngblood?"

"What is it?"

I identified myself and said that I was there at the request of his mother and would he give me a few minutes of his time. No answer. Five seconds later the squawk box shut off. Thinking it over, probably. I stood there waiting. It was a windy day, clouds chasing one another across the sky to the east; I pulled my coat collar up against the chill. Out on the bay a freighter from the Port of Oakland was moving slowly under the arch of the Bay Bridge, heading toward the Gate. I wished I was on it—not alone; with Kerry, my brand-new wife—instead of standing up on a hill watching it drift on its way toward some exotic port of call. We'd talked about taking a freighter trip someday, Kerry and I, down through the Panama Canal to one or more of the Caribbean islands, before that mode of travel became completely obsolete. Kerry knew somebody who'd taken a cruise like that and it was—

The intercom made chicken noises again. And the staticky voice said, "All right, come on up."

The door buzzed and I opened it and went into a tiny foyer and then up a flight of carpeted stairs. Another door at the top opened as I reached the landing. The young man who stood peering at me through a pair of wire-rimmed glasses was thin, pale, nondescript. His hair was thin and pale too, as fine as cornsilk. His mother had said he wasn't nerdy but he looked that way to me, if not to her. There wasn't much resemblance between them.

I handed him one of my business cards, and his eyes widened when he read what was printed on it. "A detective?" he said. Without benefit of intercom static, his voice was as thin and pale as the rest of him. "You didn't say you were a detective. Why would my mother send a detective to see me?"

"She's concerned about you, the trouble you had last week. She thought I might be able to help."

"I don't think—"

"Brian, for Christ's sake," a woman's voice called sharply from somewhere inside. "Don't talk out there—bring him in here."

He winced slightly; his expression shifted, took on an almost hunted aspect. He wouldn't meet my eyes any longer. "We'd better go in," he said, and turned stiffly and led me into a big, open front room.

The room's windows would have provided the impressive view I'd speculated on outside if heavy drapes hadn't been drawn across them. It was darkish as a result, palely lit by a desk lamp and a table lamp, and dominated by computer hardware—not just one terminal or work station or whatever they're called, but three of them, plus all sorts of other high-tec paraphernalia that took up one entire wall and part of another. An armchair, a recliner, a two-seat couch, and some chrome-and-glass tables accounted for the rest of the furnishings.

Lounging on her spine in the armchair was a long-haired blonde about Brian's age. She was the tall, lean, slinky type, wearing spike heels and black net stockings and a shiny red dress that ended at midthigh and was stretched tight across high breasts. The hard-faced type, too: smears of bright crimson lipstick and so much purple-black eyeshadow she might have been made up for one of the zombie roles in *Night of the Living Dead*. I made an effort to conceal my surprise, thinking: Hooker, and not one of the high-priced variety. Either that, or Brian Youngblood has friends a hell of a lot odder than his mother led me to believe.

He said to me, "This is Brandy. She's . . . a friend."

Brandy. Right.

I nodded and said hello, but she didn't return the greeting. I impressed her about as much as a sewer worker would have; she favored me with a brief up-and-down glance, sneered, and transferred her gaze to Brian. "Who is he?" she demanded in one of those affected whiskey contraltos.

He went over and presented her with my card. She sneered at that too. "A 'confidential investigator,' " she said, "of all the goddamn things. And not even a young, good-looking one. What's the matter with that silly-ass mother of yours, Brian?"

He still wore the hunted look, shaded now with embarrassment. "Brandy, please . . ."

"The old bitch. You told her you'd handle it, didn't you? You told her it wasn't anything serious."

"Yes, I told her."

"Damn meddling old bitch."

Some piece of work, this one. I paid her the same discourtesy she'd paid me by ignoring her. I said to Brian, "Handle what, Mr. Youngblood? Just what kind of trouble are you in?"

"You don't have to tell him anything, Brian. Not a thing."

"I asked you," I said to Youngblood, "not your friend. If you'll talk to me, there might be something I can do."

He shook his head. He wouldn't look at me; his gaze was fixed on Brandy.

"Do?" the blonde said nastily. "What can a fat old fart *do* for anyone?"

"Your mother cares about you, Mr. Youngblood. That ought to count for something."

"She—she shouldn't have gone behind my back," he said. "I don't need a detective. I don't need anyone's help."

"Except mine," Brandy said. "Tell him to leave us alone, Brian. Tell him to go apply for Social Security. Tell him to join Jenny Craig and lose some of his lard."

I'd had just about enough cheap Brandy. I turned slowly, treated her to the same kind of up-and-down glance she'd given me, sneered the same way, and said, "You're part of the trouble, sweetmeat."

"What?"

"You heard me. Any so-called friend with a mouth like yours is part of anyone's trouble."

"Fuck you."

"Right," I said. "Sweetmeat dipped in poison."

The bloody lips peeled back away from her teeth. She started to lift herself out of the chair, changed her mind, and sank back with her mouth twisted and hate leaking out of her eyes. I laughed at her before I turned to Youngblood again.

"Is she the reason you got beat up?"

"Brandy? No. No, she . . . it had nothing to do with her."

"What did it have to do with?"

Headshake.

"Come on, Mr. Youngblood. For your mother's sake, if not for your own."

He was still staring at the blonde. "Brandy . . . ?"

"No, goddamn it!" she yelled. "To hell with that bitch. You say one word to fatso here and you'll regret it. I mean that, Brian. You'll regret it."

Youngblood laid his eyes on me again. Now he looked scared as well as hunted and embarrassed. "You'd better leave," he said.

"Is that what you want? You, not her."

"Yes. Leave. Just leave and don't come back."

The blonde, behind me: "And tell Mommie Dearest to mind her own business from now on."

There wasn't anything I could do except put a tight lid on my anger and walk out of there. Shutting my ears on the way downstairs to another stream of poisonous Brandy.

I went over to the playground and took a turn through it, to cool down before I did any more driving. The anger I felt was directed as much at myself as at Brian Youngblood and his dragon lady. This was what I got for taking on a worried mother job. Well, I'd done as much for Rose Youngblood as I could. Now I was out of it; now I could go back to tracing skips and ferreting out insurance frauds and doing all the other routine and reasonable tasks that come to a man in my profession.

Sure. Except that I couldn't get the scene the three of us had just played out of my mind. In retrospect it had a vaguely surreal, vaguely ludicrous quality, and yet its hard and nasty edge hinted at all sorts of hidden tensions, hidden meanings.

Brandy had some kind of hold on Youngblood—that seemed clear. But what kind? Sex? Probably, but I had a feeling there was more to it than that. She seemed to hate his mother without even knowing her personally: If Rose Youngblood was aware of Brandy she'd have given me an earful about her. So why the animosity on the blonde's part? And why the tacit acceptance of that animosity on Brian's? And what was Brandy's connection to the beating he'd taken?

Nagging questions, puzzling questions—the kind that would keep on bothering me unless I did some digging for the answers.

So all right, I *wasn't* out of it yet. Not just yet.

I drove back to O'Farrell Street. I would've preferred an immediate talk with Gary Myers and/or Paul Janssen, but such would have to wait until later, when both men returned home from their jobs. Workplace discussions of personal problems are usually a bad idea; if people are going to be candid with a detective, they're much more likely to do so in the privacy of their own homes.

Meanwhile, a background check on Brian Youngblood seemed like a good idea. Even if it didn't shed any light on his trouble, it might give me a better handle on the sort of person he was. Tomorrow morning my new part-time assistant, Tamara Corbin, could use her Apple PowerBook to access the California Justice Information System's computers and find out if Youngblood had a criminal record or outstanding warrants of any type. As for a standard credit check . . .

I stopped in at Bay City Realtors, on my building's ground floor, to talk to Martin Quon. A few years ago a new state law had gone into effect prohibiting detectives and other private citizens from using credit services like TRW for investigative purposes. This made my job more difficult and invited a certain amount of ethical compromise. One way to get around the new law was to have a realtor request the credit pull, since realtors are in the buying and selling business and therefore allowed to subscribe to credit-monitoring services. Martin Quon didn't much like being part of a private cop's quasilegal corner-cutting, but in consideration of reciprocal favors and the fact that we'd known each other for a lot of years, he was inclined to go along with it. I asked him to pull Brian Youngblood's credit history. He said he would, but not until he'd indulged in his usual series of face-saving grumbles.

Half an hour later I had the report on my desk. And it added yet another batch of puzzling questions. According to Rose Youngblood, her son was at the top of his profession and made piles of money. According to the report, Brian Youngblood had spent most of the past thirteen months mired in debt. Credit cards maxed to the limit, with not even the minimum being paid. Two and three months in arrears on his rent. PG&E and telephone bills unpaid and service shut off once by Pac Bell. All of this had built up over a ten-month period, until three months ago when he'd come into enough money—nearly ten thousand dollars —to pay off what he owed in back rent and utilities and to lower his credit card balances enough so that he was permitted to keep the cards. But the credit fix had been only temporary. In the ninety days since, he'd managed to thrust himself right back into a money trap: credit cards near maxed out, rent and utility bills unpaid. If he didn't do something about it soon, he was facing eviction and bankruptcy.

So where did all his earnings go? Brandy? She was the golddigger type, all right. Thirteen months ago . . . was that when he'd taken up with her? Before then he'd had a fairly stable credit rating, so the overextension was a new pattern. I wondered, too, if Brandy and/or Brian's financial problems had had anything to do with Ginny Lawson walking out of his life.

Brandy . . . Brandy what? Well, maybe Myers or Janssen could provide her last name. And some idea of just who and what she was.

I stayed late at the office, closed up at six o'clock, and then drove down to Gary Myers' apartment building in Noe Valley. He wasn't home. I considered leaving my card in his mailbox, decided against it. Better to wait and catch him in person, without advance notice.

With Paul Janssen I had better luck. He lived in an old brown-shingled building on Funston, across from the narrow panhandle strip on Park Presidio Boulevard, and he was home alone and inclined to be cooperative when I showed him the photostat of my investigator's license and explained why I was there.

"So Brian's in trouble," he said.

"His mother thinks so. So do I."

"Well, I can't say I'm surprised." Janssen sighed and rumpled his thatch of lank red hair. "I don't know that I can tell you much—I haven't seen or talked to him in months. But whatever I can do . . ."

When we were inside and seated in his cluttered living room I said, "Mrs. Youngblood led me to believe you and Brian were good friends, played computer chess together regularly."

"All in the past. That's the way he wanted it."

"Why?"

"Wish I knew. You know somebody most of your life, you think you know them pretty well, right? And then all of a sudden something happens and they weird out and you realize you didn't really know them at all."

"When did Brian start to weird out?"

"Over a year ago."

"In what ways?"

"Well, it started with buying things—expensive computer hardware that he didn't really need. State-of-the-art stuff. The last time I saw him he had *six* pcs and *five* printers. His spare bedroom looked like a Compaq warehouse."

"How did he explain it to you?"

"He didn't even try," Janssen said. "Just said he wanted the stuff so he bought it."

I asked, "How else did he change?"

"Grew distant, withdrawn. Started holing up in his flat. I'd try to get him to log on for chess but he wasn't interested. I'd call him up and get his machine and he wouldn't call back."

"Did you know he was in debt, not paying his bills?"

"Yeah, I heard. I can tell you part of the reason: He lost two of his consulting jobs."

"Oh? How come?"

"He wasn't doing his work. Just didn't seem to care any more."

"Why?"

"Not a clue."

"When was it that he lost the jobs?"

"About four months ago."

"Is he the one who told you?"

"No. I found out from Gary Myers."

"You know Myers, then."

"Not well. Brian introduced us, but we didn't hit it off. I ran into him at a computer trade show at the Cow Palace and we got to talking. He was concerned about Brian too. But neither of us could figure out what to do about it."

"You consider contacting Brian's mother?"

"We discussed it, yeah. Myers said he'd told Brian he was thinking of doing that and Brian threw a fit, told him to mind his own business. He and his mom are close, real protective of each other—I guess she told you that. I probably should've gone ahead and got in touch with her anyway. But I didn't want to make things worse by butting in."

The old code of noninvolvement. Not that I blamed Janssen much; a situation like this is always ticklish for the parties involved, both directly and indirectly.

He said, "I guess Mrs. Youngblood finally found out some other way. But why'd she go to a detective? I mean, there's nothing you can do about weird behavior or financial problems, is there?"

"No, but that's not why she hired me. She doesn't know about any of that. All she knows is that somebody beat him up last week."

"Beat him up? Brian?" Janssen looked and sounded amazed. "Who?"

"We don't know yet."

"Man, that doesn't make sense. Brian's totally nonviolent. If you'd met him . . ."

"I did meet him. This afternoon, at his flat. His girlfriend Brandy was there too."

"Brandy?"

"You don't know her?"

"No. I never met anyone named Brandy."

I described her and her foul mouth, provided a capsule summary of the scene at Youngblood's flat.

"That doesn't make sense either," Janssen said. "I can't imagine Brian letting *anybody* talk that way about his mom. He didn't stand up to her at all?"

"Not for a second."

"Man." He wagged his head. "I never knew Brian to be attracted to a woman like that."

"Not his type?"

"No way. His mom tell you he was engaged to Ginny Lawson?"

"Yes."

"You haven't talked to Ginny yet, right? When you do you'll see she's the total opposite of this Brandy. Ginny's about as tight-assed conservative as they come."

"Why'd she break off the engagement, do you know?"

"He wouldn't say, but I figured it had to be the weird way he was acting."

"So it wasn't the breakup that caused his erratic behavior."

"No. The weird shit started a couple of months before."

"And for no apparent reason that you could see."

"None."

I told him about Brian paying off most of his debts three months ago, only to backslide again since. "Where could he have gotten the ten thousand dollars? Certificate of deposit or IRAs, maybe?"

"Uh-uh, not Brian. He's never been much on future planning. He and Ginny used to argue about that all the time."

"Loan from a friend? Myers, for instance?"

"Not Myers—he doesn't have that kind of money. And if Brian has any other friends with that much cash lying around, I don't know who they are. Maybe he got it from a bank or finance company?"

"He didn't." It would have been on the credit report if he had. "New consulting work?"

"That's out too. Even if he hustled two or three new jobs, it'd've taken him a lot longer than a month to raise that much cash."

Which left what? A couple of possibilities, one of them—

"Brandy," Janssen said, as if reading my mind. "Could *she* have loaned it to him?"

I shrugged. "No way of telling until I find out more about her."

"It'd explain why he let her talk about his mom that way, wouldn't it? Why he let her walk all over him?"

"Partly, anyway."

Janssen wagged his head again. "Weird, man—totally weird. How does a guy like Brian, a good guy, let himself get so screwed up?"

Rhetorical question. Most of us can't even explain to ourselves why we screw up or get screwed up in all the ways we do.

Things got even weirder at eleven the next morning.

I was at my desk, going over the CJIS printout Tamara Corbin had just handed me—Brian Youngblood had no criminal record, and not so much as an outstanding parking violation—when the telephone rang. A half-muffled voice said rapidly in my ear, "If you want to know who hurt Brian Youngblood and why, ask a man named Kinsella. Nick Kinsella, Blacklight Tavern." That was all. *Click*, and the line went dead.

My mouth was doing a flytrap imitation; I shut it as I cradled the receiver. He'd tried to disguise his voice with a handkerchief or the like, but he hadn't done much of a job of it. Enough of the thin, pale tone had come through to make it recognizable.

Brian Youngblood. And why in hell would Brian Youngblood want to tell me something anonymously that he could have volunteered straight out, over the phone or over a cup of coffee?

I knew Nick Kinsella. And I knew the Blacklight Tavern. Both operated on San Bruno Avenue, off Bayshore Boulevard west of Candlestick. Kinsella owned the bar, but it wasn't his primary source of income. He'd made his pile in the fine old time-honored trade of loansharking. He was rough trade, too; you had to be pretty desperate or pretty naive to go to him for money. He charged a heavy weekly vig, and if you missed a payment or two you could expect a visit from one of his enforcers. If Brian Youngblood was into Nick Kinsella for ten thousand plus, he'd been lucky to get off with nothing more than bruised ribs and bruised kidneys. Miss another payment and he'd find out the hard way just how brittle his bones were.

I picked up the car and drove south on the Bayshore Freeway to the San Bruno Avenue exit. This was one of the city's older residential neighborhoods, working-class, like the one I'd grown up in in the Outer

Mission. During World War II, and while the Hunters Point Naval Shipyard humped along for twenty-five years afterward, it had been a reasonably decent section to live and raise a family in. But then the shipyard shut down, and mostly black Hunters Point began to deteriorate into a mean-streets ghetto. Now, with the crack-infested Point on one side and the drug deli that McLaren Park had become on the other, the neighborhood had suffered an inevitable erosion. Signs of decay were everywhere: boarded-up storefronts, bars on windows and doors, houses defaced by graffiti and neglect, homeless people and drunks huddled or sprawled in doorways.

The Blacklight fit right in: from a distance it looked like something that had been badly scorched in a fire. Black-painted facade, smoke-tinted windows, black sign with neon letters that would blaze white after dark but looked burned out in the daylight. I parked in front and locked the doors, not that that would stop anybody who thought the car contained something tradeable for a rock of crack or a jug of cheap sweet wine.

Inside, the place might have been any bottom-end bar populated by the usual array of daytime drinkers. A couple of the men and one of the women gave me bleary-eyed once-overs, decided I wasn't anybody worth knowing, hustling, or hassling, and turned their attention back to the focal point of their lives. The bartender had a head like a redwood burl and a surly manner. All he said when I bellied up was, "Yeah?"

"Nick Kinsella. He in?"

"Who wants to know?"

I passed over one of my cards. He didn't even look at it.

"Mr. Kinsella know you?"

"He knows me. Tell him it's a business matter."

He took the card to a backbar phone, did a little talking and a little listening, and came back without the card. "Okay," he said in less surly tones. "Over there. First door past the ladies' crapper."

I found the door and knocked on it and walked in. Mostly barren office that stank of cigar smoke and had two men in it—Kinsella, and a lopsided, balding guy with the build of a wrestler who was no doubt one of the shark's enforcers. Kinsella sat bulging behind a cherrywood desk. He'd grown a third chin since I'd last seen him, added another couple of inches to his waistline. That last meeting had been five years ago, after I'd tracked down and brought back a bail-jumper for a bondsman named Abe Melikian. The jumper was somebody Kinsella had a grudge against. He liked me for ushering the guy back into the slammer.

I shut the door behind me. "Long time, Nick."

"Long time," he agreed. "How they been hangin'?"

"Low and inside."

He thought that was funny. The enforcer didn't crack a smile.

The shark said, "So what brings you around? Don't tell me you got money troubles?"

"Not your kind. But I might know somebody who does."

"Yeah? Who'd that be?"

"Young guy, works in computers—Brian Youngblood."

His face showed me nothing. He leaned back in his chair, clasped sausage fingers behind his neck. "Maybe I know him, maybe I don't. How come you're interested?"

"He's in over his head. I'm trying to find out how deep."

"Working for him?"

I hesitated before I said, "No, his mother."

Kinsella's lips twitched. Don't laugh, you bastard. He didn't; he sat forward again. "I don't like to talk about my customers. Bad for business."

"Only if word gets out. I'm a businessman too, Nick. I know how to keep my mouth shut."

"Just a couple of businessmen schmoozing, huh?"

"That's right."

"No hassles?"

"Not from me."

"Okay. So what you want to know?"

"How much Youngblood borrowed initially, how much he's into you for now. And whether something can be worked out in the way of accident insurance."

"He already have an accident, did he?"

"Just last week. Laid him up for a couple of days."

"That's too bad," Kinsella said. "But you got expect something like that when you don't pay attention."

The fat son of a bitch was enjoying himself, playing this little game. Maybe someday I'd have a chance to play a different kind of game with him; it was a good thought and I held onto it. "The original nut, Nick," I said. "How much?"

"Ten thousand."

"Pretty hefty amount. What'd he use for collateral?"

"Personal property. I took a look, I was satisfied."

All the computer hardware, probably. I asked, "What does he owe you now, with the vig? Thirteen, fourteen?"

"Five."

"Wait a minute—five thousand? How'd it get cut that low?"

Kinsella's smile widened. "Your boy walked in here two days ago and laid eighty-five hundred on me. Cash. He's a good boy, your boy. Teach him a lesson, he learns real quick. He don't need no accident insurance, not any more."

"Where'd he get the eighty-five hundred?"

"Who knows? He don't say, I don't ask."

Not from another shark, I thought, not with the size of the original nut and the fact that Kinsella had had to send out an enforcer. Loan sharks are like their salt-water relatives: When one spills some bad blood, the rest smell it and keep their distance.

"What about the five thousand balance?" I asked.

"What about it?"

"If his source is dry he'll start missing payments again. Then he will need that insurance."

"Not if he shows up next week with the full five K plus interest."

". . . He told you he was going to do that?"

"Guaranteed it." Kinsella laughed. "Swore it, in fact. You want to know what he swore it on?"

"No."

He told me anyway. "His mother. Your boy swore it on his love for his sweet old mama."

Gary Myers wasn't at Kelleher Electronics. Twenty miles down to Redwood City, telling myself that the time had come for a workplace discussion, telling myself that if anybody had an idea where Brian Youngblood had got the eighty-five hundred to pay off Kinsella, it was Myers—and "I'm sorry, sir, Mr. Myers is out of the office today."

Grumbling, I got back into the car and headed north.

Myers wasn't home, either.

And didn't that just figure?

Sausalito, across the Golden Gate Bridge on the northwestern rim of the bay, has been a lot of things over the years: fishing village, artists' colony, San Francisco bedroom community, real estate agent's wet dream (its wooded hills are dotted with million-dollar and near million-dollar homes), and expensive tourist trap. I used to go over there fairly often in the pre-trap days; now, not much at all. It's still a pretty little town, it still has some good restaurants, but I never did enjoy vying for street space with poorly driven rental cars and sidewalk space with camera-laden gawkers from Houston, Peoria, and Tokyo.

The Wells Fargo branch where Ginny Lawson worked was on Bridgeway, on the north end of town. She was on the job today, at least. A bank officer, she occupied one of half a dozen desks on a carpeted area opposite the tellers' cages. The nameplate on the desk said *Ms. Virginia Lawson*. Nobody was sitting in the customer chairs in front of it, so I went straight on over.

She glanced up from a computer screen as I approached, showed me a prim professional smile as I sat down. "Tight-assed conservative," Paul Janssen had called her, and she looked it: gray skirt and jacket, white blouse, minimum amount of makeup, brown hair drawn up into a tight bun. Her gray eyes had a remote quality, as if they were looking at you through a self-imposed filter.

"May I help you?"

"I hope so." I laid my card in front of her. "But I'm not here on bank business. It's a personal matter.'"

"Yes?" She glanced at the card, frowned, and said the word again with a flatter inflection. "Yes?"

"It's about Brian Youngblood."

She froze. Almost literally: All of her flesh seemed to harden before my eyes, like water turning to ice in one of those time-lapse photographic sequences. In a strained voice she said, "I have nothing to say to anyone about Brian Youngblood."

"It's important, Ms. Lawson. I'm afraid he's in serious trouble."

Silence for at least fifteen seconds. It occurred to me that she intended to keep on sitting there like that, frozen and silent, for as long as it took me to leave her alone. But then, as I leaned forward to make another plea, she said abruptly, "I'm not surprised."

"That Brian is in trouble?"

"He's sick. He has been for a long time."

"Sick in what way?"

"Mentally. He's mentally ill."

"Would you elaborate on that?"

Tight little headshake.

"Is that the reason you wouldn't marry him?" I asked. "Because you think he's mentally ill?"

"I won't discuss my private life."

"Ms. Lawson, please. If you know something—"

"I said I won't discuss it."

"I can understand it must be painful for you. But if you'll let me tell you just how serious—"

"No. I don't want to hear it."

All right, I thought, one more shot. "Brandy," I said.

She jerked as if I'd slapped her. The tight little headshake again, then the frozen silence.

"You know her. Tell me about her."

Nothing.

"She's the root of Brian's troubles, isn't she?"

Nothing.

"The reason for his sickness? The reason you ended your relationship with him?"

Still nothing. But the ice was beginning to crack. She sat just as rigidly, but muscles had begun to twitch in her face—an effect like fissures forming and spreading.

"Ms. Lawson?"

She started to laugh. A low, bitter, humorless sound that settled a coldness on my neck. The facial muscles kept on twitching, as if they were acting as a pump for the dribbling laughter.

"Brandy," she said. "Oh God, *Brandy*."

"Ms. Lawson?"

"Sick," she said, "sick, sick," and went right on laughing.

It was as if she were alone somewhere, all alone in a place I couldn't get to and wouldn't want to be if I could. I got up and went away from her, away from the empty, bitter sounds of her pain.

As I drove back across the Golden Gate Bridge I used the car phone to call information for Gary Myers' home number. It was after four by then; he had to come home sometime. But I didn't want to go chasing over to Noe Valley again on the chance, and to hell with worrying about advance warning. I was going to talk to him sooner or later, whether he liked it or not.

I punched out his number while I was waiting in line at the toll booths. Three rings—answering machine. "This is Gary Myers. I'm not available right now, but if you'll leave your name and number at the tone I'll call you back as soon as I can."

I sat there holding the receiver. Somebody behind me beeped his horn, did it again and then laid on the thing until I realized I was holding up traffic.

Under my breath I said, "Sweet Christ," because I'd also just realized the truth about Brian Youngblood.

The front door to his Douglass Street flat stood wide open. That didn't have to mean much of anything—doors get left open for all sorts of reasons, even in security-conscious neighborhoods like this one—but it made me even edgier than I already was. I hurried up onto the stoop, poked my head inside. The door at the top of the stairs was shut. No sounds came from up there. I pulled back out and thumbed the bell button above the mailbox.

The intercom stayed quiet. So did the door buzzer.

I hesitated. Open door, open invitation—right? I went all the way in and slowly up the stairs to the landing. If this door was locked . . . but it wasn't. The knob turned under my hand. I pushed it inward until I had an angled view into the center hallway and part of the kitchen. No one in sight. No one talking or moving around.

"Hello? Anybody home?"

Silence.

I called Youngblood's name, called it again and added my own. Thin echoes faded into a stillness that seemed heavier now, as if I had somehow thickened it with my presence. I walked soft and wary into the hallway, around to where I could see into the front room. Empty. The window drapes were closed, as they had been on my previous visit; in the half light the row of computer screens glowed, three square greenish faces that seemed to pulse faintly as if with an inner life of their own.

The way the flat was laid out, there figured to be a bedroom, at the front and another at the rear beyond the kitchen. The one in front, adjacent to the living room, would be the larger of the two; check that one first. I crossed to a closed door in the inner wall, prodded it open. Drawn drapes in there, too, but a lamp burned on a table beside the bed—

Ah, Jesus.

He—they—lay in a backward sprawl across the bed, a small hole such as a .22 makes leaking dribbles of coagulating blood above the left eye. Brian. And Brandy. One body, but for months now it had contained two individuals—the quiet hacker and the foulmouthed blonde bimbo. Half him and half her, even now in death: black net stockings and an ice-blue silk dress that had twisted open in front to reveal one of the foam-rubber falsies underneath; lean, ascetic face without makeup, nothing concealing the black hair cropped close to the skull. The blond wig was on the floor next to the bed. Shot while in the midst of one of his trans-formations from Brian into Brandy or Brandy into Brian.

I went in long enough to press two fingers against the artery in his neck, even though there was no point in it. He'd been dead at least half an hour. From next to the bed I could see inside an open walk-in closet. Racks of women's clothing, four or five times as many garments as there were of men's wear, two expensive fur wraps and a sable coat among them. No surprise there. Brandy had been the dominant personality for some time.

I backed up, turned out of the bedroom into the living room. And drew up sharp, with my stomach kicking and a crawling sensation across my scalp.

He was standing in the hallway fifteen feet away, the pistol in his hand a .22 Colt Woodsman. He'd been in the flat all along, hiding somewhere in back when he heard me come in. Thin, pale, nondescript, peering at me through a pair of wire-rimmed glasses. The elusive Gary Myers.

"Stay where you are," he said in his thin, pale voice. "Don't come near me."

"All right, Gary."

"So you know. Everything, I guess."

"Most of it, not all. Why don't you put the gun down and we'll talk about it."

"No. You stay there."

I watched the piece; it was loose and jumpy in his fingers. I didn't like that and I didn't like the look of him. Face the color of bacon fat, sweat coating it in beads and runnels. Eyes like peeled grapes in curdled milk. On the ragged edge and teetering.

"I killed her," he said. "Brandy. I shot her."

"Why?"

"I couldn't take it any more. She kept hurting me. All my life people have been hurting me but nobody as badly as her."

"How did she hurt you?"

"Made me do things."

"What things? Not sexual—"

"No! Brian wasn't gay and neither am I. And Brandy . . . she didn't want anything but control. Mean, evil control freak. She deserved to die."

"What did she make you do, Gary?"

He shook his head and then moved sideways a couple of paces, leaned his left shoulder against the wall as if he needed the support to remain standing. The movements were stiff, as his movements had been yesterday—a natural stiffness, not what I'd taken to be the result of a beating. Brian as Brandy, in the chair the whole time, starting to lift out of it when I stoked her rage, sinking back with a grimace not of hate but of pain from bruised ribs and kidneys—

"She made my life a living hell the past three months," Myers said. "I didn't know Brian was a transvestite until then. He kept it a secret from everyone, until Brandy began to take over. She'd been with him for years, he said, getting stronger and stronger. She made him buy her expensive presents, clothes and jewelry and computers . . . made him spend more and more time with her. She didn't want him to marry Ginny, she was jealous of Ginny, so she told Ginny all about Brian and her."

"And three months ago she told you."

"She had to. I was Brian's friend, I wanted to help him, but he couldn't make me do what she wanted. Neither could she, not then. But I was afraid of her from the first. Terrified. Always putting me down, calling me names, threatening me . . . I hated her too. You heard her yesterday, the way she talked to me, the things she said about Brian's mother. She was jealous of her too."

I didn't say anything, still watching the .22.

"It was her idea for me to pretend to be Brian yesterday. She thought it was funny. She wanted to see if she could fool you. And she did, didn't she?"

"Yeah," I said, "she fooled me."

"Evil. She *deserved* to die."

"You still haven't told me what she made you do, Gary. Give her money so Brian could pay off Nick Kinsella?"

"Yes."

"Your money?"

"I don't have any money. My company's . . . she made me steal it, embezzle it. She said it was the only way to save Brian. She said if I'd stolen it three months ago, when she wanted me to, he wouldn't have had to go to a loan shark. Her fault, but she twisted it around so I was to blame. She hounded me and hounded me until I did it . . . three days ago."

"What happened today?"

"She wanted me to steal *more* money. Another five thousand to pay off the rest of what Brian owed. I couldn't . . . I couldn't do it again. That's why I called you this morning . . . I thought if you knew about Kinsella—I wasn't thinking clearly, not then and not later. I let it slip that I'd called you. She went crazy . . . hit me, kicked me, threatened to kill me . . . I couldn't stand it any more. I went home and got my pistol and came back—I almost didn't use it because she was changing back into Brian. But she was still in control, she laughed at me, dared me. . . ."

"Gary, listen—"

But he was beyond listening. He made a liquidy sobbing sound. "I killed her and I'm not sorry. But Brian—he was my best friend and I killed him too. I can't live with that. I'm a coward, a miserable damned coward. . . ."

And in the next second he did what he must've been nerving himself to do the past half hour: He proved just how much of a coward he was. Before I could even think about trying to stop him, he yanked the Woodsman's muzzle up against his temple and fired.

I turned away, stood for fifteen or twenty seconds with the sound of the shot like a frozen echo in my ears and my hands fisted so tightly I could feel the nails gouging skin from my palms. When the tension in me finally began to ease a little I went over and squatted next to Myers' crumpled body. Dead—what the hell else? All three of them now.

I listened. Quiet in the flat below; nobody home down there, probably. At one of the front windows I peered through a slit in the drapes. The street below was quiet too. The .22 hadn't made much of a bang, this time or when Myers had fired his earlier fatal shot. For the moment, the only person who knew what had happened here was me.

Back in the bedroom I stood for a little time looking down at what was left of Brian Youngblood. I could almost see the headline in tomorrow's *Chronicle*: BIZARRE TRANSVESTITE MURDER-SUICIDE. Oh yeah, the media would love this. Even in jaded San Francisco, where bizarre happenings are part of the norm, it was just kinky enough to get a certain amount of play—the kind that provokes smarmy comments and sick jokes.

He's my only child. . . . I don't have anyone else. . . .

It'll tear her up, I thought. She'll never get over it. His death, even the money troubles and the collusion in Myers' embezzlement—that she can learn to live with. But the rest of it . . .

I kept staring at the body lying there in the ice-blue dress and the black net stockings. No lipstick or eyeshadow—he'd scrubbed that off. Just the dress and stockings and whatever feminine underwear he had on. Blood on the dress? No—just on his forehead and the one eye. Blood on the wig? I bent to look at it. No—he'd either had it in his hand when Myers shot him or it had gotten knocked off the bed when he fell. All those clothes in the closet, bottles of makeup on the dresser . . . but he could've been living with a woman, it could look that way in the preliminary stages. Only two people knew different, Ginny Lawson and me, and she wasn't talking to anyone about Brandy. Sure, it might come out later that he'd been a cross-dresser, but it wouldn't have any media appeal by then. It was what he was wearing when he died, and the dual personality angle, that made it sleazy media fodder. With man's clothing on instead of the dress and feminine undergarments, with some of the details left out or glossed over . . .

What's the matter with you? Cardinal rule, for God's sake: Never under any circumstances tamper with evidence in a homicide case. You could lose your license, you could go to jail. Call the cops now!

But if I was careful, there wasn't much risk. Not with my long-standing reputation as a cooperative straight arrow. And did it make any real difference to the law, to justice, if the details were altered slightly? No. Would it make a difference to a bereaved mother and her memories of her only son? Definitely. All the difference.

Bleeding heart, prize sucker . . . yeah. It had been that kind of case from the beginning, hadn't it?

Quickly, before I could change my mind, I began tampering with the damn evidence.

ZERO TOLERANCE

T HE little girl in the polka-dot playsuit was a holy terror. So was her mother. In fact, the kid wasn't all that bad—just spoiled and rambunctious—compared to the mom-thing that had spawned her.

The whole sorry business was the mother's fault. You couldn't lay any blame on the child; she hadn't been taught any better. You could lay a little of the blame on me, I suppose, but not much when you looked at it all in perspective. No, by God, the mother was the villain of the piece. An even nastier villain in some ways than the pudgy guy in the leather jacket.

It started with the little girl. She kept finding me out of all the other shoppers crowding the Safeway aisles, like some sort of pint-sized heat-seeking missile. First she charged out from behind a bin full of corn in the produce section, accidentally banged my shin with one of her cute red pumps, and then charged off without so much as an upward or backward glance. Next she showed up in the meat department, standing directly behind me when I turned with a package of ground round in my hand; I had to do a nifty juking sidestep to avoid tripping over her, but it wasn't as nifty as it might have been because I dropped the package and the cellophane wrapping split and the right leg of my trousers took on the sudden appearance of clothing in a splatter movie. And finally there was the collision in the cat- and dog-food aisle.

I was pushing my cart near the end of the aisle, minding my own business, looking down unhappily at the hamburger-stained pantleg, when she came flying around the corner with her arms outflung at her sides—playing airplane or some damn thing. Neither of us saw each other in time; she banged into the cart with a startled yelp. Just as this happened, the mother—an attractive doe-eyed blondee in her twenties—pushed her cart around the corner. She let out a yelp of her own when the kid bounced off and flopped down on a chubby little backside. She wasn't hurt; her face scrunched up but she didn't cry or even whimper. But the way the mother reacted you'd have thought her daughter had been mortally wounded. She rushed over, picked the child up, brushed her off, examined her with a probing eye, clutched her possessively, and then glared at me as if I were something she'd just found caked on the bottom of her shoe.

"What's the matter with you?" she said accusingly. "Why don't you watch where you're going?"

Under ordinary circumstances I would have diffused the situation by smiling, muttering a polite comment, and sidling off to continue my shopping. But the circumstances tonight were not ordinary. There was my sore shin, and my bloody pantleg, and the facts that I'd had a long tiring day and Kerry was working late and it was my turn to do both the shopping and the cooking of dinner, and the additional fact that I have zero tolerance for parents who allow their children to run wild in supermarkets, department stores, and other public places. I managed the smile all right, a tight little one, but not the polite comment or the sidling off.

"And why don't you curb your kid," I said, "before she really gets hurt?"

"What?" It came out more like a squawk than a word.

"Just what I said, lady. This is the third time your daughter's run into me—"

"How dare you!"

"How dare I what?"

"Talk to me that way. Accuse Amy of attacking you."

I wasn't smiling any more. "I didn't say she attacked me—"

"Of all the insane things. A six-year-old child and an old brute like you."

"Old brute?" I said. "Listen—"

"You practically run Amy down with your cart and then you . . ." Words failed her. She sputtered and said, "Oh!" and then realized that we'd drawn a small group of onlookers. This spurred her on; she was the type that would always play to a crowd. "Did any of you see it?" she asked the gawkers. "He almost ran my little girl down with his cart."

Nobody admitted to having seen anything, but there were angry mumbles and a couple of hostile looks thrown my way.

"She lets the kid run loose," I said, "play games in the aisles—"

"I never runned loose!" cute little Amy said. "I never did!"

Some guy came up and poked me on the shoulder. "Why don't you pick on somebody your own size?"

"I wasn't picking on anybody."

"Nice family like this," a henna-rinsed woman said. "You ought to be ashamed of yourself."

The nice family stood hating me with their bright doe eyes. The baby holy terror stuck her tongue out at me.

The finger-poker did his annoying thing again. "Apologize to them, why don't you?"

"Apologize? I'm the one who—"

I stopped because nobody was listening; I didn't have a sympathetic ear in the bunch. Tiny warning bells went off in my head. A no-win situation if I'd ever found myself in one. Let it go on much longer and it would turn ugly and escalate into an incident. So? So I bit my tongue. I took a tight grip on my offended pride. And I lied and dissembled like a coward.

"Okay," I said, "it was all my fault. The child's not hurt. Suppose we just forget the whole thing."

That satisfied the gawkers. Within ten seconds they were gone, though not without a few parting glances of dislike in my direction. The mother set the little girl down—as soon as Amy's feet touched the floor she was off again like a Piper Cub taking wing—and turned back to her cart. She tried to jockey it past mine at the same time I tried to jockey past hers. This produced a mutter on my part, an exasperated sigh and another angry glare on hers. We finally managed to clear each other without clashing, and she went her way and I went mine—but not until we'd traded a couple more barbs, trite but heartfelt.

Hers: "The stupid jerks you run into."

Mine: "No truer words, Mommie Dearest."

I finished loading my cart in a dark funk, wheeled it to the checkout stands and into the shortest line. I had just transferred the last item onto the conveyor thing they have when something banged hard into the backs of my legs. I swung around.

The blondee with her cart, naturally. "Oh," she said in a voice like maple syrup over arsenic, lying through her teeth, "I'm so sorry, I didn't mean to bump you like that."

I swallowed eight or nine choice words. Sweet young Amy was clutching mommy's skirt; she showed me her tongue again. I resisted an impulse to answer in kind, reminding myself that I was above such childish behavior, I really was. I put my back to the nice family and kept it there the entire time my purchases were being rung up and paid for. I didn't look their way as I left the store, either, for fear that I wasn't as far above childish behavior as I cared to believe.

It was a cold, foggy night outside, but the air tasted good and it had a soothing effect on my abused feelings. The parking lot at the Diamond Heights Safeway is almost always full in the evening, and tonight was no exception; I'd had to park toward the back of the lot, near the exit onto Diamond Heights Boulevard. All I could see over that way, through the swirls and eddies of fog, were vague shapes and outlines.

I spotted the pudgy guy in the leather jacket at about the same time I located my car. He was wandering around in the general vicinity, about three cars north of mine. He stopped when he saw me, turned his head partway as I neared with my rattling cart. When I was close enough for him to get a good look at me, his head turned again and he moved away. Not far, though, just over to a backed-in Ford Econoline van new enough to still be wearing dealer plates. He bent and peered at the van's front end, as if something about it had snagged his attention.

There was a furtiveness about him that I didn't like. I kept watching him while I put the groceries away in the trunk. He straightened after about ten seconds, went around on the far side of the van without looking my way again. I shut the trunk and approached the driver's door. The van was bulky enough and the fog thick enough so that I couldn't tell where the pudgy guy had gone. He might have continued on toward the far north end of the lot, or he might still be lurking somewhere near the Ford.

I got into the car. The fog had laid thick films of wetness over the windows; I couldn't see through them. I scooted over on the passenger side, rolled the window down about two inches. The van was visible again through the narrow opening, as was the empty asphalt lane in front of it. There was still no sign of the pudgy guy.

Nothing happened for about three minutes. I was still trying to make up my mind what to do when somebody materialized out of the fog over that way.

It was the blonde woman pushing her grocery cart, little Amy skipping along beside her.

And where they went was straight to the Ford van.

The thing had four doors; the woman unlocked the rear one and began shoving sacks inside while the baby holy terror ran back and forth in front. It's all right, I told myself, nothing's going down. But I had my hand on the door handle, my shoulder butted up against the door itself.

The woman finished loading her groceries, slammed the rear door. As she unlocked the driver's I heard her call, "Amy, you come here this instant. I've had enough of your—"

That was as far as she got. The pudgy guy appeared around the front of the van, something dark and pointy in one hand that could only be a gun, moving with such suddenness that Amy shrieked and ran to her mother. He got there at the same time she did, yanked the keys out of the woman's hand and then slugged her hard enough to pitch her backward into the grocery cart.

I was out of the car by then, running. The guy was half inside the van when he saw me; he tried to squirm back out instead of going all the way in and locking the door, and that was his mistake. I hit the half-open door with my shoulder before he could slide clear of it, knocked him back against the side of the van. He struggled to get the gun up on me, but I pinned his arm with my left hand, slammed him in the belly with my right and brought my knee driving upward at the same time. He made a thin squealing noise that blended right in with the screaming of the woman and the shrieking of the child. I smacked him in the belly again, twisted the gun out of his fingers, then punched him on the jaw as he was starting to sag. It was a good, solid, satisfying punch: He went all the way down and lay twitching at my feet.

Things stayed somewhat chaotic for the next couple of minutes. Some people came running up out of the fog, three or four of them asking alarmed questions. The woman had quit yowling and was on her feet again, tending to Amy who was still going off in up-and-down riffs like a busted fire siren. I stuffed the gun into my coat pocket, started to lean down to make sure the pudgy guy wasn't going to give me any more trouble, and somebody pushed in close enough to jostle me.

It was the finger-poker from inside. Glowering, he said, "What's going on here? What'd you do this time—"

I gave him back his glower and told him to shut up.

"What?" he said. "What?"

"You heard me. Shut up and go call the police."

"The police? What—"

It was my turn to do the poking, hard under his sternum. It gave me almost as much satisfaction as the punch to the pudgy guy's jaw. "The police. Now."

He spluttered some, but he went.

I glanced at the blonde woman, who was clutching her daughter and staring at me with one eye as round as a half dollar; the other, where the guy had slugged her, was already puffy and half closed. Then I returned my attention to her attacker. He was lying on his side, moaning a little now, his legs drawn up and both hands clutched between them; there was a smear of blood on his jaw and his pain was evident. I felt mildly sorry for the woman. I didn't feel a bit sorry for him.

Carjackers are something else I have zero tolerance for.

The cops came pretty quick, asked questions, put handcuffs on the pudgy guy and hauled him off to jail. The crowd that had gathered gradually dispersed. And I was alone once more with a calmed-down Amy and her calmed-down mother.

The woman hadn't said a direct word to me the whole time, and she didn't say anything to me now. Instead she pushed the kid into the van, hoisted herself in under the wheel. Well, that figures, I thought. I walked away to my car.

But before I could get in, the woman was out of the van again and hurrying my way. She stopped with about four feet separating us. Changed her mind, I thought. Thanks or an apology coming up after all. I smiled a little, waiting.

And she said, "I just want you to know—I still think you're a jerk."

After which she did an about-face and back to the van she went.

I stood there while she fired it up, switched on the headlights, swung around in my direction. The driver's window was down; I saw her face and the little girl's face clearly as they passed by.

Amy stuck out her tongue.

And the mom-thing gave me the finger.

Right, I thought with more sadness than anger as I watched the taillights bleed away into the fog.

Zero tolerance night in what was fast becoming a zero tolerance world.

AFTERWORD:
RANDOM CHUNKS OF MUDDLE

AFTERWORDS to short-story collections in which the author dis-
cusses the various selections have always struck me as superfluous,
and in some cases mildly insulting to the reader. So I'm not going to
indulge in that sort of thing here. Presumably any person who has
picked up and read this tome is an astute, clever individual who doesn't
require postmortem dissections or explanations. If the stories don't speak
for themselves, nothing I can say about them will give them any more
point, credibility, or value.

Instead I'll use this space to offer a few cogent words on world
disorder. That is, the disordered worlds of "Nameless" and his creator.

Most writers of series crime fiction, it seems to me, are people who
possess orderly minds and who lead reasonably orderly lives. Take
Marcia, for instance. In all ways that matter she is this type of person,
and her Sharon McCone series reflects the fact: Its chronology is exact,
as is the linkage of events which make up Sharon's professional and
personal life. Each novel takes place within a carefully structured time
and date frame that adheres to actual times and dates and incorporates
actual happenings; each short story fits more or less perfectly into the
interstices between novels and also follows the same careful structure. By
a close reading of the entire McCone canon you can follow the changes
in her career and private life step by developmental step.

Not so "Nameless."

Read his canon and you run into inconsistencies, anomalies, and
random chunks of muddle.

Unlike Marcia, I am not an organized person. I do not have an
orderly mind or lead an orderly existence. (I don't mean to make her
sound anal retentive; she has her undisciplined moments too. But
compared to me she is a paragon of order and rectitude.) My brain is as
cluttered as my office, my daily routine. My approach to fiction writing
is to sit down with a theme and a half-formed idea and wing it from start
to finish. I seldom plan or structure anything in advance, because when
I've tried doing that the plans all too often went awry and the structures

all too often collapsed. If there is such an animal as a literary loose cannon, I'm it. And this is not a good type of person to be when you write series detective fiction. No indeed.

There is a certain order to the "Nameless" novels—connective tissue from book to book, a mostly consistent chronology of events that make up his life and career—but it owes mostly to the fact that I know him so well; that he is, in all important ways, a mirror image of me. Which is also why, no doubt, there are inconsistencies, anomalies, and random chunks of muddle. For example: The series is now nearly thirty years old (good God!), and "Nameless" was already a little long in the tooth when I introduced him; so I've had to retard his aging process at an increasingly slower rate, and unto the bargain ignore certain background details which I built into the series early on. Such as his alleged service in World War II, and the period he supposedly spent in Hawaii as a military chauffeur *before* the bombing of Pearl Harbor. If I had aged him at a normal rate, and hadn't ignored such details, he'd be pushing eighty now and I'd have a hell of a time justifying such traits as an active sex life and the ability to hold his own in hand-to-hand combat.

(The age factor isn't the only large anomaly, I'm ashamed to admit. There is another which Marcia gleefully reminds me of whenever she's in one of her sadistic moods. Seems that in the first novel, *The Snatch*, "Nameless" is alleged to be godfather to Eberhardt's two daughters. In subsequent novels, however, his godfather status and the two putative daughters seem to have mysteriously vanished without a trace and Eberhardt is said to be childless. Stranger things have happened, but probably not in any detective series past or present.)

Confusion of a different sort exists in the "Nameless" short stories. His short cases do not, as with Marcia's McCone tales, fit neatly into the intervals between novels. Some can be more or less placed in sequence in his career by internal references to characters and events. Others, no matter when they happen to have been written, exist in a nonspecific time zone (if not twilight zone) and have no correlation to the rest of the series. In large part, this is a consequence of their scattershot nature.

The McCone stories have a uniform style, tone, and vision in keeping with the novels. But the "Nameless" stories have different approaches, different tones, and reflect not so much his life as mine—the overly fecund imagination and unfocused range of interests of a literary loose cannon, and the loose cannon's mood, world view, and state of mental health at the time they were perpetrated. Hardboiled shockers, offbeat whodunits, exercises in ratiocination, impossible crime puzzles, attempts

at social commentary, light-and-wry near-cozies, pure slapstick farce . . .
only a confused mind could allow his series character to hop all over the
crime fiction landscape as I've done and retain even a glimmer of hope
that readers will respond favorably to each and every tale.

Still, as undisciplined as the stories are in a series context, I like to
believe that they work on an individual basis, both as stories and as
"Nameless" stories. (I also like to believe the same is true of the novels.)
Some are better than others, to be sure; but each has a plot that doesn't
stretch credulity *too* far, each has a definite point, and each in its own
way makes use of some facet of "Nameless's" rather complex character—
mostly his strengths, now and then his weaknesses. In these respects the
same degree of order exists in the stories as in the novels. No matter
what type of case he investigates, *he* remains a constant—acting, reacting,
and interacting in a fashion commensurate with who and what he is.

Whatever their positive qualities and their shortcomings, the tales in
these pages—most of the ones I've concocted featuring "Nameless" over
the past dozen-plus years—were written with enthusiasm and pleasure (for
the most part), and I'm satisfied with most of them as entertainments.
But in any case, they are what they are and I'm stuck with them. Just as
I'm stuck with the overly fertile imagination and untidy mind that
spawned them.

My world and welcome to it. "Nameless's" world and welcome to it.
Random chunks of muddle and all.

Petaluma, California
December 1995

A "NAMELESS DETECTIVE" CHECKLIST

NOVELS

The Snatch. Random House, 1971.
The Vanished. Random House, 1973.
Undercurrent. Random House, 1973.
Blowback. Random House, 1977.
Twospot (with Collin Wilcox). Putnam, 1978.
Labyrinth. St. Martin's Press, 1980.
Hoodwink. St. Martin's Press, 1981. (Recipient of Private Eye Writers of America Shamus Award for best novel of 1981.)
Scattershot. St. Martin's Press, 1982.
Dragonfire. St. Martin's Press, 1982.
Bindlestiff. St. Martin's Press, 1983.
Quicksilver. St. Martin's Press, 1984.
Nightshades. St. Martin's Press, 1984.
Double (with Marcia Muller). St. Martin's Press, 1984.
Bones. St. Martin's Press, 1985.
Deadfall. St. Martin's Press, 1986.
Shackles. St. Martin's Press, 1988.
Jackpot. Delacorte Press, 1990.
Breakdown. Delacorte Press, 1991.
Quarry. Delacorte Press, 1992.
Epitaphs. Delacorte Press, 1992.
Demons. Delacorte Press, 1993.
Hardcase. Delacorte Press, 1995.
Sentinels. Carroll & Graf, 1996.

SHORT STORY COLLECTIONS

Casefile. St. Martin's Press, 1983.
Spadework. Crippen & Landru, 1996.

SHORT STORIES

[*Included in *Casefile*; **included in *Spadework*]

* "Sometimes There is Justice." *Alfred Hitchcock's Mystery Magazine*, August 1968. (Reprinted in *Casefile* as "It's a Lousy World.")

"The Snatch." *Alfred Hitchcock's Mystery Magazine*, May 1969. (Expanded into the novel of the same title.)

"A Cold Day in November." *Alfred Hitchcock's Mystery Magazine*, November 1969. (Incorporated into the novel *Labyrinth*.)

"The Crank." *Mike Shayne Mystery Magazine*, January 1970.

* "Death of a Nobody." *Alfred Hitchcock's Mystery Magazine*, February 1970.

"The Way the World Spins." *Alfred Hitchcock's Mystery Magazine*, May 1970. (Incorporated into the novel *Labyrinth*.)

* "The Assignment." *Alfred Hitchcock's Mystery Magazine*, February 1972. (Reprinted in *Casefile* as "One of Those Cases.")

"Blowback." *Argosy*, September 1972. (Expanded into the novel of the same title.)

* "Majorcan Assignment." *Mike Shayne Mystery Magazine*, October 1972. (Reprinted in *Casefile* as "Sin Island.")

"The Scales of Justice." *Alfred Hitchcock's Mystery Magazine*, July 1973. (Incorporated into the novel *Labyrinth*.)

* "Private Eye Blues." *Alfred Hitchcock's Mystery Magazine*, July 1975.

* "The Private Eye Who Collected Pulps." *Ellery Queen's Mystery Magazine*, February 1979. (Reprinted in *Casefile* as "The Pulp Connection.")

"Thin Air." *Alfred Hitchcock's Mystery Magazine*, May 1979. (Included in the novel *Scattershot*.)

"A Nice Easy Job." *Ellery Queen's Mystery Magazine*, November 1979. (Included in the novel *Scattershot*.)

* "Where Have You Gone, Sam Spade?" *Alfred Hitchcock's Mystery Magazine*, January 30, 1980.

* "Dead Man's Slough." *Alfred Hitchcock's Mystery Magazine*, May 21, 1980.

"A Killing in Xanadu." Waves Press limited edition chapbook, 1980. (Included in the novel *Scattershot*.)

* "Who's Calling?" *Casefile*, 1983. (First published in Japanese collection of four original "Nameless" novellas, 1982.)

* "Booktaker." *Casefile*, 1983. (First published in Japanese collection of four original "Nameless" novellas, 1982.)

"The Ghosts of Ragged-Ass Gulch." (First published in Japanese collection of four original "Nameless" novellas, 1982; expanded into the novel *Nightshades*.)

"Quicksilver." (First published in Japanese collection of four original "Nameless" novellas, 1982; expanded into the novel of the same title.)

** "Cat's-Paw." Waves Press limited edition chapbook, 1983. (Recipient of Private Eye Writers of America Shamus Award for best short story of 1983.)

** "Skeleton Rattle Your Mouldy Leg." *The Eyes Have It,* 1984.

** "Sanctuary." *Graveyard Plots*, 1985. (Reprinted in *Spadework* as "Twenty Miles to Paradise.")

** "Ace in the Hole." *Mean Streets*, 1986.

** "Incident in a Neighborhood Tavern." *An Eye for Justice*, 1988.

** "Something Wrong." *Small Felonies*, 1988.

"Cache and Carry" (with Marcia Muller). *Small Felonies*, 1988.

** "Here Comes Santa Claus." *Mistletoe Mysteries*, 1989.

** "Stakeout." *Justice for Hire*, 1990.

"La Bellezza delle Bellezze." *Invitation to Murder*, 1991. (Expanded into the novel *Epitaphs*.)

** "Bedeviled." *Cat Crimes*, 1991.

** "Souls Burning." *Dark Crimes*, 1991; *New Crimes* 3, 1991.

"Kinsmen." *Criminal Intent*, 1993. (Expanded into the novel *Sentinels*.)

** "One Night at Dolores Park." *Ellery Queen's Mystery Magazine*, April 1995.

** "Home is the Place Where." *Ellery Queen's Mystery Magazine*, November 1995.

** "Bomb Scare." *Ellery Queen's Mystery Magazine*, December 1995.

** "Worried Mother Job." *Spadework*, 1996.

** "Zero Tolerance." *Spadework*, 1996.

♠ SPADEWORK ♠

Spadework: A Collection of "Nameless Detective" Stories by Bill Pronzini, with an introduction by Marcia Muller, is set in 11 point Garamond Antiqua, except for the title page which is in Revue and Futura Bold. The book is printed on 50 pound Glatfelter supple-opaque paper. The cover painting is by Carol Heyer and the design by Deborah Miller. Thomson-Shore, Inc., Dexter, Michigan printed and bound the first edition comprised of one thousand, one hundred fifty copies in trade paperback, and three hundred fifty copies in Roxite-B cloth, signed and numbered by the author. Copies one through eighty-nine contain a tipped-in typescript page from the author's files of a story or the afterword in this book; copies ninety through three hundred fifty contain a tipped-in typescript page from the author's files of the "Nameless Detective" novel *Demons*. *Spadework* was published in May 1996 by Crippen & Landru, Publishers, Norfolk, Virginia.